Complete Creation by Andy Riedlinger

Edited by Patty Schaff

Black & White Edition 2024

www.identityofoliver.com

# Andy Riedlinger
## About the Author

Andy Riedlinger was born and raised in Williston, North Dakota, and has many fond memories of growing up in his hometown. He still has several good friends living in western North Dakota and often returns to see them. This rural atmosphere provided plenty of inspiration for Hometown Chronicles, the first novel in the Identity of Oliver Series.

Andy has wonderful parents, whose mother worked as a schoolteacher and whose father worked as a manager in a bustling oil patch called the Bakken. After raising their family, they moved to a retirement community in Ft Myers, Florida, which they absolutely love. He also has two younger sisters, who are each enjoying great careers and family life. One of his younger sisters, who now lives in Tennessee, has four wonderful children and a loving husband who has blessed their family with a thriving chiropractic business. His youngest sister became a pharmaceutical doctor and is raising one delightful child with her charismatic husband, with whom Andy enjoys fishing with when visiting North Dakota.

Andy moved to Fort Collins, Colorado, immediately after graduating high school in 1997 to pursue new adventures and his love for the mountains. In 2001, he graduated from college with a degree in video production and has since become a respected video systems engineer for many of the largest productions in Colorado. He is also a successful entrepreneur who has pursued many business interests in the city of Denver, where he currently lives. He has owned businesses in Colorado's marijuana industry, real estate market, and audiovisual industry, as well as two laundromats and a small vending business.

Andy enjoys fishing, hunting, snowboarding, snowmobiling, billiards, oil painting, writing, and traveling in his free time. He began writing at a young age and has continued to chase his dream of being a successful author. Remarkably, he had written some short stories, several poems, and a novella before he even graduated from high school. He published his first novel in 2007 and has written a number of unique pieces of literature, including five novels, two novellas, short stories, an autobiography, and over one hundred poems.

# The Identity of Oliver Series

Author

Andy Riedlinger

# The Identity of Oliver Series

**Hometown Chronicles** is the first book in The Identity of Oliver Series. This remarkable story will introduce you to a handful of exciting characters and their unique relationship with Oliver. Each one of these characters has its own tantalizing story to tell, and unique influence over the many anomalies Oliver faces. This book explains an incredible love interest and friendships whose futures hang in the balance of small-town injustice. Hometown Chronicles is a philosophical think piece with an intense narrative of true love, unique integrity, and a goal for revenge served ice cold. Be prepared to experience a whirlwind of emotions as this amazing tale of bizarre fate is told. This story will be sure to make you laugh and cry as you read what causes Oliver to embark on extraordinary journeys around the world.

**West Coast Chronicles** is the second book in The Identity of Oliver Series. This story follows the twisted fate of a young man fleeing from corrupt law enforcement. Oliver takes you up and down America's West Coast on an exuberant adventure in search of his evil nemesis and hippy friend to help save the life of the father to his love interest. However, this isn't a story that only explains physical exploration. It will also lead you on a quest to understand some of life's most intriguing questions and difficult problems to solve. The unique subplots of this book are guaranteed to leave you rolling on the floor with laughter, wiping away tears of sadness, and pondering over the many complex issues Oliver faces. Interactions with punk rockers, ravers, and hippies explain their unique subculture dancing in the lives of ordinary people. West Coast Chronicles will leave you with an intense cliffhanger with its philosophies standing on first, second, and third base. Finally, the Identity of Oliver pitches the next book in the series, which is guaranteed to be a grand slam hit.

**Chronicles of Heart and Revenge** is the third book in The Identity of Oliver Series. The glitches in Oliver's profound journey through life have finally been exposed. Now all the fantastic pieces of this obscure puzzle come together to form one final enigma to solve. Oliver plans to marry his beloved, but impossible goals must be achieved before the father of the bride walks her down the aisle. These obscure tasks provided a fantastic opportunity to develop the most gripping storylines of the entire series. This leads you to embark on a sequence of anomalous adventures around the globe as Oliver is forced into the seedy underworld of black-market crimes. Prepare yourself to venture into the inner-city slums of some of the world's most dangerous places, as well as tropical islands and beautiful beaches at some of the most exotic destinations on earth. You'll travel to the Philippines, Mexico, Columbia, Switzerland, Denmark, Brazil, the Czech Republic, Costa Rica, Thailand, Nicaragua, Germany, Indonesia, Guatemala, Honduras... fourteen countries in all before Oliver finally meets his nemesis for the last time.

# Chronicles

# Heart of & revenge

# Chapter I

THE HIPPY CARAVAN PULLED into a truck stop for gas at Barstow, California around 4 pm on September 14th, 2001. This was a small town located at the largest intersection I had ever seen. It was where Highway 247, Highway 58, Interstate Highway 40, and Interstate Highway 15 all converged. We were approximately thirty miles away from Mojave National Preserve and forty miles from Death Valley, which explained the intense heat we were experiencing that day. Not only were we very close to a location that is often considered the hottest place in America, but it was also just scorching hot with no cloud cover that day. Temperatures easily reached 120 degrees Fahrenheit.

Jessica, one member of the Psychedelic 40, and I rode with Anika in her 1999 Ford Taurus, and we were doing just fine, seeing that her car was almost brand new. To combat the intense heat, all we had to do was turn on the air conditioning. Unfortunately, this was not the situation for Anika's two friends, Tracy and Melissa, who were driving the transport vehicles. I had some serious concerns that the two older model trucks they were driving would blow up and not make it all the way to Nebraska. My concerns about the vehicles themselves kept me distracted from the human aspect of actually having to drive them.

The difference between the modern comfort of Anika's car and the older model trucks her friends were driving was a constant reminder of the challenges we faced. Given these unbearable conditions, both of Anika's friends had good reason to complain when we stopped for gas. They had likely experienced temperatures over one hundred degrees since we left Venice Beach. The heat was so insufferable that Tracy threatened to quit and said she would rather hitch a ride home with a total stranger than continue onward when we initially arrived in Barstow. After some intense deliberation, I ended up having to add another four hundred dollars to convince the girls to continue onward to Nebraska.

Thankfully, I was happy to see that the eight members of the Psychedelic 40 riding with Fredrick all appeared to be doing just fine. Although Fredrick's van was an older model, it was an incredibly well-maintained vehicle. Not only did his air conditioner work just fine, but it was obvious that they all had been indulging heavily in the suitcase full of drugs. This was the first time I realized how much they stood out in a rural area. This helped me organize my thoughts of keeping them contained at Billy's farm in Nebraska and not letting them roam free in town.

There was also the fact that they wore clothes that would indicate they were pale-skinned Rastafarians, and all but one of them had dreadlocks. What I was worried about the most was that it didn't appear that there would be any gaps in their prolific drug abuse. This didn't seem to matter much at the gas station where we decided to fuel up. However, it would matter in my hometown, where ten thousand ultra-conservative people lived. This was a concern I would need to address for several reasons before showing up in Nebraska.

In any case, once all the vehicles were filled with gas, the crazy hippy caravan continued west down Interstate Highway 15 until about eight o'clock that evening when we stopped again for gas in Las Vegas. I just figured this would be a quick pit stop on the outskirts of the city, and I had no intentions of staying there very long. Anika and her friends didn't have any extended plans to stay in Las Vegas, either.

Unfortunately, one of the hippies had somehow figured out that a band called Umphrey's McGee was playing at the Colosseum Theater at the Caesars Palace Hotel. Once the rest of them found out about this, our caravan was forced to take a detour. When they realized there was an opportunity to see this band perform that night, there was no way I could persuade any of them to continue onward. Anika, her friends, and I were unfamiliar with this band, so it would have seemed to just be an unanticipated distraction along the way for us.

While passing through Las Vegas on my way to Portland earlier in the summer, I mostly just hung out in smaller hotels during the day and was pretty wasted drunk the one night I went to the bigger casinos. Given the limitations of this experience, I was still unaware of how luxurious some of these big gambling hotels actually were, so when we arrived at Caesar's Palace, I thought it was the nicest hotel I had ever seen. Looking around at how extravagant the lobby was, I initially assumed our hippy caravan would stick out like a sore thumb. However, this was far from the situation that we ascended upon. The entire hotel was full of people who looked just like the Psychedelic 40 riding in the hippy caravan. After making this discovery, it didn't come as any more of a surprise to smell a profound odor of marijuana proliferating from every square inch of the hotel.

I promised to pay for everything while on this expedition, but I told Fredrick that the Psychedelic 40 would have to pay for their hotel room since this concert was not something I had planned for. Regardless, I still had to pay for two double bedrooms for myself and the girls. Anika and Jessica insisted on having a room to themselves, so I ended up in the other room with Melissa and Tracy. Fredrick and the hippies got five hotel rooms in the same hallway as the girls and me.

The girls were excited to change out of their clothes and go down to the pool after sitting in the hot sun all day. I just planned on going down to the first floor to get some food and maybe plug some quarters into the slot machines. Once the four women were all changed into their swimsuits, they met in my room to smoke a joint before continuing to the pool. This was when I noticed how much Anika, Tracy, and Melissa fit the stereotypical hot girl from southern California. Until this point, I only observed them talking like orthodox valley girls, often embedded into Hollywood's list of cinematic impressions. They all had long blond hair that was curled and made up like they were going to a dance club or something. I found this odd because they were headed to the pool, where I assumed they planned to get their heads soaked in water.

Tracy and Melissa also wore sunglasses on their foreheads, which I didn't see any reason for considering the fact that it was dark outside. The most obvious thing that stood out to me was the fact that all four of the girls were wearing the smallest bikinis that money could buy, and not a single one of them had a noticeable tan line. Even Jessica was wearing a bikini, which I would not have expected. It wasn't that Jessica was ridiculously fat or anything, it was just that she was a humongous woman. She was over six feet tall and was built like a professional football player.

After we smoked the joint, the girls cleaned out my mini fridge full of shooters and headed down to the pool. At this point, I headed down to the lobby to get something to eat. I ended up at the largest of the three restaurants on the first floor. This restaurant seemed to be a catch-all for people like me who were not interested in fine dining. After I ate, I continued to sit at the bar, drinking beer and watching TV. I can't remember for sure what I was watching, but I think it may have been an episode of *Steve Irwin the Crocodile Hunter*. This was the first time I had seen anything besides news coverage of the Twin Towers terrorist bombings since the morning of September 11th. Unsurprisingly, the other three TVs that hung above the bar were turned to 9/11 news, so I felt pretty fortunate to be sitting in front of the only TV not hashing over 9/11 bullshit. I thought I had gotten so lucky to get my seat that I ended up abandoning my plans to go gambling.

Around eleven o'clock, I randomly met up with Anika and her friends, who showed up at the restaurant bar to get some drinks. At this point in the night, Anika and Jessica had changed into some clothes that seemed appropriate to wear in this establishment. In contrast, Melissa and Tracy just put on nearly matching tank tops over their G-string bikinis, which gave off the appearance that they were wearing no bottoms at all if you stood directly behind them. These were two very small bleach-blond women with absolutely nothing wrong with their bodies. Their bare-naked asses, combined with stunning looks and twenty-something personalities, made them sexually alluring to almost any guy that passed by.

This quickly resulted in all four of the ladies being surrounded by a bunch of men wanting to buy them drinks in a matter of minutes, which was kindly reciprocated by each one of them. They were so into this situation that Anika and Jessica made no indication that they were lesbians. The only thing that would make this apparent at all was that Anika made whatever men were buying her drinks to also buy Jessica's. There weren't any men standing who were as tall as Jessica or as large as her in general. This contributed to my best guess as to why I didn't see her getting hit on. In contrast, Anika and the two little blond girls I shared a room with had a completely different story to tell. Each of the girls had somehow gotten pretty drunk before arriving at the restaurant bar, and they were now proceeding to get plenty more drunk.

The men who were buying the ladies their drinks were a unique cocktail of hippies, dressed-down businessmen, and college alpha males who talked really loud. When the Umphrey's McGee concert was over around midnight, the bar became completely packed. This is when things seemed to get out of control. There were guys taking body shots off of Melissa and Tracy's stomachs, and one guy even laid out a line of cocaine on Tracy's ass after giving her a couple of lines to snort. The bartender got pretty pissed off about this, but this was far from the only thing he was concerned about at this point in the night. The hippies were all sorts of intoxicated on every kind of drug known to man, except for Crystal Meth. Hippies seemed to stay clear of this particular drug.

I noticed Tracy continued to drink heavily and snort additional lines of coke for the next hour or so. Around two in the morning, I noticed that Melissa had left and was no longer in the restaurant. I was concerned about this because she was blackout drunk and was attempting to dance on an island bar the last time I saw her. I tried my best to watch over her, but there were so many people and distractions that she was impossible to keep track of.

Tracy, on the other hand, was drunk, but the coke she had snorted seemed to keep her drunkenness out of the weeds. Shortly after I noticed that Melissa was missing, Tracy and I decided to go up to our room to see if she had wandered up there by chance. When we opened the door, we found Melissa lying spread eagle on the nearest bed with a rather large man who was taking full advantage of her drunkenness. When this man saw us walk into the room, he jumped up and started yelling, "Holy shit? Ever thought about knocking?"

"Shut the fuck up Asshole!" I yelled back at him, "Just put on your clothes and get the hell out of here."

"Why should I leave?" the man aggressively asked. "You should be the one leaving." Around this point in our short conversation, I saw that Melissa was completely passed out. Tracy had walked over to the bed and tried to talk to her, but she only managed to mumble a few undecipherable words.

That's when I started turning on all of the lights in the hotel room while intentionally ignoring whatever the naked rapist was saying to me. Then I gathered his clothes up in a ball and threw them at his face as hard as I possibly could while yelling, "Put on your clothes and get the fuck out of here before I get angry!" This man stood there staring at me after I said this as if to make it a point that he had no intentions of obeying my demands. I'm not sure why he felt entitled to rape blackout-drunk women. It might have been because he was shitfaced himself, or maybe he was just being an absolute douchebag. Either way, he showed no signs of backing down from this unusual feeling of entitlement. That is when I aggressively got right in his face. Standing only about a foot away, I told him again to put on his clothes and leave.

This was about the time this naked man started to make a series of bad decisions. I was 5'10" and probably only weighed a hundred and sixty-five pounds, where he was at least a few inches taller with a significantly larger build than myself. His raging testosterone and clear size advantage provided him with enough blind confidence to feel unthreatened by me. Despite being completely naked, he seemed ready to fight when he looked directly into my eyes and said with a shit-eating grin, "What are you going to do about it if I don't?"

# Chapter II

THERE WAS A VERY critical flaw in the drunken rapist's decision to want to pursue a fight with me. To his credit, this flaw was in no way obvious to him at the time. However, he was about to learn in a real quick hurry that I was incredibly good at fighting. I talked a little about this earlier, but I need to elaborate further on how good I actually was at fighting because it becomes very relevant later in this story.

You should know by now that Erica, my two little sisters, and I were endlessly tormented in grade school because we smelled like cowshit as a result of growing up on cattle ranches. My sisters stopped getting picked on once we moved into the town of Ogallala. Erica moved away around this same time when we were twelve, and by the time she moved back to town at the beginning of our junior year, the issue had been resolved. This meant that Erica and my sisters didn't continue to get tortured like I did.

I continued to get picked on and plagued with nonstop aggression up until the beginning of my second year in high school. Unfortunately, dozens of bullies had gotten so used to starting playground brawls and picking on me that it had become a daily routine. This resulted in me getting into hundreds of fights growing up. When I was in grade school, I lost nearly all of them and only won a few in middle school. Even though I got involved with boxing and Karate during my freshman year, it didn't appear to significantly change the outcomes of the fights I would get into.

However, this all changed my sophomore year when I developed some manly physical features and an uncanny ability to beat the shit out of people. I'm not in the least bit joking when I say that I spent the entire summer after my freshman year watching Rocky Balboa, Bruce Lee, Chuck Norris, and Karate Kid movies. When I wasn't watching the inspiring 80's fight plot cinema, I spent up to ten hours a day lifting weights, practicing boxing, and going to Karate lessons.

I will never forget the first fight I got into in my sophomore year. It was after gym class when some bullies thought it would be funny to steal my clothes. I remember standing there in my underwear, asking six giggling kids where they had put them. Then I yelled, "Come on, guys... just give them back."

Interestingly enough, the largest of these six bullies walked over to me and said the exact same thing as this naked rapist standing in the corner of my hotel room in Vegas, "What are you going to do about it if I don't?"

This is when I would usually start to get my ass kicked, but this was not how it was going to go down anymore. I walked over to a giant basket of red dodge balls and proceeded to chuck one of them as hard as I could at this kid's head. This took him completely by surprise since no one had ever seen me instigate a fight before, so he didn't even attempt to protect himself. Suddenly, everyone in the locker room heard the distinctive noise of a red rubber dodgeball hitting someone in the face. If they had been smart, they would have paid more attention to what happened next and run away.

The rubber ball hit this kid so hard in the face that it caused him to grab his nose and bend over, yelling, "Fuck, fuck, fuck..." That was when I walked up to him, put one of my legs in the air, and held up my hands just like Daniel LaRusso did in the first <u>Karate Kid</u> movie. The reason for me doing this wasn't because I thought it was the best way to beat someone in a fight. I did this because I wanted to make my actions look as elaborate as possible. I stood like this for a second or two, waiting until the kid looked up at me, and then I kicked his face so hard he almost did a complete backflip.

I want to clarify two things before telling you what happened next. The first is that I never intended to seriously hurt anyone during any of the high school brawls I got into. Once I figured out how good I was at fighting, I actually spent countless hours training and educating myself on exactly where to hit someone to avoid causing injury. This same research also taught me exactly where to hit someone if I did want to cause a serious injury.

What happened during this brawl in the locker room that day was unique because it was before I understood any of this. The previous fights I got into would typically result in me getting my ass kicked. Incidentally, the only thing I had gotten good at was preventing myself from getting seriously hurt while fighting so I had no idea about the lasting effects of injuries that could occur from a fight.

The second thing I need to mention is that I got in so many fights growing up that it is hard to remember what exactly happened during these brawls and this one is not an exception. However, what I seem to remember is that the other five kids formed a single file line, each taking turns getting their ass beat down. This was not just a schoolyard scuffle where someone got a bloody nose and some feelings were hurt. This was an absolute massacre! I managed to break the nose of the first kid to fight me and knocked two front teeth out of another. There was one poor kid whose jaw I hit so hard that he had to get these weird rubber band things stuck inside his mouth, and as far as I know, he still had the rubber bands in his mouth when we graduated high school. The rest of them were lucky in comparison. They walked away with some black eyes or minor cuts and bruises.

Because I was the same person who was nothing more than a punching bag to them for the past nine years,  they were so embarrassed about getting their ass beat by me that they never told anyone the truth about what happened. Incidentally, this one event profoundly changed my reputation and future. It began with these six kids wanting revenge. This caused six more fights and six more times that they each got their asses handed to them by my bloody fists, but it didn't stop there.

A true anomaly occurred at this point when pretty much every boy in our school seemed determined to try to beat me in a fight. This wasn't because they all wanted to gang up on me in a violent attempt to teach me a lesson. The majority of the fights that I got into my sophomore year weren't about revenge. In fact, it wasn't like that at all. Some real organization transpired in their efforts to beat me in a fight. I might be exaggerating here, but these bouts seemed to be arranged in alphabetical order according to their last name. They each took turns fighting me in an attempt to secure the ultimate prize of high school popularity.

During the first two months of my sophomore year, I was immediately surrounded by about one hundred kids in the high school parking lot once class was let out for the day. They were expecting to see some brawls. Typically, three or four kids wanted to fight me each day. Somedays, there would be more, and other days, less. Regardless of how many kids there were lined up to fight me, I never lost. I came close to losing a fight several times, but it never actually happened, nor did I ever back down.

I won so many fights that no one dared to fight me after Christmas break during my sophomore year. As a matter of fact, I never got into one single fight for the rest of high school aside from boxing and Karate. All this fighting only elevated my interest in these sports. I fought people from all over the state during my junior and senior years in high school and only lost one single match. During my junior year, I placed second in the black belt class at the Nebraska State Karate Tournament, narrowly missing my opportunity to advance to nationals.

However, I handily took first place in the state tournament the following year. I think this would have caused most kids my age to become a bit cocky, but I remained humble when I advanced to nationals for two reasons. The first was that I thought back to all the times I got my ass beat down while growing up, and the second reason was that I thought that the competition at a national level would be much harder.

When my family and I flew to Ft. Worth, Texas, to watch me compete at the National Youth Karate Championships during my senior year, it was only the second time we had ever been on a plane. Aside from going to Disney World when I was in grade school, we had never even traveled past the neighboring states of Nebraska. This was enough to make everyone excited to attend this tournament, but it wouldn't be the only thing they got excited about. I remember my mother telling me several times that she would be proud of me no matter how I performed at the national level. My Dad also mentioned something like this too, thinking I didn't have a chance of winning this tournament. My folks obviously thought the competition at a national level would be much harder, just as I did. This assumption may have been accurate, but it didn't materialize in such a way that I noticed much difference.

A Karate tournament features two disciplines, which are Kata and Kumite. Kata is a demonstration of Karate techniques using pre-defined movements judged on speed, strength, focus, balance, and rhythm. Athletes choose from an official list of roughly one hundred Kata and must perform a different Kata each time. Technical and athletic performance are given separate scores using the same scale from 5.0 to 10.0. An athlete must achieve at least 5.0 in order to advance, and 10.0 is considered a perfect score. There are three rounds of competition in Kata: the elimination round, the ranking round, and medal bouts.

I scored a perfect 10.0 in the first round, 9.4 in the second round, and another perfect 10.0 in the final round of competition. My nearest competitor also scored 10.0 in the first round, but he scored 8.8 in the second round and 9.6 in the final round. Not only did I win in this area of discipline, but only one athlete in the history of this tournament ever scored as high as I did in Kata.

The Kumite discipline is very different from Kata. This is what most people envision a Karate match to look like, as I assume that the only education they have about this sport would have likely come from watching The Karate Kid movies. In this area of discipline, you actually fight head-to-head against an opponent using punching and kicking techniques performed on permitted parts of the body. All legal hand techniques that score are awarded one point.

All legal kicking techniques that score are awarded two points. All jump-spinning kicks to the head are awarded three points, and all penalty points are awarded one point. To win, an athlete must either reach an eight-point advantage within the three-minute round or have the most points at the end of the bout. There is also an elimination round, a ranking round, and a medal bout in this area of discipline.

The reason that I was so good at Kumite was that I spent at least an hour each day working on blocking and jump-spinning kicks since I started taking Karate lessons. I developed an unusual ability to block a punch while simultaneously performing a jump-spinning kick. This was such a deadly move that I rarely used any other technique to score points. With this said, I can say with almost 100% certainty that I would have won this tournament without using this combination because there was only one point collectively scored by my opponents throughout the entire tournament.

Interestingly enough, as good as I was at Karate, I was likely even better at boxing. I never even came close to losing a boxing match at the state level. Not only did I easily win the middleweight state title during my junior and senior years in high school, but there was only one fight that even made it to round two. Almost all of the boxing matches I fought in during my senior year ended with only a few punches. Remarkably, there was no exception when I fought at a national level. At least not until I reached the championship fight at the National Youth Boxing Tournament in Ft. Lauderdale, Florida.

I didn't expect much competition after winning handily so many times over the past couple of years. I seemed to easily beat my opponent regardless of who I fought against. The championship fight at this particular tournament made me realize that I wasn't as invincible as I thought. I got knocked down several times during the championship match and nearly lost by a technical knockout, aka TKO, during the first round. I remember the referee counting up to five as I stared at the ceiling while suffering from swirling double vision. This is generally what people see before losing consciousness after being punched extremely hard on the cheekbone, temple, or lower forehead if it's not lost immediately upon impact. I have no idea how I managed to stand up during the ten-second count yelled out by the referee, and my vision didn't seem to change much when I did.

The only reason I didn't lose this fight in the first round was because I heard my coach yell, "There are only four seconds left in this round, so for the love of God, just put your gloves in front of your face and block." Thankfully, I heard this and followed my coach's instructions, or I would have lost that match the very moment I stood up. I didn't even come close to winning this boxing match. If I didn't lose by TKO in the fourth round, I would have eventually lost by a majority decision. This happens if TKO does not win the fight and all three judges score a draw for the same boxer. I was knocked down six times, and I didn't knock down my opponent even once during this fight. I was getting beaten up so badly that I looked like Rocky Balboa when he fought Ivan Drago in Rocky IV, but instead of coming back to win, I just kept getting my ass beat.

At this point, there are likely two questions regarding the fights I was involved in. I will answer the question as to why I was knocked out during the fight against Ogallala's star quarterback after he found out that I nearly had sex with his girlfriend. If you remember, this occurred at the keg party following the funeral for the morbidly obese man whose death caused the incarceration of my friend Adam.

The reason I lost that fight had nothing to do with Troy's fighting ability and very little to do with the fact that two of his teammates helped him by ganging up on me. So long as my opponents stayed in front of me, it wouldn't really make any difference how many people ganged up on me if they weren't world-class fighters. The only reason Troy knocked me out was that I got sucker punched in the back of the head, and after turning around to see who had hit me, Troy had a haymaker already lined up. There are few fighters in the world who could have avoided this punch, and anyone as small as me would have been knocked out just the same.

The next question you might have is that if I easily won both disciplines at the Youth National Karate Championships, then how could I have been better at boxing than I was at Karate when I got my ass handed to me during the championship round at the Youth National Boxing Tournament? This can be answered by simply telling you who my opponent was. His name was Jermain Taylor. This guy was a better boxer than me, hands down. He was an absolutely incredible fighter! He hit harder than I did. He dodged punches better than I did, and his one-two combination punches were significantly quicker and more powerful than mine. The only reason I even made it to the fourth round of our boxing matchup was because of some sort of miracle delivered directly from the hands of God for reasons that only he could explain.

Jermain Taylor was so good at boxing that he started competing at a professional level immediately after he graduated from high school and won the bronze medal at the 2000 Olympics in Sydney, Australia, only a year later. Jermain continued to box at a professional level for the next thirteen years and still remains the champion of the world. He won his first professional boxing match only two months after high school graduation and went on to win his first twenty-five bouts, which included victories over former champions, Raul Marquez and William Joppy. He undisputedly won the World Boxing Association, World Boxing Council, International Boxing Federation, World Boxing Organization, and THE RING middleweight titles in 2005 by beating Bernard Hopkins, and in doing so, ending Hopkins' ten-year reign as middleweight champion. This made Taylor the first and, to date, only male boxer in history to claim each title from all four major boxing-sanctioning organizations in a single fight. He once again defeated Hopkins six months later, making him the only fighter to have defeated Hopkins twice.

I was good enough at boxing to easily become a professional, and maybe I would have if I wasn't such a confused kid, but there wasn't a snowball's chance in hell I'd ever come close to winning a world title match at a professional level. I could have fought against Jermain Taylor a hundred more times on his worst days and me on the best day of my life, and I still would have never won a single match against him. Looking back at all the boxing matches I ever fought in, my proudest moment moment by far was getting my clock cleaned by Jermain Taylor during the title match at the Youth National Boxing Tournament.

# Chapter III

"So, what are you going to do about it if I don't?" the naked date rapist asked. Before he had time to finish his sentence, I slapped him across the face so hard he fell onto the table and chairs behind him, but this didn't seem to faze this idiot because he surprising stood right back up, and walked over to me with his fists in the air.

At this point, I remember giving him a fair warning that he was about to make a big mistake, but he found my threat funny, and then he chuckled while attempting to throw a jab at me. I moved my head to the right only about three inches to avoid being hit. This was the beginning of a series of failed attempts at hitting me in the face. He didn't even come close to landing a single blow. I could have dodged his punches all night or ended the fight immediately if I wanted to.

My ability to dodge punches eventually made this naked man super pissed off. He clenched his teeth while repeatedly attempting to hit me. This charade finally ended when he thought he would let me have it with a giant haymaker. However, instead of landing this punch, he became familiar with a move I learned from Mr. Bruce Lee while watching <u>Game of Death II</u>.

This was to grab his arm as he extended it toward me, and then I would pivot and turn, flipping him into the air and throwing him against what I figured would have been the wall. Unfortunately, my back was turned just slightly more than I thought, so this minor miscalculation caused him to fly into the TV rather than the wall. The date rapist was thrown with incredible force inverted and upside down when he hit his head against the TV screen, but he never managed to break it. What is even more surprising than the TV not being damaged is that this didn't seem to phase this drunken idiot either. He jumped right back onto his feet and tried to square up again.

As much as I admired this man's ability to sustain hitting his head on the TV, and then again when he landed upside down on the floor, I was finished playing games. After giving him a few moments to recover, I quickly landed an uppercut and a right hook, which knocked him to the floor again. I absolutely thought that this ended the fight because he seemed to be knocked the fuck out, but I guess he was just taking a short nap because thirty seconds later, he woke back up and started to crawl toward the door on his hands and knees. That was when Melissa and I took turns kicking him in his naked ass while telling him to get out.

The drunken rapist made it all the way to the door and then proceeded to defy logic by somehow standing back up. I expected him to grab the door knob or his clothes and leave after what had just happened, but he was still determined to fight me. I didn't want to provide any more false hope that he had a chance at winning this fight at this point, so I ended it. I hit him just above his eye so hard that he was instantly knocked out with no chance of regaining consciousness any time soon.

I couldn't believe this coincidence. For the second time this summer, I had to figure out what to do with a drunken naked pervert taking advantage of a woman that I had only known for one day.

Unfortunately, I didn't have any duct tape this time around, so Melissa and I dragged his sorry ass down the hallway and put him into the elevator, which sent him down to the lobby for someone else to deal with.

I woke up the following morning to an earth-shaking rumble caused by Tracy snoring her head off. Melissa was also awakened by this at about the same time as I was. We tried to get Tracy to wake up or quit snoring, but it was useless. At this point, I planned to ask one of the Psychedelic 40 to drive the truck, but this idea was also squashed shortly after I knocked on Fredricks's door that morning. "Hey, are you and your friends getting ready to leave?" I asked. "It is almost ten o'clock already."

"Ahhh... I am ready... I guess," Fredrick answered. "Wanna come inside my room and smoke a joint?"

"Sure but let me see if the girls want to burn one before we get going." A few minutes later, I returned with only Anika, Jessica, and Melissa because we were still unable to wake Tracy up. We sat down on the bed while Fredrick opened the suitcase containing his supply of drugs. I expected him to pull out a large bag of weed from this suitcase and it to be still filled with the copious amount of drugs he packed up before leaving Venice Beach, but this was not the situation that transpired.

I quickly noticed that the two-pound bag of mushrooms was considerably smaller than it was twenty-four hours ago, and less than half of the two-pound bag of weed remained. As shocked as I was to see the amount of drugs the eight members of the Psychedelic 40 had already consumed, this didn't seem to come as any surprise to Fredrick because he initially fished through the suitcase for some papers to roll a joint without saying much. However, after about thirty seconds, he suddenly yelled, "Damnit! I knew I should have brought more acid!"

He continued to mutter some indistinguishable words while holding up the same bag that contained twenty sheets of LSD just before we left California. From where I sat, all but ten gel tabs had already been eaten. This meant that Fredrick and the eight members of the Psychedelic 40 ingested a little over a sheet of acid each in less than twenty-four hours. This was in addition to a half-pound of mushrooms and what appeared to be over a pound of weed.

After twisting a joint to smoke, Fredrick asked me if I had more money for drugs. I didn't exactly want to let him know that I did, but it didn't seem like I had much of a choice. I came to the West Coast with roughly fifteen grand and made thirty grand on my T6 Cartel contract, so I still had plenty of money. I reluctantly told Fredrick that I could cover the hippies' drug problem.

This was when Fredrick started to call a bunch of people, who I figured must have been the eight members of the Psychedelic 40. He seemed really upset about the fact that they had already eaten his entire supply of LSD. He continued to make call after call, trying to track down more acid. Meanwhile, some of the hippies started coming to his room, and by eleven o'clock, almost the entire hippy caravan had been assembled. The only people missing were Tracy, who was still passed out, and one single hippy who apparently reunited with his long-lost hairy hippy girlfriend during the concert and now planned to go with her on the Umphrey's Mcgee tour.

The fact that only two people were missing from the initial group of people I hired for the harvest was nothing short of a miracle because nearly every person from this motley crew came together despite the majority of them eating over a sheet of acid. They lacked the ability to think, reason, or comprehend reality but still somehow managed to find their way back to Fredrick's hotel room. These people were profoundly fucked up!

One hippy had been rolling on the floor laughing for the past twenty minutes and had turned completely purple from the inability to catch his breath. A female hippy kept reaching into the air with her hands as if she were trying to catch a butterfly or something. There was another hippy who had a bad case of the hick-ups and was trying to remedy his problem by attempting to stand on his head and drink water. Another one of the female hippies put her legs behind her head and started to roll around the hotel room. There was another hippy sitting on a long dresser in front of the hotel room, who had been licking the mirror that hung on the wall since he walked in the door, and this wasn't the only hippy licking a mirror at this point. There was another one in the bathroom doing exactly the same thing. It was absolute chaos!

That's when Fredrick stood on a chair in the middle of the room and yelled, "Everyone, you need to stop what you are doing and listen to me. This is important! We all have a terrible drug problem." As he said this, everyone who wasn't in the middle of doing something downright bizarre immediately began to look around the room with puzzled looks of bewilderment on their faces. "Okay, as some of you might know already, I completely underestimated how much drugs would be consumed on this expedition to Nebraska, particularly the LSD, which means we need to find more acid before we leave here today."

That's when one hippy yelled out, "It's not just the LSD... we are going to need more mushrooms, too."

Then another hippy yelled, "Yeah, and you completely forgot to bring mescaline, ecstasy, molly, and ketamine." These comments seemed unanimously agreed upon, with nodding heads as I looked around the room.

"You also forgot about valium and DMT," one hippy added.

"Ya, how the hell did you forget about valium and DMT?" another hippy yelled out.

"Nobody forgot about valium and DMT, for Christ's sake! Anyway, it appears that you all seem to understand the gravity of this situation," Fredrick replied, waving his arms around in an animated attempt to secure his balance. This is when Fredrick fell off his chair and stumbled over to the suitcase of drugs. This was when he pulled out the untouched one-pound bag of cocaine that he had packed and stood back up on the chair.

At this point, even the hippies that were hallucinating their asses off started to pay attention, particularly after he started waving this giant bag of cocaine around while yelling, "I'm going to set a big pile of coke on the table, and I want you all to start doing lines to clear your heads. We need to face the facts about our drug problem. There is no way that we have enough drugs to last us three weeks. This means that we need to figure out how to find a lot more drugs before we leave Las Vegas."

After Fredrick said this, he climbed off the chair and poured a gigantic pile of coke onto a table at the front of the room. I watched everyone, including Anika and her friends, snorting several giant lines of cocaine, attempting to come up with some ways to solve their drug problem. Unfortunately, an entire hour passed without anyone even coming remotely close to coming up with any good ideas. Everyone seemed to be only slightly less fucked up than they were an hour ago, and it was now noon, which was our scheduled check-out time. At this point, I walked back to my room to see if I could wake Tracy up, but my best efforts failed again. This was when I realized I had no choice but to go down to the lobby and pay for Fredrick's and my room for one more night.

When I approached the front desk to pay for these rooms, I was far from confident that my plan to harvest the weed back in Nebraska would work out. By this time, I figured we would have already arrived in Nebraska. Unfortunately, we didn't even make it three hundred miles before the hippy caravan flew completely off the rails. I decided to grab some lunch after paying for the rooms and thought hard about abandoning my plans to harvest the weed altogether. By the time I finished my meal, I was convinced there was no way the hippy caravan would ever make it out of Las Vegas, and I definitely didn't think it was possible for us to harvest the weed on Billy's farm. I was now prepared to call this crazy expedition off and planned to drive the rest of the way to Nebraska by myself.

When I went back up to Fredrick's room, I expected to see thirty thousand dollars worth of failed expectations and eight members of the Psychedelic 40 rolling around on the floor, confirming a complete failure to move forward with my plans. However, when I walked through the door, it was nothing like I imagined. In the hour I spent eating lunch, the atmosphere in Fredrick's hotel room completely changed. Apparently, the effects of cocaine caused vastly different behavior than hallucinogenic drugs because Fredrick and the Psychedelic 40 were now sitting around the room looking like geniuses. They were all concentrating heavily on a dedicated effort to locate more drugs.

I remember most of the hippies having notebooks and pens in front of them. Some of them were suddenly wearing shoes and eyeglasses. Many were on their phones, having serious conversations with their drug dealers. One hippy was sitting in front of a computer creating a spreadsheet, while another sat beside him with a calculator. For the next four hours, I witnessed the most intense brainstorming session I had ever seen in my life. It was absolutely incredible!

Not only had Fredrick and the Psychedelic 40 transformed into a bunch of intellectual wizards, but they seemed to have formed some sort of union that followed a ridiculously organized voting procedure. At about five o'clock in the afternoon, Fredrick stood back on the chair in the front of the room with the balance of an Olympic gymnast and announced, "Okay, ladies and gentlemen, may I have your attention, please? It appears we have come up with a plan. After I explain this plan to everyone, we will vote by show of hands on the proposed solution to our drug problem. If the vote passes by a two-thirds majority vote, it will be ratified and put into action."

When he said this, the hippies put down their pens and closed their laptop computers to give Fredrick their full attention. "We have found someone that a few of you might know right here in Las Vegas who also attended the Umphrey's McGee concert last night," Fredrick said. "His name is Pimp Daddy. This man can locate forty sheets of acid, another half-pound of cocaine, two more pounds of mushrooms, and an extensive cocktail of Mexican pharmaceuticals.

This will include both ketamine and valium. Pimp Daddy has decided to come with us to Nebraska with these drugs so long as we are willing to pay him slightly more than the going rate for them."

"Hey, I know Pimp Daddy," one hippy yelled. "That asshole stole my girlfriend during the West Coast Phish tour back in 1999."

"I was on that tour too," another hippy said. "What was your girlfriend's name?

"Shela."

"I know Shela," the hippy replied. "She is that girl with a sleeve tattoo with a bunch of giraffes."

"Okay, enough about Shela and her goddamned tattoos," Fredrick said. "We need to concentrate on solving our drug problem."

"Our drug problem is worse than you think, Fredrick," yelled the hippy who was licking the bathroom mirror earlier in the day. "Pimp Daddy doesn't have enough drugs. We will need more acid than that!"

"Please, everyone! Wait till I am finished," Fredrick replied. "String Cheese Incident is playing two nights at Red Rocks in Denver, Colorado, beginning tomorrow night. We have a plan to attend this concert so we can pick up thirty more sheets of acid and two hundred Tweety Bird ecstasy pills. We may even be able to find some Mitsubishi's." I had no idea what Tweety Bird or Mitsubishi ecstasy was, but this seemed to be something the hippies were all pretty interested in.

"This all sounds great," one hippy said, "but how in the hell are we going to come up with enough money to pay Pimp Daddy?"

"Yeah, I don't even have enough money to buy lunch," another hippy added.

"And what about DMT, mescaline, and molly?" another hippy yelled.

"Settle down, everyone," Fredrick responded, "Oliver has plenty of money, and he has agreed to pay for the drugs. We are still working on DMT, molly, and mescaline, but I'm sure we will have something figured out by the time we get to Denver. Now, does anyone have any questions or concerns before we put this to a vote?"

"How many eight balls are in one and a half pounds of cocaine?" a hippy asked.

"One-hundred and ninety-two!" Fredrick answered.

"How many days is this going to take?" another hippy questioned.

"It has been estimated that it will take around three weeks to harvest and process the weed, assuming that there are six hundred pounds to farm."

"How much of that time will be spent trimming?" another hippy asked.

"Our goal is to get the first fifty pounds of weed cut down within two days of our arrival. I have a plan to begin to quickly cure and dry this weed. If all goes as planned, some of you will pivot and begin trimming on the sixth day of farming. Are there any more questions?" Fredrick asked, as he looked around the room. "Okay, all those in favor, raise your hand. I see one, three, seven hands raised. This means we have the votes to move forward."

# Chapter IV

Once all the votes were cast and the plan to solve the drug problem was ratified, I ordered room service to bring me a cheeseburger for dinner. I asked if anyone else was hungry, but everyone was too high on cocaine to eat anything. My mind was completely blown by what I had just witnessed. I didn't think it was possible to consume that much drugs and still be able to function. I figured all the hippies would be dead by now, but I guess I was wrong.

Fortunately, everything worked out perfectly when we arrived in Denver. The girls and I ended up getting baked before going to see *Scary Movie 2*. We stayed at a Holiday Inn in downtown Denver, while the hippies all went to see String Cheese Incident at Red Rocks. I fell asleep immediately that night feeling wonderful and woke the following morning feeling even better. After grabbing a donut and some coffee in the hotel lobby, I found the entire hippy caravan waiting outside with Pimp Daddy and a shit ton of drugs.

We crossed the Nebraska border later that evening and drove up the long driveway to Billy's house just before sunset. Erica was waiting for us all to arrive, and after some brief introductions, she came with us to go look at the field of marijuana. It took only about ten minutes to walk down the trail, through the field of corn, and down into the valley where the weed was growing.

When we looked at the marijuana field, Fredrick and the eight members of the Psychedelic 40 began to inspect the weed and quickly came up with some initial conclusions. The first thing they noticed was that there was more weed than anticipated. I had no idea how much weed was growing in this field, but Fredrick's estimate was about three acres. He also estimated that we would harvest at least six hundred pounds of processed bud. After careful inspection, the hippies concurred with Fredrick's estimate.

There were some other fortunate observations about this giant marijuana field that neither of us was expecting. One was that Billy had invested in a very elaborate irrigation system that provided the plants with water and a mixture of specialized fertilizers specific for growing weed. We also noticed that Billy was meticulous in putting plenty of space between plants, allowing buds to grow down the entire plant. In addition to the elaborate irrigation system and attention to detail, the high-quality seeds he purchased also seemed to pay off. All of these qualities together combined to help grow some fantastic outdoor marijuana. The hippies all seemed to be pretty impressed, which was saying a lot considering their profession, and all.

I went to sleep that night without knowing exactly what to expect regarding harvest. I only hoped that the nine members of the Psychedelic 40 were as good as Fredrick described. Surprisingly, by the time I woke up the following morning, the hippies had already been working on the harvest for three hours. Incidentally, I didn't know anything about this till around noon because Erica and I had spent the entire morning having marathon sex.

By the time I actually made it down to the field of marijuana, the hippies had already cut down a significant amount of weed, which was piled up into three piles about the size of a three-man tent. I stopped worrying about the performance of the Psychedelic 40 at this point, and it was only a little past noon on day one. Equipped with their specialized tools and plenty of drugs, they needed absolutely no instructions to harvest this weed. I felt so good about this situation that Erica and I just went back to the house early in the afternoon, and continued to enjoy each other's company. I think that we had more sex that day than we had all together before I fled to the West Coast. Thinking back on it, this may have been one of the best days of my life.

After Erica left for work early the following morning, I decided to square up with Pimp Daddy. I needed to get his stupid ass off the farm as soon as possible. This guy was nothing like Fredrick and the hippies, who wouldn't give a shit if the sky was falling so long as they were high as Willie Nelson having a joint smoking contest with Snoop Dogg. Pimp Daddy complained about absolutely everything, and this wasn't even the worst thing about his personality. From the time the hippy caravan left Las Vegas until we reached Nebraska two days later, he had already asked Anika, her three friends, and all three female hippies if they would suck his dick for coke.

My initial plan was to dig up the shoeboxes full of money that I buried under Erica's old house, but there was a lot that needed to be sorted out with transportation and getting everyone familiar with the farm. I also needed to get everybody fed, so I asked Anika to bring me into town to buy some pizza. When everything was sorted out, and we finally arrived back at the farm with the food, it was already after two o'clock in the afternoon.

Erica's shift ended at one o'clock, and she drove to the farm right after work. I remember pulling up into Billy's driveway and seeing

Erica running up to me before I even had time to stop the truck. "Oliver, oh my God, I am so happy to see you."

"Holy shit, Babe, what's wrong?" I asked, thinking that she saw a spider or something.

"Pimp Daddy asked if I wanted to see something about ten minutes ago."

"What?"

"Pimp Daddy asked if I wanted to see something about ten minutes ago," Erica repeated, "so I followed him into the barn, and do you know what that creep did?"

"What?"

"He threw a big Ziplock bag of coke down in front of me and pulled down his pants?"

"Where is Pimp Daddy right now?"

"I think he is still in the barn," Erica said.

"Okay, wait here until I get back."

I got out of the truck and immediately walked into Billy's house to look for a few things. First, I grabbed all my money I owed Pimp Daddy, and wrapped the wad of cash with a rubber band. I then wandered around the house, gathering a few more items. I found a toothpick, a glass plate, and two cans of beer. Then, I walked over to the barn, and there was Pimp Daddy with his dick in hand, standing in front of Jessica, of all people. He quickly zipped up when he saw me walking toward him.

"Hey, do you guys want to see a magic trick?" I asked.

"Okay," was a collective response.

"What kind of magic trick are you going to show us?" Jessica asked.

"Oh, you'll have to wait and see," I answered, while pulling out the wad of cash from my pocket. "This will be the greatest magic trick you have ever seen."

"Hey, Pimp Daddy, this is approximately fifteen thousand dollars, which is about how much I owe you, but since you are such a stud, I have decided to pay you double."

"Really?" Pimp Daddy asked.

"Yep," I replied, "but it's going to take some magic, and I'm going to need your help."

"Okay," Pimp Daddy responded with a puzzled look on his face. "What do I need to do?"

"First, I need you to put this toothpick in your mouth. Next, I need you to balance this plate on top of your head. Now, I'm going to hand you two cans of beer, one for your right hand and one for your left hand. Finally, you'll need to stretch your arms out all the way."

"Okay," Pimp Daddy replied, as he stretched his arms out.

"Are you ready?" I asked.

"I guess so," Pimp Daddy answered.

"Make sure to keep your eyes open because this magic trick happens real quick."

"Okay," Pimp Daddy said, as I kicked the toothpick out of his mouth and punched the two cans of beer simultaneously just before I kicked the plate on top of his head with a spinning roundhouse. The plate flew fifty feet across the barn like a frisbee before it broke against the wall. This all happened so fast that Pimp Daddy didn't even have time to blink. Then, I grabbed him by his long stupid hair that he constantly combed, and dragged him back over to the pick-up truck where Erica stood waiting for me.

"Hey Babe, will you grab the rope and roll of duct tape sitting in the cab of the truck for me?"

"What are you going to do to Pimp Daddy?" Erica asked with a concerned look on her face.

"I'm going to explain to him why he shouldn't have showed you his dick."

"You aren't going to hurt him, are you?"

"Nope, not going to be necessary."

"Okay, here is the rope and duct tape," Erica responded. "You promise that you aren't going to hurt Pimp Daddy. I don't want you going to jail again."

"I pinky promise," I said, while holding out my pinky finger.

"Okay," Erica replied, as she locked her pinky finger around mine.

"Why don't you walk down to the marijuana field and see what Fredrick is doing?" I said to Erica. "I need to have a little man-to-man chat with Pimp Daddy."

"Take your clothes off, Pimp Daddy," I said after I saw Erica disappear behind the barn.

"What? Why do you want me to take my clothes off?"

"You've been showing off your dick so much lately, I figured you'd want to show it to me too."

"I only show it to girls," Pimp Daddy responded.

"Not anymore, you don't."

"I'm not going to get naked in front of you."

I wrapped my arm around his neck as he said this and rolled backward, flipping Pimp Daddy and myself over with a unique variation of a piledrive throw technique, which placed us back on our feet standing, more or less in the same position as we were in a second earlier. "Take off your clothes, Pimp Daddy!" I demanded. "If I have to ask you again, I'll cut your dick off and shove it down your throat."

Pimp Daddy looked into my eyes and realized that I was not someone that he wanted to upset any more than he already had, which may have been the best decision of his life. His clothes came off in a quick hurry after this. I didn't say a word for the next twenty minutes or so while attaching Pimp Daddy to the front bumper of that old F-250 pickup truck with twenty feet of rope and a whole roll of duct tape. There wasn't anything I needed or wanted to say to him. I just started up the truck and backed down the driveway until it intersected with County Road 10. Then, I revved up the engine, put it in gear, and took off down the gravel road.

After upshifting four times, I pressed the gas pedal to the floor for two or three minutes and got the truck going down the gravel road at almost ninety miles an hour. Going that fast on gravel was incredibly dangerous, but I didn't slow down or stop for several miles. I wasn't afraid of death, gravel, or country roads, and I figured at least one of us deserved to die that day.

I sped north down a series of gravel roads for about forty-five minutes till I reached the jeep trail that led over to the spillway of Lake McConaughy. This is when I took out my buck knife and cut Pimp Daddy loose from the bumper of my truck. On the way to the lake, he had shit and pissed himself. It got all over the bumper, so I used his hair to clean it off. I then tied the rope around his ankle and dangled him over the 120-foot tall dam for a few minutes. When I pulled him back up, he was so terrified that he couldn't talk. He just laid on the ground vomiting and reeking of human biomatter.

"How many wads of cash do you see, Mr. Pimp Daddy?" I asked, while pulling him up off the ground by his leg. Unfortunately, Pimp Daddy couldn't answer me. He was speechless. "I see that you are having some trouble answering my question, Pimp Daddy, so just nod your head if you see two wads of cash." I stood there looking at Pimp Daddy for about thirty seconds, and he didn't move an inch. He was so scared of me that his face was pure white. This asshole wasn't even able to blink. "You don't see any wads of cash, do you Pimp Daddy?" I stood there looking at him for another thirty seconds or so. I had never seen anyone go this long without blinking their eyes. "There is your magic trick."

I don't know what happened to Pimp Daddy after leaving him naked next to the Lake McConaughy dam, but I told him not to show his dick to women without their permission. Since I've never seen him again, I can't be certain if he followed my instructions, but I'd bet the wad of cash I owed him that he never flashed his dick at another woman ever again.

I want to explain that what I did that day is not how I'd handle the situation now, but I was a country boy with little understanding of laws when I was eighteen years old. I didn't know how they pertained to seeking justice for not only what Pimp Daddy had done to Erica, but what he had likely been doing to nearly every woman he met. Back in 2001, you'd find yourself in a world of hurt if you attempted to sexually persuade Erica with a bag of drugs. Pimp Daddy learned this the hard way. Sometimes laws don't understand justice, and sometimes justice didn't understand me. I don't know what I'd do if this same thing were to occur today, but I can tell you that I don't regret what I did that day. I made Pimp Daddy think really hard about what he had done to Erica and the females that came out to help with the marijuana harvest. I left him naked, penniless, and incredibly frightened of not just me, but the whole world around him. Most human beings will never experience the level of terror I bestowed on that man, but I can guarantee that he eventually found some clothes and left Nebraska a better person.

I was getting really tired of dealing with drunk, naked perverts. It was as if I won the world's reverse lottery with these asshats. I dealt with more perverts that summer than I've encountered ever since. I have had to deal with a dozen or so assholes who needed to be taught a lesson about respecting women, but not many more perverts. To be clear, this doesn't include my nemesis and his horrible acquaintances, but I will get to that later.

When I got back to the farm, I walked down to the field of marijuana to look for Erica. I wasn't surprised to see her helping out Fredrick. She really liked Fredrick, which was understandable. Fredrick is one of the most awesome and polite people I have ever met. When I walked down into the valley, they were laughing and giggling about something that beautiful people think about after they smoke a joint. After kissing Erica and fist-bumping Fredrick, we started to discuss what needed to happen to make everyone happy for the next three weeks.

Fredrick's input was perfect, "Oliver, we are going to need a lot of beer, some bottles of water, rolling papers, and more pizza."

"Is there anything else you can think of?" I asked.

"Mmmm.... nope. I think that'll do it, Buddy."

"Okay, I will drive into town to grab these things for you," I replied. "What kind of toppings do you want on your pizza?

"Onions, pepperoni, green peppers, olives, jalapenos, mushrooms, sausage, pineapple, Canadian bacon, normal bacon, spinach, pesto, shrimp, pickles, and extra cheese," Fredrick responded as he looked up at the sky, seeming to search for answers. "Oh, and would you mind getting some breadsticks?"

"Sure, not a problem."

"And there is just one more thing if it's not too much to ask," Fredrick said with a look of concern.

"What's that?"

"Will you get some extra marinara sauce?" Fredrick asked. "I always seem to run out of sauce before I finish my breadsticks."

"You got it," I replied.

"You're the best, Buddy."

When Erica and I went back into town to get the short list of things that Fredrick thought would make him happy, Erica had a little more foresight into the human aspect of this situation. These logistics, in particular, were some of the most important to work out. All of the workers who were employed to help harvest the marijuana field would need blankets, shelter, and food, so we stopped by Walmart to buy these things.

We ran by the furniture store after picking up the necessities, and I bought a lot of furniture. I loaded up the long bed of the truck with as many couches, chairs, and La-Z-boy recliners as I possibly could. If you live in a metropolitan area, you've had to have seen a few crazy ass junk collectors driving around. These are a unique group of eccentric people who stack so much shit up on their trucks that it looks like they are trying to win a million-dollar contest to see who can look like the biggest dumpster-diving meth addict.

Anyway, that's what my truck looked like going back out to the farm.

For some reason, I initially just imagined everyone crashing at Billy's house, but there was nowhere close to enough room for this. Erica and I also spent an awful lot of time having sex in there while we were out at the farm, so it wasn't an ideal situation to crash in Billy's house much during the first few days anyway. The fact that Anika had a car and her friends could stay in a hotel helped with logistical issues regarding sleeping accommodations.

Unfortunately, I didn't feel comfortable bringing any of the hippies into town. This was partly due to the fact that their appearance would make them stick out like a sore thumb, but it was mostly because there was no way to stop them from smoking copious amounts of weed. It would be a decade before any state would vote to end the prohibition of weed. Nevertheless, laws did not seem to exist in the minds of the hippies, and so it was already more than legal in their minds. I could see a redneck calling the police just based on their appearance. Then there were people like my dad, who were loose cannons when reacting to subcultures. I had no idea what he would do if he saw a hippy walking around town smoking a joint.

The good thing was that none of this mattered to the hippies. They were perfectly content staying on the farm. It helped that they didn't all seem to go to sleep at the same time. This was largely due to a vast difference in what drugs they had decided to do that day.

I put all this furniture in the barn for them to crash and hang out on. They loved to sit around and smoke joints on this furniture, but I rarely saw them sleeping in the barn. When the hippies got tired, they laid down wherever the hell this happened and went to sleep. This was a fascinating group of people, and their bazaar culture grew on me over time. I really started to like having them around. In addition to being badass marijuana farmers, their obscure habits were a constant form of entertainment.

In addition, several other overall logistics needed to be worked out, but by the second or third day, everything seemed to be working like a well-oiled machine. I didn't even get involved much with the harvest. When I realized just how incredibly efficient the Psychedelic 40 were at their jobs, my best effort would appear to be a joke.

Anika and her friends also initially seemed to lack purpose. By the time one of the marijuana farmers from the Psychedelic 40 explained what the girls should be doing, that single farmer could have completed more work than all four of the girls combined. Fortunately, this all seemed to be worked out by the third day as well. This was when some of the harvested weed was transported back to the barn in preparation for processing. The girls filled the back of the old F-250 pickup truck with the harvested weed and then brought it over to the barn to be processed.

The girls also catered food for everyone. This was a huge undertaking because there were seventeen of us, including Fredrick, all the hippies, Anika, her friends, Erica, and myself. Occasionally, our friend Sherly would even stop by. She didn't participate in helping out with the harvest at all. She mostly sat around smoking joints and petting Fredrick's dog, but she ate plenty of food when it was available.

All this, in addition to a few other minor tasks, kept the girls busy for six to eight hours daily. They never seemed to start work earlier than ten, nor did I see them work much past dinner time. This was in contrast to the hippies who seemed to work around the clock, wanting to stop only to take bathroom breaks or short naps.

This didn't necessarily mean the girls returned to their motel rooms in Ogallala right after work, particularly after figuring out Fredrick's unique talent. I noticed that the girls all started to call Fredrick by his nickname, Mr. Magic Tongue, after only a couple of days. In addition to the three female hippies, Anika and her friends hung out around him like a bunch of groupies accosting a rock star.

Jasmine, the girl I met in Seattle, told me about this nickname and that he was a legend amongst the females on the Phish tour, but I only partially believed her. Apparently, she wasn't lying because I even saw Jessica hitting on Fredrick, and as I understood, she had a very strict lesbian diet. In any case, the girls constantly walked around the farm with obscure smiles of sexual satisfaction, which made them all pleasant as hell to be around. This was just another great thing about Fredrick. He kept female tempers at bay like nothing I'd ever seen before. I kept this information in the back of my head for the rest of my life and went down on Erica as many times as possible to keep her good mood elevated.

# Chapter V

By the end of the third day, I was so ecstatic about how smoothly things were going that, outside of a little supervision, Erica and I completely stopped participating in the farming operation. This gave us plenty of time to concentrate our efforts on having sex multiple times a day. We managed to go two years without having sex, and now we wanted to make up for that lost time. We had only three weeks to satisfy two year's worth of sexual cravings, and we tried our best to make sure our sexual goals were accomplished.

Erica seemed to have a better handle on things than I did when it came to sex. Incidentally, she was not afraid to tell me exactly what she thought of my prowess and how to make it better. I wasn't into porno videos, so I collectively only watched about ten minutes of porn in my life. This all changed the night that our hippy caravan arrived in Nebraska.

Erica kept her porn fetish a secret from me for the past two years because I never heard her mention a word about watching porn before, so it caught me by total surprise when she brought in an entire backpack full of porno videos the night I arrived. The results of watching all this porn caused us to try all sorts of new things sexually. I remember one particular conversation that occurred on the fourth night that heavily influenced our sex life.

"Hey, Oliver, do you think I am good at sex?" Erica asked.

"Yeah, you are really good at it," I replied.

"What about me?" I asked. "Do you think I am good at sex?"

"I think you could get better if we practiced enough," she replied. I wasn't sure if that was what she intended to say or not, but I suddenly felt inadequate.

"What could I get better at?" I asked, curious to know if it was something easy to remedy.

"Lots of things, actually," she replied. This statement made me feel even worse. I felt like maybe I was really doing something wrong.

"Please elaborate. I didn't realize I was that bad at sex," I replied baffled by my underperformance.

"Okay, so the first time we have sex, you know, in the morning, when we first wake up...you always want to face me for some reason. It's not that I don't want to look at you or anything, but I'd really like it if I woke up being spooned with your dick poking me in the ass."

"Every morning?" I asked.

"No, not every morning, but maybe some mornings," Erica replied. "There are sometimes I think I would like to really get fucked aggressively and hard in this position. I think I'd probably like it if you even pulled my hair sometimes or even slapped my ass, just like in some of the porno videos we watch."

"Really," I responded, like a deer in headlights.

"Yes, really."

"When you say you want to be fucked hard... umm... aahhh... how hard do you want me to fuck you?"

"As hard as you possibly can, Oliver, and I'll answer your next dumb question because I can see it written on your forehead," Erica said, with a slightly annoyed look on her face. "When it comes to pulling my hair and slapping my ass, start off gently and get more aggressive as we continue to have sex. I will tell you if it hurts. Oh, and talk dirty to me sometimes, too. Say the nastiest things that you can think of but don't ever call me slut. Remember that, Oliver. If you ever call me a slut during sex, I'll slap you so hard that your teeth will go flying out of the back of your head."

"Okay... pull your hair, slap your ass, and talk dirty, but don't ever call you a slut. Got it." I replied, feeling very impressed with Erica's ability to read my mind and oddly thankful that she answered my questions without me even asking them.

"And instead of turning me over to cum on my stomach like you always do, I'd like you to pick some other places to cum," Erica said, with an oddly commanding yet polite tone in her voice.

"Like where?" I asked, like an absolute idiot.

"Anywhere but on my stomach," she replied.

"Like on your legs or tits?"

"Yeah, my tits would be ok, but not my legs. Oh my God, Oliver, do you watch porn with your goddamned eyes closed or something?" Erica replied. "On my tits if you are fucking me in a missionary position. Or even on my face if you want, or if we are fucking doggy style, you don't even have to turn me over. You can just cum on my ass, or for that matter, in my ass."

"Are you serious?" I asked. "That's what you really want?"

"Maybe... I don't know yet because we haven't tried this stuff."

"Well, I guess... just tell me what you want me to do, and I will do it," I replied.

"I'm going to fill you in on a little dark secret of mine," Erica said, "but I don't want you to freak out, okay."

"Okay," I responded, now wondering how many dark secrets she had when it came to sex.

"When I watch porn with you, it's not because I need extra help getting horny. If I needed extra help getting horny, I'd just ask you to lick my clit, which is one thing you are really good at. Okay, before I put my foot in my mouth, I should probably ask... why do you think I like to watch porn with you?"

"I don't know, really," I reluctantly replied. The guys have really big dicks, I guess... girls seem to like big dicks."

"See, that's what I thought," Erica responded. "You're an idiot sometimes!"

"Why am I an idiot," I asked. "So, you don't like big dicks?"

"The reason why I want to watch porn with you isn't that I like to watch slutty women getting fucked by a big dick... well... this is very little of the reason anyway. The main reason I want to watch porn with you is that I'm hoping that we learn how to have better sex." A lightbulb in my head went on when she said this. Erica is a little ditzy in cute little ways pertaining mostly to worldly affairs, but she is very insightful when it comes to things that apply to practical life. She just has a way of making things better, and this was a perfect example of this.

The fourth day of harvest was one of the strangest days I had ever experienced, at least up until this point in my life. I would say that it was one of the strangest days of my life, period, but as you read on, you'll understand the competition this had. How that morning started out would make it seem like I was destined to have a fantastic day. I woke up at about 5 am from Erica giving me a blowjob. I don't know how long Erica had been sucking my dick or how I ended up with an erection in my sleep, but she was really going at it. She didn't even look up for at least ten minutes.

At this point in my life, this was the best blowjob I had ever received for two reasons. The first was that it set a new record for the longest blowjob Erica had ever given me. She usually made me cum in three minutes or less. The other reason was she seemed to be getting as much pleasure from this blowjob as I was. After listening to sounds of slurping, sucking, and intense sexual pleasure since the moment I woke up, she finally paused to ask, "Do you want to cum on my face?"

"Yeah, if you want me to."

"I definitely want you to, Oliver."

"Okay, how do you want me to do this?"

"Ummm... let me lay down... ah... then straddle my chest and jack off."

This new sexual experience ended with fun-loving, horny teenage giggling and giant wads of cum on Erica's face. This caused us to quickly jump in the shower to wash the jizz off. After several minutes of passionately kissing and rubbing soap on each other's bodies, Erica guided me back to her bedroom by gently pulling me by my cock down the hallway and back onto her bed.

This turned into aggressive doggie-style sex while trying to fulfill another one of Erica's recently described sexual fantasies. With the assistance of dirty talk, slapping her ass, and tugging her hair, my pulsating cock brought Erica to a screaming orgasm in a quick hurry. This was the first time she ever reached an orgasm while having sex. Erica left her bedroom experiencing a new level of satisfaction, and I felt like an absolute fucking stud.

I had no idea why we were up so early, and I also didn't have any idea why Erica's father was up so early. The sun hadn't even thought about hitting the horizon yet. I remember walking down the stairs and into the kitchen, following the aroma of freshly brewed coffee. This is when our giggling love and happy hearts met Erica's Dad sitting at the dining room table. We sat down at this table, grinning from ear to ear, with the expression of sex written all over our joyful teenage faces, and this was when Erica's father greeted me,

"Good morning, Oliver," Erica's dad said. "How are you doing this morning?"

"I'm doing great," I replied. "How are you doing?"

"Just fine, thanks for asking, Oliver. Would either of you like a cup of coffee?"

"I would," Erica said.

"I would like one too," I answered.

Moments later, I sat with Erica and her dad, drinking coffee. I sat at one end of the table. Erica's Dad sat at the other end of the table, and Erica sat on a chair in the middle. For several minutes, little, if any, conversation transpired. We just sat there peacefully, drinking our cups of coffee. In the abundance of silence, I sat across from Erica's dad, reflecting on my efforts to pay for his heart transplant. While pondering this noble goal, a feeling of vindication was observed through Erica's love for her father.

That morning also made me realize that Erica's Dad admired his daughter with no less than all the love in the world. This affection he felt for Erica was a specific type of love that I couldn't understand yet. This would be something I would learn in time, particularly after Erica and I had our first child. Nevertheless, on this day, we each shared a common interest. This was to love Erica. The realization of this common interest enriched my dedication to saving this man's life and verified this specific goal of mine to be righteous. I will never forget how inspired I felt to run away with this goal and never look back as the silence was finally broken.

"So, Oliver, it sounded like you did a really good job at having sex with my daughter this morning because I heard her yell, "Fuck me harder," and you did because I heard this terrifying sound all the way down in the basement where my bedroom is. Of course, there is an air vent that goes straight up from my room to hers, which helps to amplify things a little bit. Hell, who am I kidding? It amplifies things a lot." This bone-chilling moment wasn't something I would ever want to relive. I remember Erica's Dad looking into my eyes as he asked, "Do you know what woke me up this morning, Oliver?"

"Umm... your alarm clock?" I said after spending about thirty seconds trying to clear the lump out of my throat.

"That's a good guess, Oliver, but I'm retired, and I also suffer from severe heart complications, so I don't set an alarm out of an abundance of caution that I don't suffer another heart attack from the loud sound they make," Erica's Dad said all this very calmly. Then, he turned toward Erica, "Maybe you might know what woke me up this morning?"

"Did you have to go pee really bad?" Erica said after a long pause.

"That's a good guess, too, but it is also a wrong answer," Erica's Dad replied. "What actually woke me up this morning was when I heard Erica yell, "I want to feel your hot cum all over my face!" It sounded like you also did a pretty good job at this, Oliver."

I nearly died when I heard this comment. These words left me petrified! I had no idea what to do or say. Erica turned toward me with her eyes wide open. The look of terror on her face was a reflection of what I felt at that moment. Her mouth started to move, but no words came out.

"You are a multi-talented young man, Oliver. You didn't just pleasure my daughter this morning. You taught me things about her that I didn't even know about. Since I'm Erica's father, I thought I knew everything about her, but I guess I didn't. Thanks to you, now I know that my daughter has a tight vagina. If I didn't hear you describe this particular body part three or four times this morning, I might have gone my entire life without knowing a damn thing about my daughter's vagina. Since you taught me so much about my daughter this morning, I'd like to return the favor by teaching you something as well." This is when Erica's father stood up from his chair and looked deep into my eyes. His voice suddenly changed from being calm to a horrific tone of terror as he said, "If you get my daughter pregnant, you are going to regret ever being born."

After these terrifying words were spoken, Erica's Dad looked at me with the creepiest smile I had ever seen. His expression was telling me to get the fuck out of his house, and these feelings were reciprocated by my intentions to leave and never come back. Erica and I beat greased lighting in a foot race out the front door.

When we got inside my truck, I hit the gas pedal so hard that I made the tires squeal on a 1986 long-bed pickup truck, which I wouldn't have thought possible unless I heard the sound of its screeching tires. As I tore off down the road and passed the city limits, Erica and I didn't know if we should cry, cry harder... or drown ourselves in Lake McConaughy. Rather than making a decision about this and potentially committing to something we might regret, we agreed to completely avoid any further thoughts on the matter. We pinky promised never to talk about this horrific glitch

matrix or anything about what we experienced during what, otherwise, would have been a perfect morning.

50

# Chapter VI

I DIDN'T PAY ANY attention to where I was driving when I drove away from Erica's house. At some point, I turned off the highway and started to drive down a series of long dirt roads. This place on planet Earth created an interesting trifecta of farmland. There were fields of wheat, fields of corn, and fields of sunflowers. At this time in my life, I didn't consider Nebraska to be a particularly beautiful place. I felt that this was especially true when I compared the sandy beaches of the Pacific Ocean to the shores of Lake McConaughy, for instance. I didn't think any place in Nebraska matched the beauty I saw while driving through the Rocky Mountains or traveling up the West Coast on Highway 101.

However, there was one glaring exception to my jaded perception of America's heartland. This was during the three months of fall when the lackluster scenery hiding in the fields of Nebraska came into bloom and suddenly became known as God's country. Red spring and durum wheat would begin harvest in August and continue all the way through September. If the wind blew hard enough, it would create golden waves of exquisite beauty all across these wheat fields. This incredible phenomenon was truly something amazing to see.

I never found the corn fields to be attractive until after the corn was finished being harvested. These fields would then become a pheasant and deer hunter's paradise. During the late fall and early winter, people who enjoyed hunting found incredible beauty in rural Nebraska. This obscure attraction may have been in the eye of the beholder, but I thought there was nothing more splendid than seeing Daisy, our well-trained English Springer Spaniel, working a cornfield and retrieving pheasants for my dad and me.

Moreover, the fields I found unrivaled and exceptionally beautiful were when the sunflowers were ready to be harvested. This would start mid-August and last as late as the third week in September. It was the fourth day of this expedition on September 18th, 2001. While on the way to the marijuana farm, Erica and I passed by a few of these sunflower fields that hadn't been cut down yet. It couldn't have been much past six thirty when we decided to park alongside one of these fields and watch the sunrise.

I remember opening the passenger door and helping Erica climb out of this old Ford F-250 pickup truck. We held each other's hand as a faint orange glow and the night sky were still casting shadows. It seemed to take only minutes for a deep purple horizon to turn into a brilliant blue and burning amber. We watched the fiery fire of sunlight rise into the eastern sky and illuminate millions of yellow sunflowers.

Erica and I stood there looking at all these joyful plants dancing in the wind for several minutes on that warm summer morning until we were suddenly distracted by a giant butterfly fluttering its wings above the sunflower field. We watched as it began to fly toward us, and then it landed right on top of Erica's head. This is when I said to Erica, "Don't move!"

"Why?" Erica asked.

"Because the butterfly just landed on your head."

"Really?" she replied.

"Yes, really!"

Then Erica held out her arms while trying to remain completely still. There was no way for her to see this butterfly, but I could tell by her pretty smile and rolling eyes that she really wanted to see the butterfly on her head, "Is it still there?" she asked.

"Yes," I told her, and for that moment, I swear that I stood in heaven looking at an angel with a butterfly on her head.

After watching the sunrise, Erica and I returned to the truck and continued driving to Billy's farm. When we drove up the long driveway, I was pleased to see that Anika and her friends had already made breakfast. After breakfast, Erica and I walked down the trail that led to the marijuana field. I was happy to see how much progress had been made. It appeared that nearly half the field had already been cut down and organized into piles.

Anika and her friends had already transported several of these piles to the barn to get ready to be processed. Two members of the Psychedelic 40 were supposed to pivot later in the day and begin to process the harvested weed that was brought to the barn. Fredrick anticipated that Anika and her friends would be able to help out with some simple tasks when it came to processing. I wasn't clear on what processing entailed, but it was my best guess that we were ahead of schedule. Since everything appeared to be going very well, I started to think about a tentative list of tasks I planned to complete that day. However, before Erica and I started back up the trail, Fredrick ran behind me and tapped me on the shoulder.

"Hey, Buddy, I have a few concerns that need to be addressed, and I am hoping you can help," Fredrick said.

"Sure," I answered. "What can I do?"

"Some of the Psychedelic 40 farmers forgot to bring gloves and are getting sore hands," Fredrick said. "I was wondering if you could maybe go into town and pick up six or seven pairs of gloves."

"Yeah, absolutely," I responded. "Erica and I can leave right now. What kind of gloves do you need?"

"Gardening gloves," Fredrick said. "If you can't find gardening gloves, then look for some sort of thin utility gloves."

"You got it," I replied. "I'll leave as soon as we get back to the truck."

"Wait, there is more!" Fredrick responded.

"Okay, sorry," I replied. "I'll get whatever you need."

"Alright, cool. There really isn't anything major here," Fredrick said. "We also need some band-aids, more toilet paper, some toothpaste and toothbrushes, a couple of cartons of cigarettes, and maybe ten cases of beer."

"Okay, I need to find a piece of paper and a pen to write all this stuff down," I replied. "I thought that Anika and her friends were handling this type of thing."

"They were, and they have been," Fredrick said. "These issues just surfaced this morning, and I already made a list for you. Here it is."

"Awesome!" I responded. "Is there anything else?"

"There is one more thing," Fredrick said with heightened sympathy and concern. "A couple of the farmers lost their shoes somewhere on this farm and have no idea where they put them. Would you mind picking them up some new shoes?"

"Yeah, no problem," I replied. "What size do they wear?"

"That is also on the list I gave you."

"Hell, yeah, thanks for being on top of it. Erica and I will go into town and come back this afternoon as soon as we gather these things up for you." I said, somewhat surprised at Fredrick's commitments and wanting to make sure the rest of the hippies were well taken care of.

"Do you have enough money for all of this?" Fredrick asked. "I noticed your giant wad of cash wasn't a wad anymore."

"I think I will have enough money for this," I answered. "Actually, that was one of the things I had planned for today. When I get back, I will have to dig up my secret stash of cash."

"Okay, cool... I guess that I will see you this afternoon."

"Oh, wait, before I go," I said after taking a few steps back up the trail. "Hey, do you have that one hitter you like so much? Erica will likely have to do most of the shopping because I'm still on the DL. This means I will spend a lot of time chilling in the truck, and I don't have any inconspicuous way to smoke weed."

"Alright, I guess I'll loan you my one-hitter," Fredrick reluctantly answered. "Here you go, Buddy, but whatever you do... DON'T LOSE THAT PIPE! I have had it forever. It's one of my most cherished possessions."

"Don't worry," I responded. "I'll give it back to you later this afternoon. Oh, and one more thing... If I take the truck into town for a few hours, will that set us back in any way?"

"It shouldn't," Fredrick replied. "We will be in full swing by tomorrow and ready to start processing, so you'll have to figure out some other way to get around because that box van won't work."

"Yeah, and that could raise some suspicions with the local farmers," I replied. "My old truck flies under the radar pretty easily, so I'll have to figure out something else. We will see you in a few hours," I said, as I turned around and started back up the trail hand in hand with Erica. When we got back to the barn, I thought of asking Anika and her friends to take care of the errands for Fredrick. I stopped short of doing this because a couple of hippies were still eating breakfast, and they looked pretty busy dealing with the catering. It also sounded like Fredrick had some projects for them in the afternoon.

I didn't have enough time to think everything through, so I wasn't opposed to chipping in on the work for a few hours. It was convenient that Erica also had the entire day off, so I didn't have to go into the stores. I planned to sit in the truck and smoke pot while Erica did the actual shopping. It wasn't like this was a super extensive list or anything. It required quick stops at one or two places, depending on how many things could be purchased at Walmart.

Everything was going according to plan it seemed. Within an hour of getting back into town, we bought everything on the list that Fredrick had given me, except for their beer and shoes. We decided to pick up the beer last, so we headed to the shoe store. After buying the shoes, Erica and I felt a little hungry, so we stopped at the Taco Bell drive-through.

Right after we ordered our food and were asked to pull ahead to the drive-through window, I noticed a police car pull up behind me. At this point, the officer didn't seem to have any interest in my truck or me, but I started to panic anyway, so I grabbed the bag of weed out of my pocket and tried to eat it all. I even convinced Erica to grab a handful to eat. There was only about a quarter ounce in this bag, so consuming the whole bag wasn't a big problem. We had it all eaten before our food was even ready, and the police officer still didn't seem to be paying any attention to us.

Unfortunately, I noticed his lights come on just as we were handed our food, but since I didn't hear any sirens, I pulled away, hoping his lights were turned on by accident. Unfortunately, this was not an accident because he turned on his sirens and peeled around the corner after us. Before the officer had time to get to the window, my paranoid thoughts convinced me to reluctantly put Fredrick's pipe in between my butt cheeks.

"Well, well, well... if it isn't Oliver. I was planning to warn you that your tags were put on backward. The way you stuck the tags on your license plate would indicate that it was the year 120 and not 2001," the officer said. This happened to be Deputy James O'Hare, the officer involved in my arrest. "Unfortunately for you, I will not be able to let you go with a warning today. You should have accepted my offer because you wouldn't have any pending charges."

"What charges do I have pending?" I asked, acting dumb while experiencing a minor panic attack. "I thought the charges were dropped."

"Yeah, well, you have some interesting parents, I can tell you that much," the officer replied. "I never formally met your Mom or your Dad before all this... and, well... they... anyways, you still have a warrant for misdemeanor possession of marijuana. If you cooperate and don't make a fuss about your arrest, the other charges are likely to be ignored. Go ahead, wait here for a minute, and don't try any funny business.

At this point, I saw the deputy walk back to his police cruiser and appear to make a phone call for backup. When I saw him walk into Taco Bell, I started freaking out pretty bad. This would have been a great time to discuss a plan for her to bail me out and return the truck to the marijuana farm in the meantime. Unfortunately, the short conversation we managed to have didn't amount to anything constructive.

A few minutes later, the deputy walked out of Taco Bell and back to his police cruiser with a bag of food. This was about the time two other police officers arrived on the scene. I then watched the deputy get out of his police cruiser with a burrito in his hand and have a short conversation with the other two officers. It didn't take long before this conversation led them to my window.

"Alright, Oliver, step out of your vehicle and put your hands behind your head," the deputy said before he proceeded to pat me down and put handcuffs on me. "You are under arrest for an outstanding warrant for the possession of one ounce, or less, of marijuana. You have the right to remain silent. Anything you say can and will be used against you in a court of law. You have the right to an attorney. If you cannot afford an attorney, one will be provided for you. Do you understand the rights I have just read to you? With these rights in mind, do you wish to tell me anything?"

"Not that I can think of," I answered.

"Well, if you think of anything, just let me know," the deputy said before leading me to his police cruiser and putting me in the back seat.

I had a tough time walking without Fredrick's pipe falling out from my butt cheeks, but I ended up making it. I thought at this point that I would be brought into jail without much further to do, but the police forced Erica out of the truck as well. They then searched through the vehicle and patted Erica down before letting her go. Just before the officers returned to their cruisers, I saw her walk down the street.

When the deputy got inside his car, he asked me what all the shoes and gloves were for. I stumbled over my words for a few seconds before I said, "I don't know, it's something to do with a volunteer project my girlfriend is involved with."

"Okay, that's interesting," the deputy replied. "Well, maybe you also know who Anika is and why the truck you were driving was registered in her name out of California."

"That is Erica's friend," I answered. "She just moved here."

"Alright, we might have to ask her a few questions if we run into her again."

"Are you sure there is nothing else you want to tell me about before we take you into custody? It seems like you are pretty nervous."

"No, I have nothing to say," I responded.

"Okay, then," the officer said, as he started to drive out of the Taco Bell parking lot. "You know that your Dad was just in jail. You missed him by only a week."

"Yeah, I heard about that," I answered.

"Oh, I thought he would have told you himself," the officer said. "When did you get back into town? I heard some rumors that you went out to California."

"A few days ago,"

"Haven't you been home yet?"

"I have been staying with my girlfriend," I said. "I was planning to go home tonight."

"I see," the deputy shrugged. "Well, you might be happy to know that your friend, Adam, is still in custody. You might even get to see him if you make it into the general population."

"Why would that make me happy?" I asked.

"I just figured that you might enjoy shooting some hoops or playing spades with him," the officer said.

I was asked if I wanted to make a phone call when I arrived at the Ogallala Detention Center. This would have been an excellent opportunity to call a bail bondsman or my folks. I could have even called Erica to ask her to bail me out, but I would have been afraid of her Dad answering the phone. The biggest reason I never made a phone call was that I didn't understand the booking process or know my rights. The last time I was in jail was not a typical experience. In any case, I never took advantage of this opportunity to make a phone call.

I ended up getting put in a standard, low-risk jail cell with one other person. When I first was put into the cell, there was an old man on the floor making noises that would indicate he was in pain. He had a scruffy beard with nappy hair and looked like he had never seen a shower before. He was lying in a pile of puke, which had gotten on his shirt and beard. I could see that his pants were also soiled. In addition to the disgusting smells of piss and shit, his body reeked almost as bad as the fat person I sat next to on the bus ride from Seattle to San Francisco.

This cell was tiny. It had one bunk bed and a toilet with a drinking fountain attached to the back of it. The bottom bunk bed, as well as the toilet, had puke and shit all over it. When I climbed up to the top bunk bed, I thought about this horrible situation and tried to devise a plan. One tiny window right next to the bed let in some sunlight and offered a partial view of the police station parking lot. I spent the rest of the day looking out this window for answers.

I was provided a dinner meal, but I never touched any of it except for a small carton of milk. My stomach was in knots, and the food looked awful. I finally fell asleep around midnight. This was not a very good night of rest. I tossed and turned until early the following morning when another tray of food was provided. Shortly after this, the door to my cell was opened, and a couple of officers came into it. One of the officers started to tend to my cellmate. The other took me out of the cell and led me down to the first floor. After walking through a series of doors, I was eventually led into a small internal police station courtroom.

Five other inmates, along with myself had a court appearance that morning. This was something that I had no idea was going to happen, and I also didn't know how to respond to the judge when she asked me if I wanted to plead innocent or guilty. If I had pleaded guilty, I likely would have been let out that day with a small fine and some community service. Unfortunately, I didn't know this, so I made the mistake of pleading innocent.

I noticed that some of the other people in court were offered a recognizance bond, which let them out of jail with the promise to return on their next court date. I was not given this opportunity, likely because I fled the last time I promised to return to the police station. I figured this was also why the judge issued me such a high bond. I usually would have been given a five hundred dollars or less bond, but I was given a five thousand dollar bond.

After court, I was brought to another large jail cell with ten other inmates. Everyone was still in the clothes that they were arrested in. We all sat in this cell for about an hour without an official explanation for what we were doing there. The people in the cell had speculations, and the most agreed-upon explanation was that we were about to get dressed in clothes provided by the Department of Corrections. One person seemed familiar with this process and noted that it was Friday. He said they were likely trying to get us into the general population before the weekend because the opportunity to make bail wouldn't resume until Monday. They did this to clear out the holding cells in order to make room for the people who would get arrested over the weekend.

After about an hour, we were all given a brown bag of food containing an apple, a bologna sandwich, and a small carton of milk. Someone asked the officer what we were doing in this cell at this point, and he replied, "You are about to get your ass searched." Then he walked away without saying anything else.

I started to panic when he said this because I still had Fredrick's pipe hiding between my butt cheeks. Throughout this whole ordeal, I somehow managed to keep it from falling out by repositioning it several times and clenching my ass muscles together when I walked. If what the officer had just said was the truth, I needed to remove it before the impending cavity search, or else I would get caught with it.

I didn't know what would happen to someone who got caught with a pipe in their ass while in police custody, and I didn't want to find out. After some quick thinking, I moved into the corner and inconspicuously removed the pipe from my ass. Then, I quickly shoved it into the brown paper bag and hid it between the two slices of bread from my sandwich. After I put the sandwich back into the Ziplock bag, I put all my food back into the brown bag and tossed it in the corner. Finally, I moved to the other side of the room.

I managed to do all this without anyone noticing, and it was just in time. Less than a minute after sitting back down, an officer opened the cell door. I was freaking out! Plagued with a panic attack, I was sweating profusely as we were all led down the hallway and around the corner of the detention center. From there, we were all placed in a single file line in front of an officer sitting on a chair wearing some plastic gloves. One by one, we were all going to get asked to pull down our pants and spread our butt cheeks apart.

I don't know what this guy did to get this job. I can't imagine that he planned to become a cavity search specialist, but he appeared to enjoy what he was doing for a living. At the very least, he didn't seem to mind looking at sweaty butt cracks and hairy asses. He got his flashlight out. Then he'd say with a big smile, "Let's spread'em." At this point, he would shine his flashlight up someone's ass and start to make verbal observations to the rest of the people standing around. As if a cavity search wasn't embarrassing enough already, we all had to listen as he cracked jokes about everyone's ass.

He started belly-roll laughing when he got to the second person in line, while telling the man to turn around and show his bare ass to everyone, "Look at this guy's ass, everyone. Doesn't it look like Bob Ross? It's so fucking hairy I bet it could paint a picture of happy trees and shit." I was the last in line, so I had to stand and listen to every disgusting observation and stupid joke about everyone's ass before he finally got to me.

"Okay, spread'em," the officer said, as he continued with inappropriate comments. "Goddamn, that has got to be the sexiest ass I have ever seen! You better not drop the soap, my friend. I'm telling you that some big guy will jam his cock up your ass so fast you won't know what hit yeah... well.. actually, you probably will 'cause it's going to be someone's giant dick! Okay, pull your pants back up, and good luck. Trust me, you're going to need it."

# Chapter VII

Immediately following the cavity search, I was led around the corner and down the hallway until we arrived at a concrete window. When I looked through the window, another officer was handing the inmates big clear bags to put their clothes in. After this, he assigned us a yellow jumpsuit, a pair of underwear, some socks, and some bright orange plastic sandals. In addition to the jailhouse uniform, we were assigned one small blanket and pillow.

Once our personal clothing was gathered, and we were wearing our jailhouse attire, all ten of us sat on two long archaic benches built with a combination of metal and concrete. I sat on this bench holding my bag of clothes, a blanket, and the shittiest pillow I had ever seen for only a minute before I was told to get in another line. The officer who was just in the concrete window collected all our bags of clothes in a basket on wheels. We met with the Department of Correction nurse after this. She took our vitals, discussed our ailments, and asked about prescription information. Finally, we were led to a giant locking steel door, which opened with rudimentary motorized mechanics and let us into a gigantic jail cell called the general population.

This room was two stories tall! It had about fifty beds on the top floor, where you could look down at a big, police desk in the middle of a large open space called the general population area. There were some TVs, books, basic weights for bodybuilding, and a basketball court attached to it. The basketball court was on the top floor and surrounded by a giant half-globe made of the same thing the chain link fence was made of. I had observed this basketball court from the street while passing by the police department many times, but I never expected to witness it from the inside. After being assigned my bed, I walked out to this basketball court, where I discovered my friend, Adam, playing basketball.

"Holy shit, Oliver, what are you doing in here?" Adam asked as soon as he saw me.

"It's a long story... do you really want to know?"

"Well, yeah," Adam answered. "To hell with playing basketball... let's hear it."

"Okay, so about a week after you got arrested, Billy and I were tripping on mushrooms out in the country somewhere."

"Were these the mushrooms that Billy was growing?" Adam asked. "He told me about how he had bought something out of High Times magazine called the PF Guide to Growing Mushrooms. Then he followed the instructions and had a ton of mushrooms growing in that secret room in his basement."

"What secret room?" I asked.

"You mean you don't know about this?" Adam asked. "I thought you were his best friend, and he told you everything."

"He never told me much about his drug operations," I replied. "I think he was paranoid that I'd tell Erica, and that she'd tell Sherly, who would likely tell everyone because she's a big blabbermouth."

"You don't know anything about the secret room?" Adam asked.

"Nope!"

"I shouldn't be telling you this because Billy told me not to tell anyone, but after all his corn was harvested, some migrant farm workers from California were working in the area and were just about ready to head back home. That was when Billy asked these guys to dig out a giant room in his basement. I guess it took almost the whole winter to complete. The entrance is behind a bookshelf somewhere in his storm cellar. After Adam explained all this to me, he continued to ask about Billy, "Okay, so you and Billy were tripping on some shrooms in the country... go on."

"Billy started slamming a handle of tequila after tripping on mushrooms all day, and I told him that he was too fucked up to drive, but he insisted that he was fine. Unfortunately, he wasn't fine at all, and he continued to slam the rest of the bottle of tequila just before we left to go back home. A few minutes later, we were cruising down a dirt road, and Billy was swerving all over the place. He drove right through a stop sign and went flying through a highway intersection. That's when we got into an accident. I was horrible!"

"Holy shit! Did anyone get hurt?" Adam asked.

"Billy got hurt really bad. His face got all fucked up, and he may be in a coma," I replied. "I haven't heard any updates lately."

"No way, poor Billy," Adam said. "That's the worst news that I have heard since I got locked up in jail. It's a good thing you are ok. Did you fly into the ditch or something?"

"I wish that is all that happened," I replied. "We crashed right into the side of a minivan filled with an entire family. Neither one of us saw the stop sign."

"Holy shit!" Adam yelled. "So, what happened to the minivan?"

"It was totaled along with Billy's truck, and I think everyone in the family got injured. Either the Dad or the Mom ended up dying."

"Is Billy in trouble?"

"Yeah, big fucking trouble!" I answered. "He's facing like twenty felonies. I almost went down with him because I ran out into the field to ditch the drugs Billy still had in his truck. That's right when the police showed up and arrested me."

"That must have been what you were doing in jail when you were dragged past my jail cell a couple of months ago," Adam said. "I was wondering what happened."

"Unfortunately, since I was a key witness, the police asked me to rat on Billy," I explained. "I was asked to rat on you, too."

"For what?" Adam asked. "You didn't do anything."

"Ya, but I still got locked up for a week, and they told me that if I didn't help with your prosecution, then I would be charged with an accomplice to murder, or manslaughter... something really bad in any case."

"What?" Adam asked. "That doesn't make any sense."

"Yeah, that's what I thought," I responded, "but I ditched town and went to California instead of ratting on you and Billy."

"So, what the fuck are you doing in here if you ditched town?"

"That's another long story," I said. "Long story short, my Dad nearly beat the shit out of the officer that put me into that situation. Then my mom went berserk and took out an ad in the paper, which got everyone at church all pissed off. I guess it got the whole town pretty upset, so my charges were somehow dropped to a misdemeanor possession of marijuana. I had to come back home for something completely unrelated, and then Erica and I were in the Taco Bell drive-through yesterday, and the same douchebag police officer that initially arrested me pulled up behind me and arrested me again!"

"That's fucking nuts!" Adam replied. "To add to this pile of insanity, I saw your dad in here just recently. His bed was only a few bunks down from mine. We even played a few games of chess, but he didn't say much. As a matter of fact, I can't remember him saying anything the whole time he was here. I don't think he even said "checkmate" when he beat me at chess. I heard that he beat the shit out of everyone in the police station."

"My dad didn't beat the shit out of any police officers," I replied. "From what I understand, he just threatened to beat them all up up."

"Still, Dude, these are some of the craziest goddamned stories I have ever heard in my life!" Adam said, as he picked up the basketball and tossed it at me, "Think fast!"

Over the next couple of days, Adam and I hung out pretty much the whole time. Incidentally, we played some basketball and spades, just like the deputy had mentioned. We also played a lot of chess and we were always hanging out with each other. There were things about our conversation when I first saw him on the basketball court that I needed to follow up on once I got out of jail. I wanted to check out Billy's basement and look for the hidden room Adam told me about.

I also forgot that Billy had bought a new truck before the accident. I didn't see it in his garage or around his farm, so I didn't even think about it. However, I did remember that he picked me up in his dad's old truck the day of the accident, and he told me it was because his truck was in the shop. I remember that it was getting lifted, and some bigger tires were being put on it. There were only two car repair shops in town at the time, so I didn't think it would take much to track it down.

Adam told me that he had a fifty thousand dollar bail, which was a lot of money in 2001, especially in rural Nebraska. His parents never even tried to get him out of jail for a couple of reasons. First of all, there wasn't a bondsman in Ogallala willing to pay that amount, and even if there was, they would have expected 10% upfront. Adam's parents didn't even have enough money for a reasonable defense attorney. He said they hired a local attorney to delay his case as long as possible. They wanted to save money and figure out how to pay for a good defense attorney.

He also told me about how I better figure out a way to post bail, or otherwise I would be stuck in jail till my next court date, which wasn't until the end of October. I had two choices of places to call. I could call my folks and face the music. I had no idea what they would say, but I knew it would be a very awkward conversation, or I could also call Erica's house and run the risk of talking to her dad. Adam told me that if you called someone, a recording asks if they would accept a collect call from the detention center and whoever made the call. This was not something I was willing to risk.

I decided that I would call my folks on Sunday night and spent all weekend thinking about a bunch of bullshit ways to explain everything that had recently happened. I stopped short of telling Adam about harvesting the weed on Billy's farm because I was afraid that he would tell someone in jail, and it would somehow get passed along to law enforcement. I was already nervous about Sherly knowing about the operation.

Somewhere in my mind, I thought about ways to get him and Billy a reasonable defense attorney. He also shared the last of his commissary with me, which was only a few candy bars and bags of chips. He told me that his parents had stopped putting money toward his commissary to save as much money as possible for an attorney. I already felt horrible about Adam's legal issues, but I began to feel even worse after I saw what we were expected to eat in that shithole. I made a promise to myself to add a thousand dollars to his commissary before I left Nebraska. I couldn't imagine being stuck in jail for as long as he was. The food in jail was absolutely disgusting! I never even touched any of it the entire time I spent in custody. However, Adam got used to jail food, and wanted to eat most of the food on my tray and also what was on his tray. He would try to trade whatever he didn't eat for bananas and apples. By the end of the weekend, he had acquired a pretty good stash of fruit. Everyone in jail called him, "Banana Boy."

I remember on Saturday night, some of the inmates made something called a "spread." This consisted of peanut butter and jelly packets they collected throughout the week and a bunch of random snacks collected from everyone's commissary. There were Raman noodles, cheese dip, all different types of chips, an assortment of cereals, and other weird shit you'd never think about mixing together. All these random snacks were spread out over a table covered in newspaper. Anyways, it looked fucking gross, so I never ate any of that shit either, but I watched Adam munch pretty hard on it.

I didn't learn much while in jail, at least not anything that applied to the real world. I found it fascinating that everyone seemed to be Christians, especially the guys who were definitely going straight to hell. It was like a bad tattoo convention that I couldn't leave. I couldn't tell if these guys were so high they couldn't see straight when they got their tattoo, or if a two year old took a marker to their skin, and they thought, "Best tattoo design ever!" With this said, there were some really nice guys in the clink, but this didn't make me feel any less sorry for Adam. I understand what he did was both wrong and illegal, and it was an awful tragedy what happened, but he wasn't trying to kill anyone. He was just mad that his stereo was broken.

There were three phones in the corner of the common area that any inmate could use whenever they felt like it. I waited until after dinner on Sunday to finally call my folks. I didn't want to piss off my dad or make my mom cry, and I was frightened of what my dad would say to me if she did. If there was one thing my Dad couldn't stand, it was when my mother cried. If it were him that made her cry, he would often start crying himself and apologize like it was the end of the fucking world. If someone else made her cry, he unleashed such ferocious anger that they'd wished the world would end. I reluctantly picked up the phone, with no other options to peruse.

"You are about to make a collect call. Say your name after the beep and dial the number you wish to call," a recording explained. "Beep... please state your name."

"Oliver."

"Please wait as we connect your call," the recording said.

"Hello," I heard my mother say.

"This is [Oliver] making a collect call from Ogallala County Detention Center. Are you willing to accept the charges of ten cents per minute?" the recording was explained to my mother.

"Yes," my mother responded.

"Please note that you will be limited to a ten-minute conversation, and your call may be recorded. You will now be connected to [Oliver]."

"Mom, are you there?"

"Yes, I'm here," my Mom said, "Daaaaad, get on the other line. Oliver is on the phone."

"Does Dad have to get on the phone?" I asked.

"Yes, you are his son," my mom replied. "What are you doing in jail? You told us you were in California a couple of weeks ago, and you didn't know when you were coming back. We were told you had found a warehouse job and planned to live out there."

"I don't know," I answered.

"Well, you have to know something," my mom said. "You don't just wake up in jail without knowing how it happened."

"Erica and I were in the drive-through at Taco Bell, and that asshole, Deputy James O'Hare, arrested me again!"

"Okay, well, what happened to your job out in California," my mom asked, "and why didn't you call us to let us know you were coming back to Nebraska?"

"I still have my job," I said, preparing to explain a series of well-crafted lies that I had thought up. "I'm supposed to go back to work again after next weekend. Erica's uncle and aunt from California just happened to be driving to Nebraska to visit her family, so I asked if I could catch a ride. I came back because I was missing you, Dad, and Erica... oh, and I missed my sisters a little bit, too. The reason I didn't tell you was because I didn't want you to worry and wanted to surprise you... surprise!"

"Dad, are you listening to this?" my mom asked.

"Yes, it sounds like a bunch of bullshit," my dad said. "You know what, son?"

"What?" I reluctantly replied.

"You need to pull your head out of your ass. You turned eighteen nine months ago, and you already managed to fuck up your life. You're just lucky that your Mom stuck out her neck for you, or you'd be on your way to prison, just like your two pals. And if you think you can come back here to ask us for money to galivant around the United States, you can forget about it."

"What your dad is trying to say is that we are worried about you and would like to see you start college," my mom said. "It's probably not too late to start at the community college in the fall. The dean goes to our church. I can call to see if he can pull some strings."

"Mom, not right now. I need to go back to California," I explained. "I also need to get my car. I can't just leave it out there. I promise to come back to Nebraska before next school year if I attend college."

"What do you mean if you decide to attend college?" my mom asked. "We agreed to pay for your school and expect you to get a degree from a state college. I don't want to sit around here worrying about you or hearing about how you are throwing your future away to live in California with some hippy!"

"Fredrick is not a hippy, Mom."

"Erica says he is," she replied.

"Well, he is not a hippy," I replied, thinking to myself that if you looked up "hippy" in the dictionary, you'd likely see a picture of Fredrick. "Erica doesn't know what she is talking about."

"And, what about Erica?" my Mom asked. "I thought you were in love and were planning to get married," my Mom stated. "Dad, talk some sense into your son. I have to get a Kleenex because I have a potluck in twenty minutes, and I don't want to have to fix my mascara."

"See what you did, Oliver. You made your mother cry," my dad said with a pissed-off tone of voice. "Here is what is going to happen. We will bail you out because I assume that is why you are calling. You might have fooled your mom, but you don't fool me. I bet you are back here on your last dime and expected to borrow some money so you could go back out to California and smoke pot."

"That's not it at all," I replied.

"Yeah, bullshit, Oliver! Don't lie to me, or we will leave you rotting in jail!" my Dad said. "You are going to ride back with Erica's relatives to get your damn car, and then you are going to drive straight back here. Then, you are going to enroll in the community college or figure out a state college to attend before next semester. If you don't go to college, then you're gonna get your CDL license and start driving one of my semi-trucks."

"I don't want to be a goddamned truck driver," I replied.

"Why? There is good money in truck driving, and you could take over my business someday. Well, I'll tell you what, son, if you don't want to drive trucks for a living, I suggest that when your mother gets back on the phone, you tell her that you love her and are going to college next semester. Then, you had better explain how you plan to return from California immediately after you get your car. Got it?" my dad asked with a commanding voice.

"Yes," I answered, attempting to mollify his temper.

"Okay then, 'cause if you don't, I won't come down to post your bail. Also, if you make your mother cry again, I will post your bail just to whoop your ass. Then I'll bring you back to your pal, Deputy James O'Hare, and tell him to lock your ass back up! That's all I have to say to you. Now, how much is your bail? We can bring it down in the morning."

"Five thousand dollars," I answered.

"Five thousand dollars," my dad yelled. "Did you rob a fucking bank or something?"

"No, that's just what my bail is."

"You'll have to call a bondsman because we don't have that kind of money just lying around," my dad replied.

"Adam said that you only need 10%, which is five hundred bucks," I explained. "I don't have five hundred dollars."

"Yeah, then whoever bails you out will lose that five hundred dollars," my dad said. "So, it sounds like we might just have to leave you in there."

"No, please, Dad, my next court date isn't for a month," I pleaded. "Get me out of here!"

"Let's see what your mom has to say about it."

"Say about what?" my mom interrupted.

"I love you, Mom," I said abruptly. "I am going to college next semester. I also plan to get my car in California and come right home."

"Oh good," my mom replied. "It sounds like your dad talked some sense into you."

"He sure did," I answered, "so, do you think you can come down in the morning and bail me out?"

"We'll have to think about it," my dad answered.

"Oh, your dad is just kidding around. We will be down first thing in the morning," my mom replied. "Have they been treating you nicely in jail? I hope you've been minding your manners. What have they been feeding you in there?"

"This call is ending in thirty seconds," a recorded voice explained.

"I guess that's it. I love you, Oliver," my mom said, "and we will be down there to bail you out in the morning... right, Dad?"

"We'll see," my dad replied.

"I love you, Mom, and you too, Dad."

# Chapter VIII

The following morning, I heard my name called shortly after nine o'clock by the police officer standing behind the desk in the commons area. I was told that my bail had been posted and was instructed to return my blanket and pillow. After this, the giant mechanical door opened, and I was told to follow another police officer to get my clothes. When I finally walked out the front doors of the city jail, my folks were standing there to meet me.

On the way home, my dad informed me that I was a very fortunate person. He said that my mom decided to take five thousand dollars out of her personal bank account to post my bail. He also explained that if I didn't appear at my next court date, he'd end up in prison with my friends because he would probably murder me. This sarcastic statement was made in a serious voice, so my mom told him to shut up… and then she started to say a bunch of mom shit for the rest of the morning.

After getting breakfast at the local diner, we drove home. Once there, I went straight down to my room to play some video games for about an hour. I also sent a message to my nemesis and the T6 Cartel to confirm my delivery of guns for when I returned to southern California. In addition to thinking of some solid reasons to leave the house to get away from all the tension I felt being around my folks,

I really wanted to get in touch with Erica to see if she had been out to see Fredrick while I was in jail. I also really needed to pick up my truck at Taco Bell.

Since I never returned to the marijuana harvest to bring Fredrick the things on his list, I thought my plan may have fallen apart. Fredrick and the rest of the hippies could have gone on some crazy drug binge. I anticipated to find them naked, and running around rural Nebraska with their dreadlocks on fire, about as much as I figured everything to still be in order. After thinking through some of this, I eventually realized I didn't have the keys to my truck. I also thought that unless I got lucky and found Erica at work, I would have to call her house. This meant running the risk of her dad answering the phone. I was still traumatized by his comments about me having sex with his daughter and hoped to avoid talking to him until sometime in the distant future.

First, I called the supermarket where Erica worked to see if she was there. Unfortunately, she wasn't working, so I had to call her house to talk with her. I thought about this for quite a while and tried to come up with another option. When I finally got around to calling Erica's house, as I feared, her dad answered the phone.

"Hello?"

"Is Erica there?"

"Well, Oliver, how are you doing this morning?"

"Fine."

"I was reading in the Sunday newspaper that you got arrested again. This comes as no surprise to me. I don't understand what my daughter sees in you. About a month ago, someone named Tyler called for her, and then I saw her get in a big pickup a little while later. I hoped that might be it for you and my daughter, but you're like a rash that won't disappear."

"I'm sorry that I disappointed you, Sir. I promise to try harder," I responded. "Now, can I please speak to Erica?"

"Erica," I heard him yell. "Your jailbird boyfriend is on the phone!"

When Erica answered the phone, I frantically told her about my concerns. Surprisingly, she managed to calm my nerves down over the next few minutes by explaining how the marijuana harvest was going. She explained what she had been doing to help out while I was in jail and that she grabbed the keys to the truck before walking home from Taco Bell. She told me that she had returned the truck to the farm, and everything seemed to be running smoothly.

I was very relieved to hear this. I remember spending the next few minutes thanking her and describing how much I loved her. This led to a short debate about who loved who more, but we ultimately decided that our love for each other was equal, so the conversation continued. This was when she began to tell me several more amazing things that made me happy.

Erica had asked to take a week off work to help with whatever needed to be done, and she had used her money to keep things running smoothly. This money came from what I had left for her in the coffee can at the supermarket, but it would need to be replaced. She also brought her car in to get it fixed over the weekend. I didn't even express my concerns about Billy's new truck, and Erica told me that it was at the same auto repair shop as her car.

When this delightful phone call ended, Erica said she would pick me up in ten minutes to check on the marijuana farm. Besides having to talk to Erica's dad, this morning really couldn't have gone any better. When I went upstairs, I told my mom that I was going to go hang out with Erica and planned to come back for dinner. Then, I heard Erica honk her car horn, and about thirty minutes later, we arrived at Billy's farm.

Even though everything ran smoothly, I still needed to address several issues. I also wanted to accomplish  some important tasks that day before heading back into town to eat dinner. After checking in with Fredrick and Anika, I needed to dig up the cash I had buried under Erica's house to keep everything running smoothly. I also planned to go into Billy's basement to look for the hidden room Adam told me about while I was in jail. This was where Billy supposedly grew a bunch of mushrooms that I knew nothing about. Well, at least not until the night of the crash, anyway.

Erica pulled her car next to the barn, where we saw Anika, Jessica, and a few hippies eating lunch. I asked Anika how things had been going the last few days, and she told me everything was going well. She said that Fredrick had found a few ways for Melissa and Tracy to help process the harvested weed. She continued to explain how Jessica was going into town to do all the shopping while she was doing most of the cooking and cleaning.

I expressed my gratitude by telling Anika to keep up the excellent work, and that is when she nervously asked if I could afford to pay everyone when we got back to California. She had heard how much the nine members of the Psychedelic 40 were getting paid and did some math in her head, which she calculated to be much more than what she had expected. I tried my best to calm her nerves by telling her that I could easily cover the payroll, and I think she felt a bit better after we talked.

Once I was finished with this conversation, I walked over to the barn to see what processing marijuana was all about. I found Melissa, Tracy, and three hippies tending to piles of bud and asked them how things were going. They said they were doing great. This was likely contributed to a big pile of cocaine I saw on a table in the center of the barn.

After checking on the girls, Erica and I followed the trail to the marijuana field. As soon as we walked into the valley, we discovered that the entire field was almost finished being harvested. We also saw that a dozen or so piles in the field were covered with blue tarps. Fredrick had my truck parked next to one of these piles, where he and another hippy appeared to be hard at work. When he noticed us walking toward him, he stopped what he was doing and ran up to greet us.

"Oliver, I heard that you got put in jail for a few days," Fredrick said with an oddly cheerful voice. "I'm happy to see that you made it out."

"Yeah, I just got bailed out this morning," I replied. "It wasn't anything serious... just a misdemeanor."

"That's good to hear, Buddy. So, do you have my favorite one-hitter?" Fredrick asked. "I have been missing that pipe like crazy!"

"You are not going to want to hear this," I answered with sincere sadness in my voice. "That pipe suffered an unfortunate fate. I had to put it in between my butt cheek when I got arrested. It was left in a brown paper sack in the corner of a jail cell right before I got a cavity search so you wouldn't have wanted it back anyway."

"Shit... that sucks hard!" Fredrick responded while kicking the ground with his muddy shoe.

"I promise to get you another one just like it!" I said, putting my hand on his shoulder. "I'm so sorry!"

"Yeah, I have lots of pipes.  Remember, I make them," he replied, showing clear signs of frustration and sadness. "That one was special."

"Again, I'm sorry," I sympathetically responded. "So, how are things going with the harvest?"

"Pretty good for the most part," Fredrick replied. "It rained the last couple of days, which slowed things down and made things muddy. That's why the weed is covered in tarps," he explained, "but we are doing good. I expect to have everything harvested and over to the barn by tomorrow. Then, it's just a matter of processing."

"How long will that take?" I asked, hoping to hear that we were nearly finished and would be headed back to California soon.

"Probably another two weeks or so," Fredrick replied.

"Wow, when I saw this field, I figured we were almost finished."

"Trimming takes a long time," he explained, "but I think we will pull down almost eight hundred pounds of weed."

"That's great news!" I responded. "Hey, could you give Erica and me a ride back to the barn? The trail is pretty muddy."

"Yeah, no problem," he replied. "I was just getting ready to head up there myself."

Later that day, I planned to dig up the other show boxes of cash I left under Erica's house before I left for the West Coast. I wanted to finish with plenty of time to look for the secret room in Billy's basement, so I went straight to work digging up the three shoe boxes full of money while Erica kept me company. I was surprised at how easy it was to dig up the money, especially compared to when I initially dug the hole. The ground was soft, and the dirt was loose, so it took less than an hour to get to the loot. I predicted that uncovering the weed and guns would take a lot more time, but I could worry about that later. Once we had the three shoe boxes full of money, I was eager to count it, but this would have to wait. My estimates were somewhere between one hundred thousand and two hundred thousand.

I found the bookshelf that Adam told me about pretty easily. It wasn't that big, making it easy to move. Unfortunately, I discovered that the door behind it was locked. This resulted in a scavenger hunt to find something to smash the door open. After about thirty minutes of looking everywhere, we finally found an ax in the garage. It was hard to understand what we were looking at when we finally got the door open and walked inside the room.

We found several shelves with ten-gallon rectangular fish tanks on them. There had to be fifty aquariums or more. When we looked inside each aquarium, we found ten white, dried-up cakes with shriveled-up mushrooms attached to them. We also discovered a trash bag in the corner, half full of dried mushrooms. There were also a bunch of bags of what appeared to be potting soil. However, a closer look showed they were bags of vermiculate and powdered rice. We also found hundreds of half-pint mason jars and five large pressure cookers. This was in addition to the valuable discovery of several different drug scales. One looked like it could weigh a hundred pounds or better.

"Hey, look at this," Erica said. "There's another room over here." This room was a much smaller room that looked like Billy's office. It had some large filing cabinets and a desk. There were also several maps and posters all over the walls. Several of these posters were of women in bikinis advertising an assortment of beer. However, a closer look revealed that most of these posters were of Amsterdam and the Netherlands.

After looking around this room for a bit, Erica and I became incredibly curious about what all these filing cabinets contained. We were stunned to find thousands of important papers organized, sorted, and labeled. This was not something we were expecting from Billy. He didn't seem like someone that was organized to this extent.

We spent all afternoon looking through all these documents. He had insurance papers, utility bills, lease agreements, receipts, and vehicle titles. He appeared to have kept, organized, and filed every important document and mail he ever received. Upon closer inspection, we learned a lot about Billy's life and found all sorts of things we never expected.

We found bank statements that showed that Billy didn't seem to have any money in the bank. We also found a bunch of titles for all sorts of vehicles. What was the most surprising of the titles was that it appeared that he owned a combine harvester and two other tractors worth well over fifty grand apiece. We discovered that he leased these farm vehicles to local farmers, and also leased over two thousand acres of his land.

After a few hours, Erica sat down at the desk to look through its drawers, and that is when we made some life-changing discoveries. The first was that the bottom drawer was filled with stacks of money. We found increments of bills wrapped in official paper bands that showed how much money was in each stack. We could pull this money out and quickly count it all using a large calculator that sat on the desk. The total amount came to three hundred and forty-five thousand.

However, this enormous amount of money was far from the most surprising discovery. We found the deed to Billy's house. We also found several important correspondence letters between him and a local attorney. These documents showed that he planned to give me the deed to nearly all of his possessions at some point in the future.

I thought back to the conversation when Billy and I ate acid after the first time Erica broke up with me. We were fishing, and Billy told me how much money he had. He thought he'd have so much money at some point that he could move to wherever he wanted. He explained that he wanted to attend college in Austin, Texas, and he said he would pay for my tuition if I went with him. I asked him what he planned to do with his farm if this happened, and he said that he would give it to Eric or Adam.

However, when I told him I couldn't go to college with him because I anticipated Erica and I getting married, he continued telling me about his plans to move to Amsterdam. He said if he followed through with his plans, then he would give his farm to Erica and me for a wedding present. I didn't think much of this because we were drinking and tripping on the triple-dipped Timothy Leary blotter acid I got from Fredrick, but I was now thinking a lot more about the conversation I had with him that day.

As we continued to look through these papers, we found some quick deed documents that only needed my signature to complete the transaction. We also noticed a calendar on the wall that explained that Billy planned to travel to Amsterdam that winter after harvest, but there wasn't a calendar for 2002, so we didn't know what he had planned after this. Erica and I couldn't believe what we found and knew that we needed to talk about this to come up with some ideas for handling our new reality.

Our conversation that night led us to devise a series of plans and crucial steps we needed to take in the coming weeks. One such plan was for both of us to obtain passports. While seemingly unrelated to our mission, this was a necessary step towards our future goals. I needed a passport to accept potentially lucrative overseas T6 Cartel contracts. I also expected the remote possibility that Erica and I needed to arrange for an illegal heart transplant for her dad, which would also happen overseas. I convinced Erica to get a passport by asking her to consider going on a trip with me to Mexico that winter.

Another thing that we discussed that night was to contact the attorney in town who had prepared the quick deed documents. We planned to do this the next morning to see if he had any insight. Our plans for the next day also included convincing the auto repair shop to let us take Billy's truck. Then we talked about how we needed to open a joint bank account in Denver for the money that we found and the additional money that we were expecting from the sale of all the marijuana that was being harvested. This also included some sequential plans on how to secretly fund this account.

In addition to this, we needed to find out exactly where Billy was and what condition he was in. We also needed to find out exactly what charges were pending against him, and then we needed to find a good defense attorney. We anticipated all this would require at least a few trips to Denver. Erica had heard that Billy was being treated at the Swedish Medical Center in Denver, so we figured it would also be convenient to hire an attorney there.

# Chapter IX

THE FOLLOWING MORNING, ERICA and I ate breakfast with my family before heading straight out to the farm. We obviously needed to check on the harvest to ensure everything was running smoothly and everyone was happy, but we were mainly interested in collecting the documents from Billy's desk. When we got out there, it seemed to be business as usual. At this point, there were still a couple dozen piles of weed lying out in the field, but all of the marijuana had been harvested. Fredrick and one other hippy were still making trips back and forth from the field to the barn, where we discovered the processing to be in full swing. When Erica saw Fredrick, she ran up to him and gave him a big hug. They began to chat by the time I caught up to them.

"Fredrick is headed back down to the marijuana field," Erica explained. "Would you mind if I go with him for a little while?"

"Sure?" I responded.

"Just come get me when you are all finished up here," Erica replied.

When I walked into the barn, I found Tracy, Melissa, and the Psychedelic 40 hard at work. They were working so hard that no one except Anika even noticed me. I guessed that this was caused by their dedication to their work and the giant pile of cocaine that sat in the middle of the barn.

When I spoke with Anika, I was told that she didn't need to cook as much food anymore because everyone had lost their appetites after the weed went into full-tilt processing mode. This was when the hippies switched from daily consumption of hallucinogenic drugs to strictly cocaine and marijuana. After this short conversation, I was about to leave and let everyone do their thing, but then Anika told me something that suddenly left me with a head full of questions.

"See you later, Oliver," Anika said. "Oh, wait a second. I have a quick question."

"What's that?"

"Do you know where to get one of those drinking fountains with the plastic jug on top?" Anika asked. "I think we need one of those."

"Mmm.... I'm not sure," I replied. "I could ask Erica if they maybe have them at the supermarket where she works."

"Please do," Anika said.

"Why do we need that kind of water fountain?" I asked. "I saw several cases of water in the corner of the barn. What's wrong with that water?"

"Some of the members of the Psychedelic 40 are on a three-day cocaine binge," she said. "I'm getting a little worried about them. I think there may be one or two that are now on day four."

"You are telling me that there are people in this barn that haven't slept in four days?"

"I suppose it's possible that they took a nap, but it couldn't have been for long."

"Have they been eating?"

"Not much," Anika said. "Well, except for that guy over in the corner. His name is Bob. He eats a lot."

"Has he been doing cocaine like the rest of them?" I asked.

"Oh no," Anika replied. "He does way more."

"How come he eats so much?"

"I'm not sure," Anika replied, "but he eats about as much as the rest of them all combined."

"Huh... that's bizarre."

"It is, isn't it?"

"Getting back to the water jug fountain... why do we need one of those?" I asked.

"Every hour or so, I go around to give everyone a bottle of water, but the only one who drinks the water is Bob."

"You are telling me that some of these people haven't drank any water in three days?" I asked, concerned about the health of the hippies.

"Yep," Anika replied. "And there are two of them who look really sick."

"Erica! We need to leave right now!" I said after running down to the marijuana field.

"Why?" Erica asked.

"We need to find one of those water fountains with the jug on top," I replied. "Does the supermarket where you work sell those types of water fountains?"

"Yeah," Erica responded. "Why is it so important to get a water fountain?"

"It's the hippies... they haven't drank any water in three days!"

"Yeah, so."

"They will die if they don't drink water!"

"What?"

"People can't live that long without water!"

After this brief conversation with Erica, I told Fredrick about the water crisis and that he needed to check on his friends. After I dropped Fredrick off at the barn, Erica and I immediately left for Ogallala to get more snacks and a water jug fountain. On the way back into town, I got the F-250 going nearly 90 miles an hour, its top speed. I was really worried about the hippies. Thankfully, three jug water fountains and several jugs of water were available when we arrived at the supermarket.

After grabbing the water jug fountains and some snacks at the supermarket, I stopped at Kentucky Fried Chicken to pick up ten buckets of chicken. Then Erica and I sped back out to the farm. When we arrived, I saw Anika and Fredrick standing outside the barn. Fredrick frantically ran up to me as he saw me walking toward them with the buckets of chicken.

"Oliver, did you get the water fountains?"

"Yes," I replied. "They are in the back of the truck."

"Fuck that chicken. We can eat later," Fredrick said. "I'll open the barn door wide open. You need to drive the truck straight into the barn. We need to scare the shit out of everyone!"

"Why?" I asked.

"Two of my friends have stopped responding," Fredrick replied. "They are still trimming the weed but won't look up. I tried smacking them in the head with a bunch of things to get them to look at me, but they just won't look up from the buds they are trimming."

I ran back to the truck and drove it into the barn, just like Fredrick told me to do. This really scared everyone except the two hippies that Fredrick said were not responding. Anika, Erica, Fredrick, and I ran over to them after I drove the truck into the barn. Their skin was pale white, and they didn't appear to be breathing.

"Quick, get the water jugs!" Fredrick said.

As Erica and I ran to grab the water jugs, everyone else in the barn helped to remove the trimming scissors from the sick hippies' hands. They laid each of them down on the ground. This was when everyone started frantically running around gathering water bottles to pour into the mouths of the two hippies.

"What should I do with this big jug of water?" I asked. "How will we get these guys to drink from it?"

"Just pour it on their face!" Fredrick yelled.

Over the next two or three minutes, several gallons of water were poured into the mouths and onto the faces of these poor people. Fredrick started crying, "Please don't die, John and John. I love you guys!" Incidentally, these two hippies were both named John. Jessica was going back and forth between Fredrick's two friends performing CPR when the water wasn't being poured into their mouths.

Suddenly, one of the hippies started breathing. Unfortunately, another whole minute went by without any response from the other hippy. We all thought that this person had died, but we kept trying to do everything we could to resuscitate him. Finally, after nearly ten minutes of performing CPR and drenching him with water, Jessica felt a pulse. Moments later, water shot out of his mouth, and he started to breathe again.

John and John were alive! This caused everyone in the barn to start cheering as we ran around, giving each other hugs. This celebration went on for several minutes. When the cheers quieted down, and joints started to be passed around again, Fredrick made an announcement.

"Attention, everyone," Fredrick yelled as he climbed onto a hay bale. "I need everyone's attention! We are done working for the day. Actually, we are done for two days! I am putting the cocaine back in my suitcase, and it's not coming back out till everyone has slept, eaten, and drank at least two gallons of water!"

***

After things had calmed down and everyone looked healthy, I let Fredrick and Anika know that I would not be around much over the next week. I told them that they would have to supervise everyone and keep the operation running smoothly. Most importantly, I told them that someone needs to make sure everyone is drinking water.

Erica and I made a quick trip over to Billy's house to grab the documents we needed out of his desk before we left the farm. When we got back into town, the first stop we made was the auto repair shop to pick up Billy's truck. The mechanics and the shop owner were well aware of the accident Billy was in. Several of them could also vouch that I was Billy's best friend, so it wasn't hard to convince them that I was responsible for picking his truck up. His brand new 2001 Dodge Ram extended cab pickup truck was lifted and had some huge knobby tires.

After leaving the auto shop, we headed to the photo lab to get our pictures taken and fill out the paperwork to get our passports. I had asked Fredrick what his address was and if he would have my passport sent to his address rather than my family's house. After eating lunch at the diner, we quickly tracked down Billy's estate attorney, who had an office downtown. I'm not sure how many lawyers there were in Ogallala, Nebraska, at that time, but it wasn't many.

We spent at least an hour that afternoon talking with this attorney, who had more insight into this situation than we were expecting. He confirmed that Billy intended to move to Amsterdam in the spring or fall of 2002. He also told us that Billy didn't want to sell everything he owned and figured that if he gave his estate to Erica and me, we would look after it. He thought that since we grew up on this land, we would be familiar with farming and ranching.

This was more of an elaborate plan than we were anticipating. The attorney explained that he had created quick deeds already prepared to give all of his assets to me, expecting that we would be married or at least engaged to be married by the time he left for Amsterdam. These assets included things like his home, barn, vehicles, and all 4000 or so acres of land that he owned. He also explained the conditions under which these assets would be transferred. He said that Billy expected us to look over the land and continue operations. We would simply have to agree to pay him forty thousand dollars a year, and pretty much everything Billy owned would become ours.

This was incredible news, but it wasn't all the attorney had to say to us. He also explained how he expected Billy to lose everything he owned and would likely become bankrupt before he was released from jail. This came as no surprise to Erica and I, as we discussed this further. This was part of the reason we were so persistent in meeting with this attorney in the first place.

We asked what it would take for Billy's assets to be turned over to us, specifically me. The attorney told us that Billy was very thorough about his plans, and it would require only one signature. The bottom line was that Billy didn't want to deal with selling his assets and also didn't want to leave it all behind if he were to move.

The attorney showed us the document that needed Billy's final signature and encouraged us to get him to sign it. He was confident that if this document weren't signed sooner than later, it would result in the banks and the state eventually acquiring all his assets. He said he liked Billy and didn't want to see that happen. We ended up leaving the attorney's office with a plan to get Billy to sign a quick deed document. If we could get his signature, we needed to bring the signed document back to the attorney so he could begin working on transferring the assets.

This left Erica and I with an awful lot to talk about. We first discussed if this was something that we wanted to do. I told Erica that I didn't want to live my entire life in Nebraska, especially considering my friends' legal issues, but Erica wasn't as opposed to this idea as I was. She liked the idea of becoming a farmer and rancher, even though she hated almost as many people living in our town as I did. This was a lot to think over, particularly when we started to discuss the farm that Billy owned.

We would acquire the deeds to 4300 acres of farmland, a five-bedroom house, a massive detached garage, a giant barn, an old ranch house, a 1994 F-250 extended cab pickup, a 1987 Ford Bronco, a 1957 Chevy Hot Rod, a 1967 Notchback Mustang project car, a 1991 Claas Lexion combine harvester, a 1984 John Deer front load tractor with all sorts of farm equipment trailers, a Harley Davison motorcycle, a Honda CRF dirt bike, a ski-doo snowmobile, two 4-wheelers, and a ton of other miscellaneous items.

After a lengthy discussion, we decided to settle down on this farm south of Ogallala, at least for the next few years, until we understood more about Billy's health and legal situation. All we needed was Billy's signature. At this point, we had no idea if Billy was even conscious. If he was conscious, it didn't mean that we would be able to see him face to face, nor did it mean that he would be able to sign the document. He might not have wanted to sign it for some reason or another.

On the morning of the following day, we picked up Billy's truck at the auto repair shop and brought it to his house. Then, we checked in with Anika and Fredrick to tell them we were headed to Denver to tend to some business matters. It was Tuesday, and we anticipated leaving early on Thursday. We weren't entirely sure how long we'd need to stay in Denver. There were a lot of variables, but we expected to return sometime over the weekend or early the following week.

After leaving the farm, we drove back to my house and didn't leave for the next two days. We spent this time making love, watching movies, and doing our due diligence on our plans for Denver. We contacted several defense attorneys who didn't seem interested in helping us but eventually found someone interested in both Adam's and Billy's cases. She appeared highly recommended on the Internet, so we arranged a meeting with her at eleven o'clock on Thursday morning.

After making several calls, we eventually confirmed that Billy was being treated at the Swedish Medical Center in Denver with visitation rights. We were also able to verify that he had suffered severe head trauma, a brutal face injury, and a broken neck. We were also told that he was no longer in a coma and was conscious to some extent. This was excellent news! I was so thankful to hear that my best friend had come out of a coma. I was still apprehensive about the extent of his injuries, but this was much better news than if I heard that he was still unconscious. This also increased the chances of getting the quick deed document signed.

When Thursday morning finally came around, I said goodbye to my family before Erica and I left for Denver. I reassured them that I only planned to work at my imaginary warehouse job for another month. My Dad promised to kill me if I didn't come back to Ogallala for my court date. If I had any idea what my future had in store for me, I would have made it a point to hug everyone in my family, and I probably would have hugged my Mom for even longer than I did.

We planned to arrive in Denver when the banks opened, and we managed to deposit ten grand in a joint bank account with Wells Fargo before our scheduled meeting with the defense attorney. She had a retainer agreement ready for us to sign when we arrived. This lawyer was very thorough. She expected forty thousand dollars for Billy's case and thirty thousand for Adam's case, which we agreed to. We asked if she accepted cash as payment and were happy to hear that she would take up to ten grand in cash but expected the additional sixty thousand dollars to be wired to her account. We told her we would have this money within a couple of weeks.

According to the internet, this attorney was highly recommended. She went to law school at Stanford University and graduated at the top of her class. She had spent ten years as a Federal

Prosecutor in Illinois and had been practicing as a defense attorney in western Nebraska for the past five years and in the Denver area for fifteen.

She had a lot of information about Adam and Billy's case. Adam had a fifty-thousand-dollar bail and was being charged with the alleged crime of second-degree murder. She felt confident that Adam's charges would likely get reduced to (F3) Second Degree Assault and (F5) Second Degree Manslaughter.

We asked about Adam's possible prison sentence, and she predicted four to eight years, with a possibility of parole after two years, but Adam would have to sit in prison for only sixty percent of this time. Then she explained that this would be what a plea offer might look like, but she insisted that this case would be better off going to trial. She said that the Ogallala law enforcement screwed up by charging Adam with (F1) Second Degree Murder rather than an (F1) First Degree Assault and an (F2) Manslaughter.

To be found guilty of this crime, the state prosecutor would have to prove that Adam intended to murder the obese man and not just that he had accidentally killed him. I brought up that the victim of his alleged crime was a celebrity in my hometown because of all the eating contests that he won and that the jury may be biased. She said it would be possible to move the trial to Omaha so that Adam could be given a fair trial.

Unfortunately, Billy's case was not close to this cut-and-dry. After reviewing several news reports about his involvement in this horrific accident, she predicted that if Billy's case was available for bond, his bail would likely be well over one hundred thousand dollars. This was nationwide news due to the sad state of affairs regarding the fact that the accident involved an entire family. It was reported on for a solid week in Nebraska, so she expected no mercy in Billy's case.

She was surprised that I had only been charged with misdemeanor marijuana possession and that my name was not mentioned in the actual police report. Thankfully, for the most part, my name had stayed pretty clear of the news. I told her that the reason for this was likely because of the offer made to me by Deputy James O'Hare to rat out my friends. She found this to be intriguing information and thought it might help if the case went to trial.

The attorney explained that Billy was being charged with four counts of vehicular assault, four counts of attempted manslaughter, four counts of reckless endangerment, one count of manslaughter, DUI, possession of a controlled substance, careless driving, not obeying a stop sign, driving with expired tags, driving with a suspended driver's license, possession of a dangerous weapon while intoxicated. Then she said that once they get him back to the police station at some point in the future, he could also be facing an additional second-degree murder charge. We were afraid to ask what she thought the prison sentence would be. However, we needed a rough estimate to answer some of our questions. We also needed to know what to say to Billy. I wasn't surprised to hear that Billy could be looking at spending twenty years in the Nebraska State Penitentiary.

We ended up leaving the law office feeling miserable about Billy's future. This was my best friend, and I loved him dearly. Erica wasn't as close to him, but she had such a big heart that she seemed to be hit just as I was. We went to visit him that afternoon. This was an emotional journey that we could not prepare for.

His arm was attached to an IV, and he was being monitored by two other medical devices that I was unfamiliar with. He had a plastic brace around his neck, face, and nose. There were also special bandages to treat his skull fracture. This meant that the only parts of his face we could see were his eyes and chin. However, when we first entered Billy's room, he was tilted up in his bed and was plenty aware that we were there to visit him. Our conversation was brief due to his scheduled medical treatments, but this visit was insightful, and we were better prepared when we met with him the next day.

After driving around Denver for a bit, we found a nice restaurant to eat dinner and then checked into a Holiday Inn down the street from the Swedish Medical Center. This was the first time Erica and I had been alone in a hotel, so we made the most out of it. We woke up the following morning and deposited another ten grand in the bank, so we were one deposit closer to paying what was owed to the defense attorney. After going to the bank, we headed straight to the Swedish Medical Center.

We ended up spending the entire day in Billy's hospital room, at least until the nursing staff asked us to leave. My friend would respond to our questions with a thumbs up, a thumbs down, or a middle finger. He seemed to use this gesture the most. Considering his sad state of affairs, I was happy to see that Billy still had a sense of humor. Unfortunately, I eventually had to tell him about the miserable details regarding his case and pending charges. These were some of the saddest moments of my life. Billy began to cry so hard that he soaked the bandages on his nose with tears to the point that we were asked to leave the room so the nurses could replace them.

Erica and I were both crying as well. There is no question that Billy's tears were from emotions significantly more profound than mine, but my heart was broken just the same. Before walking into the hospital room, Erica and I discussed whether it would even be appropriate to ask about transferring the assets from Billy's estate. We decided to tell him about the defense attorney we hired for him before asking questions about his estate. These conversations continued for the next two days.

We decided to tell Billy that we were meddling through his house, trying to clear out anything illegal, and we stumbled upon the documents regarding his estate. We told him that we brought these documents to his attorney. We told him we couldn't believe this and were incredibly thankful. We spent a couple of hours expressing our gratitude before telling him about his attorney's prediction and that he would eventually lose everything he owned. Billy was prepared for this and seemed to be well aware of the legal challenges he was faced with.

We didn't even need to tell Billy that his signature was required on the quick deed document. He seemed to know that this question was coming and made a gesture with his hand to indicate writing. When I pulled this document out from my backpack, he immediately gave a thumbs-up. He signed the document without hesitation and appeared relieved that we had discovered this. Erica and I were also relieved at how all this was handled. We were predicting more of an emotional battle.

However, this was far from a pleasant experience when it came time to say goodbye. We all started crying. I couldn't stand to think about the future and what this all entailed for Billy. Unfortunately, no matter what, his life would not turn out well. This horrific thought and my best friend's terrible misfortune was an ongoing emotional battle that I dealt with for years. Do you know how when you are about to cry, you get that weird lump feeling in your chest?

I had that lump in my entire body when I said goodbye to my best friend that day.

Erica and I arrived back in Ogallala just before noon on Monday. We made it a point to drop off the signed estate document with the attorney immediately after driving past the city limit sign. During a short conversation, I gathered some insightful information. I was told that it would take some time to process all this, but it was anticipated that by January 2002, I would be the rightful owner of basically everything that Billy owned.

I walked into the barn shortly after I was dropped off. When I looked around, I saw a pile of about four hundred-gallon-sized Ziplock bags full of processed weed and some of the highest people on the planet. Nobody seemed to notice me standing in the giant doorway of this big red barn, so I went on about my business. I had all sorts of shit to work on while the hippies and the girls were finishing up processing the harvested weed.

I eventually ran into Fredrick the following day, who informed me that he predicted all the weed to be finished being processed sometime during the upcoming weekend. This left me with a few tasks to finish up before the hippy caravan drove back to California. One of the more obscure items on this list was that I needed to dig up the firearms buried under Erica's old house. I also needed to contact my nemesis and confirm an arrangement for the T6 Cartel to purchase these weapons the moment I arrived back in southern California.

Another task on my list was harvesting all the dried mushrooms I found on the white cakes inside the aquariums. Perhaps the most important task on my to-do list was disposing of anything illegal on the farm before the hippy caravan left for California. I'm not sure where making love to Erica ranked on my to-do list, but it was as unique as it was important.

I remember the last conversation with Erica before leaving for California. We were lying naked in bed after making love. We discussed all sorts of things, but nothing significant enough to change the future or have a reason to remember much of any of it. However, about thirty minutes of this conversation were meaningful to Erica and I.

"I love you," I whispered in Erica's ear, which was just a sweet nothing and nothing more.

"I love you more," Erica replied.

"I'm pretty sure that I love you more."

"Nope, I definitely love you more," Erica said.

"How is that possible when I love you the most?" I asked.

"Because I was told that it's possible," Erica answered.

"Who did you ask?"

"Everyone."

"Who is everyone?"

"Everyone in the world, and they all said I love you more," Erica said.

This debate went on for several more minutes. Ultimately, it wasn't clear which one of us won the debate. However, three solid points were made perfectly clear. The first was that Erica loved me. The second was that I loved Erica, and the third point was that we were both madly in love.

# Chapter X

The hippy caravan left Nebraska on October 8th, which was pretty much right on schedule and very close to what was initially predicted by Fredrick and me. There was only one significant modification to my plans. This was that I would be driving the three hundred firearms back to southern California in Billy's 2001 Dodge Ram extended cab pickup truck... AKA... my new truck.

Melissa drove the old box truck filled with five hundred pounds of weed and twenty-two pounds of dried hallucinogenic mushrooms. Tracy drove the 1986 long-bed Ford F-250 pickup truck filled with an additional two-hundred and thirty pounds of weed. Fredrick drove his van filled with all the Psychedelic 40. Anika drove her 1999 Ford Taurus with Jessica sitting in the front seat. Her car was simply filled with lesbian love and everyone's luggage.

Fredrick and I devised some generalized plans the morning before leaving the farm. Fredrick predicted that each pound would be sold at an average price of just over twelve hundred dollars a pound. He thought it would take roughly two months to sell all seven hundred and thirty pounds of weed. It was estimated that this would generate almost exactly a million dollars by the time everything was said and done.

We agreed to simply divide this money. Fredrick would take five hundred thousand dollars, or half of the total profits generated from the sale of the weed. He would pay the Psychedelic 40 and himself with this money. I would take the other half of the total profits generated from the weed. I planned to add the five hundred thousand dollars to the money Erica and I had found in Billy's desk.

After paying for the defense attorney in Denver and the new retainer for the estate attorney, as well as all the additional expenses that had accrued from the harvesting operations, there were around three hundred thousand dollars left. I estimated that I would have eight hundred thousand dollars after adding up all this money. Before I left Nebraska, Erica discussed an estimated cost of at least a million dollars for her father's heart transplant. This meant that I needed to make at least two hundred thousand more dollars through T6 Cartel contracts.

When it came to the sale of the three hundred firearms, I was given an address to meet for the transaction at a warehouse in Industrial District 7 in East LA. The problem was there was no Siri or Google Maps in 2001. There was just Map Quest which was very useful if you had a computer or a printer. The only other way to figure out how to get to your destination was a paper map. I was anticipating a meeting with the three-armed assailants I met during my first interaction with the T6 Cartel, and there was the off chance I would come face to face with Bile, my nemesis.

The assailants were armed to the teeth during my last interaction with the T6 Cartel. Two of them had automatic machine guns around their neck and their fingers on the trigger while the other one talked. They didn't trust me for shit and would not hesitate to blow my brains out if they even suspected something was wrong. This was the level of stress that I was currently dealing with.

When I pulled into the warehouse, the lights suddenly came on, and all the doors closed behind me. One armed assailant was at my driver's side door. Another one was standing at my passenger side door, and the third assailant stood in front of my truck. A man eventually walked out from a dark corner inside the warehouse. He was wearing a weird, crusty green suit and smoking a cigarette. This man was my nemesis. He had no idea who I really was, but he would learn I was his hellfire dryad of death, the temple of sin, and the destroyer of evil. He would one day look into my eyes and see the wrath of my revenge.

Bile was the leader of the three thugs holding automatic machine guns, and I was forced to do what he instructed me to do. He ordered two of the assailants to help me unload the weapons. They took turns aiming a gun at my head. I didn't know if he planned to kill me or if he was afraid that I was planning to kill him. During the twenty minutes that it took to unload these weapons, I had no idea if I was going to get shot.

"Oliver!" Bile suddenly yelled. "You came through on your word once again. These weapons look fabulous. How does thirty thousand dollars sound?"

"I was hoping for fifty," I answered.

"I can go as high as forty thousand, and I will provide you with an opportunity that is not common for me to give," he said. "I will let you pick your next contract."

"This still seems like a low-ball offer," I replied. "My girlfriend looked on the internet to find out how much these guns are worth, and she said that two of these weapons are worth that much money by themselves. One of these weapons is an MPADS, and another one is a Colt Paterson revolver, which is dated 1832. This gun was manufactured four years before Samuel Colt even sent the paperwork to the United States patent office."

"What is a MPADS?" Bile asked.

"It's a man-portable-air-defense-system, which is essentially a guided missile launcher. These were invented in the 1950s to provide post-WWII ground soldiers a tactical defense against low-flying aircraft," I explained. "I'm surprised that you haven't heard about these things. Al-Qaeda uses them all the time for their terrorist bombings."

"Really?" Bile responded with robust enthusiasm. "I love Al Qaeda! Osama Bin Laden is one of my favorite people! I think of him as a mentor for all the evil things that do."

"Yeah, well, if you can't come up with fifty grand, these contracts better be good, and there better be a lot to choose from," I told him.

"Oh, there are plenty," he replied. "Business is good, and crime is high. All you need to do is pick your poison. Do you want to traffic little girls, smuggle drugs, or murder someone? Maybe you are interested in something more exotic? We have contracts all over the world. All you have to do is decide what kind of criminal you want to be."

"Whatever pays the most," I responded.

"Whatever pays the most," Bile repeated while laughing. "That sounds familiar... it kind of sounds like... well... me," Bile laughed. "Are you afraid of water?"

"No," I replied.

"Do you like boats, airplanes, and cocaine?"

"Yes," I answered.

"Perfect!" Bile said. "I have a sixty-thousand-dollar contract with your name on it! All you need to do is help load up a Cessna with three or four hundred kilos of cocaine and fly out into the middle of the ocean."

"Then what," I asked after some unexpected silence.

"That's it!" Bile answered. "The plane lands on the ocean, and you jump out with the coke tied to your feet. You are going to love this, Oliver. It's going to be exhilarating. You'll come back with balls so fucking big...."

"You said boats, airplanes, and cocaine," I replied. "Where is the boat?"

"There are two boats," Bile explained. "You'll be sitting out in the middle of the ocean with a giant life jacket and the three hundred kilos of cocaine tied to your leg for a little while."

"What's a little while?" I asked.

"No more than an hour," he replied. "Then you are going to hear the roaring engines of a go-fast boat. This is when you will want to turn on the light attached to your head and set off the flares we give you. Once the go-fast boat picks you up, you'll have about an hour to rest before being tossed back into the ocean. But this time, you'll be picked up by a pleasure boat and brought into the Miami marina."

"What the fuck is a go-fast boat?" I asked.

"It's a boat that goes fast," Bile explained. "In fact, it goes so fast that law enforcement cannot catch it. Well, unless they send out a helicopter or plane. In this case, turn off the light on your head. Somebody will come to find you eventually... I promise. The T6 Cartel really doesn't give a shit about you as a person, but the cocaine tied to your leg will be worth millions of dollars, and they will care a lot about that!"

"Thanks for the reassurance that I won't be left in the ocean to die," I replied. When do I get paid?"

"You know, Oliver, I like you already," Bile said with a smile.

"Thanks, so when do I get paid?" I asked again.

"You have your money the very second you make it to the marina in Miami," Bile answered.

"Cool, I will see you in a week," I replied. "Now, do you think I can get my forty-five grand? I need to get the fuck out of here."

I spent the next week hanging out with Fredrick, smoking weed, learning how to surf, and looking for an apartment. It didn't take long for the money to start rolling in from all the weed we brought to California. We initially stacked all the Nebraska kind bud into Fredrick's basement. There was already a sizeable chunk missing after only a week. Fredrick was confident that he could sell all seven hundred thirty pounds in a month or so. I thought that this was impressive, to say the least.

When my passport showed up the following week, I made it a point to call my family and Erica that night because there was at least a slight chance that this would be the last time we spoke. I remember taking a cab to another seedy warehouse to meet with Bile and his three assailants. I was happy that the thugs were not as afraid of me as before, or at least they had some reason for not aiming automatic rifles at me. Bile gave me instructions and plane tickets to Bogota, Colombia. I was told that a man would meet me at the airport and guide me through my assignment for the next couple of days. Bile told me that once I got close to the cocaine, there would be T6 Cartel thugs following me around to protect me and to make sure that I was doing what I was supposed to be doing.

I was ready to walk out the door when Bile called me over to a table in the corner where he was sitting. This is when he took a large bag of cocaine out of his pocket and set out ten giant lines. "You are going to like this coke, Oliver. This shit is as pure as it gets!" Bile told me while the assailants crowded around the table waiting to be handed the tooter. I noticed that the goons had their guard down, and so did Bile. They still were strapped with automatic weapons, but they were not paying attention to what I was doing so much as being coke fiends.

I tried to talk my way out of taking this giant line of cocaine, but I eventually realized that there was no way out of it. I had never tried cocaine before and had no interest in it at all, particularly a line this big. I was likely going to lose my fucking mind, but I would somehow need to keep it together. The initial head rush was terrific, and I tried my best to get the hell out of there before another phase of this drug kicked in. All drugs have phases, and cocaine has some of the more profound. I couldn't talk! I tried to say something to Bile to move things along, but my mouth wasn't working. I don't know how I even left his house with my plane tickets.

Unfortunately, I didn't get very far. I walked down the road for only a block and stood in the exact same place for two hours. I was staring into the abyss. Thank God my plane wasn't scheduled to leave that night because this was just phase one of this drug. The thing with cocaine is that there are tolerance levels, and there is a huge difference between good cocaine and run-of-the-mill American cut. I had no tolerance, and this was 100% pure Columbian. A key bump of this shit would set a seasoned addict off like a firecracker. Bile just made me take a line the length of a #2 pencil.

The abyss happens with any drug if you take enough. This is when your brain quits talking to your body. You are still very much in your head, but this is a peculiar reality that floats between a dream and a type of paralysis that is both fantastic and terrifying at the exact same time. This may have been the most intense abyss I have ever experienced in my life, and I had no way to escape.

When this finally happened, I walked through this horrible neighborhood into another and then through several more. I finally figured out who I was about the time of the sunset that evening. For the next two hours, I still was incredibly high, so I felt good... really good! However, phase three of cocaine sucks elephant balls. I stopped at a bar and started taking shot after shot, hoping that this miserable feeling would go away. After about twenty shots of Jack Daniels, I finally felt somewhat sober. I remember smoking a cigarette and making a promise to myself that I would never do cocaine ever again.

# Chapter XI

I TOOK A CAB to the nearest Holiday Inn around midnight and tried to prepare my head for what was in front of me. I had never even been out of the country before, and this would only be the fourth time I had ever been on a plane. I was an eighteen-year-old with my whole life ahead of me, and here I was on my way to Bogota, Colombia, to smuggle cocaine on an international level.

I remember being paranoid from the time I arrived at the Los Angeles International Airport till... well... forever. I never stopped being paranoid this entire trip. After landing in Bogota, I was met by a Columbian man. We walked through the airport and onto the tarmac toward a long line of hangers. Inside one of these hangers was a plane that this Columbian man was about to fly. This was a two-propeller Cessna, and it was old as dirt. This airplane looked like the Wright Brothers invented it before they invented a plane that could actually fly.

By the grace of God, we somehow landed on a shitty runway in a field that was precisely in the middle of fucking nowhere... or so I thought. I realized pretty quickly that we had just landed in the cocaine capital of the world. We were literally on the equator, where Peru, Ecuador, and Colombia intersected. Surprisingly, the Columbian man offered me a tour of the plantation and cocaine processing facility. As he and I walked around this massive operation, I saw hundreds of workers and so much cocaine that I couldn't believe what I was seeing.

I saw giant piles of freshly cut coca leaves and thousands of acres of coca plants in the fields we visited. There were people on four-wheelers, pulling carts around these fields, that would bring the coca leaves over to giant vats of gasoline. After the leaves were extracted from the vats of gasoline, the residue was transported to get mixed with lime and potassium. Then, this mixture was soaked in acid, which created a paste. This paste would then be drained of any remaining liquid and finally dried into bricks of cocaine.

Less than forty-eight hours ago, I had made a promise to myself never to do cocaine again, but this was impossible when I walked through the packing plant. Everyone was wearing face masks, and I should have been wearing one as well because the cocaine dust got me high as hell. However, this was nothing like the giant line Bile gave me. It was more subtle and somewhat enjoyable.

I couldn't believe how much cocaine was in this place. There were thousands and thousands of pounds. I wondered why I had been brought here only to smuggle three hundred kilos. There was so much cocaine on this plantation and processing facility that it would probably fill a container ship full. I sat around with the Columbian man and other folks, smoking weed and drinking whiskey that night. I even did a little line of coke with everyone. This shit was addicting. I fell asleep that night fucking wasted drunk on a whole other level. I couldn't believe how much I was able to drink on this shit.

The following morning came way too early, and I had one of the worst hangovers of my life. This was when I was told by the

Columbian man that a good cure for hangovers was cocaine. Sure enough, he was right. I was a new man by noon and loving life. Incidentally, this was when about fifty people, myself included, were all preparing a giant lunch. Unfortunately, I wasn't hungry because of the cocaine. For this reason, I remember regretting the line I took that morning. This meal looked amazing, and I could barely nibble at it.

I noticed a couple of things while sitting at one of several tables where everyone sat to eat. One was that everyone on this plantation and cocaine processing facility was being overseen by roughly fifty armed assailants. These men made Bile's thugs look like three pussies. I also noticed a man walking around whom everyone admired and feared. He was called El Loco, and his real name was Daniel Barrera Barrera. This was the kingpin of this whole operation.

That afternoon, a large plane landed on the runway, which was basically some gravel and asphalt in the middle of a coca field. This plane had four propellers and was modified to land on water. I learned that this was the plane I would take back to Miami. I was surprised to see significantly more cocaine than three hundred kilos were loaded onto this plane. I had no way to estimate how much cocaine was loaded, but my best guess was three or four tons. Whoever I was delivering cocaine to was small potatoes in comparison to whoever was going to get the rest of what was loaded.

Right around the time the sun went down, we boarded this plane and flew away to an unknown destination. Four hours later, we touched down at Northwest Florida Beaches International Airport in Panama City. Considering 9/11 had just occurred, I was surprised at the lack of security when I watched about fifty huge boxes of cocaine taken off the plane and loaded into a large box truck. This was a very advanced operation. Then we refueled and flew away again.

About eight hours later, we touched down at Sangster International Airport, east of Montego Bay, Jamaica. This time, we pulled the plane into a large hangar, where fifty more giant boxes of cocaine were unloaded. At this point, the cargo was less than a third of what was initially loaded. I had no idea what time it was, but judging by the sun, it appeared midday. The Columbian man, the pilot, and I deboarded the plane for the rest of the day and took a cab into Montego Bay.

I thought this city was fabulous! I learned that it was the capital of Saint James Parish on Jamacia's north coast. Several colossal cruise ships were docked here, which were neat to look at. I had never seen a cruise ship before. I couldn't believe how big they were compared to what I imagined them to be from looking at pictures. Then, we walked down to a beach called Walter Fletcher and drank beer for the rest of the afternoon. We stayed in Deja Resort, an all-inclusive resort, where everything was free. I got pretty tanked with the Columbian man that night.

The following morning, we ate breakfast at a huge buffet that had every type of food you could possibly imagine. It was almost as big as the $8.99 all-you-can-eat buffet at the Imperial Palace Hotel in Las Vegas, but it was all breakfast food. It was amazing, and everything I tasted was incredible. We hung around for a while after we finished eating, drinking beer, and smoking joints with some Rastafarians. This continued into the afternoon.

I noticed the pilot getting pretty drunk, which made me a little concerned, considering that I was counting on him to land in exactly the right place in the middle of the ocean. I even spoke up about it, but he assured me that he had everything under control. We ate a late lunch or early dinner around three o'clock in the afternoon, and our dessert was a little blow. This sobered up the pilot quickly, which I was happy to see.

This was when we headed back to Sangster International Airport. I was nervous getting on the plane because I knew this would be the last time the plane would land at an airport with me in it. I didn't say anything during this whole plane ride out to the middle of the ocean. I was scared shitless. This may have been the most frightening experience I had ever had up until this point in my life. The plane took off around five o'clock in the afternoon, and we were airborne till sunset.

This is when the Columbian man started to prepare everything for me. First, he gave me a helmet with a light on top. He showed me how to turn it on, which made the bright red color light start strobing. Then he dug out this giant contraption that turned out to be a heavily modified wetsuit. The entire suit was a flotation device with extra life support around the shoulders and arms. I imagined myself looking like the Pillsbury Doughboy with this thing on.

In addition, I was given a backpack that would create an additional flotation device for me to be attached to. He described this as something that would almost turn into a small boat of some sort. This seemed like a lot of flotation shit, honestly. It was a bit overkill for me, and the three hundred kilos of cocaine I was expecting to be tied to my leg. I soon realized that this was because I was going to have a hell of a lot more cocaine tethered to me than three hundred kilos. It looked like a pickup truck full of coke.

This was a huge plane landing on water, and when I got into the water, it looked like the craziest form of transportation I had ever seen. The Colombian man wished me luck and said goodbye as he closed the door to the plane. When the propellors started to spin, I started to panic about getting eaten by sharks and just being left out in the middle of the ocean to die. One hour passed without me hearing or seeing anything but small waves and the night sky. The only thing lucky about this was the full moon over my head, which helped illuminate the ocean and make things slightly less scary.

I thought of the craziest shit while floating alone in the middle of the ocean. I initially thought about Erica. I thought how much I loved her and decided that I was going to ask her to marry me as soon as possible. I also thought of my family and how much my mother worried about me. I hated lying to my mother. The fact that I was hired by an international crime organization, which had me floating around in the ocean with over a thousand pounds of cocaine tethered to me, was vastly different than preparing to go to college and working at a warehouse, as I had explained to her only days before.

I also thought of my nemesis. Until now, I only made plans for revenge but had no idea what this revenge would look like. I didn't want to simply kill him... I wanted to torture him and destroy his soul. This was for exploiting Erica, of course, but now it had become an even deeper reason. It had become personal. I knew this man was pure evil and needed to suffer for what he had done to the world.

The last and most profound thoughts I had that night were about myself. Until this point in my life, I had only two goals aside from my ever-evolving plans and continuing goals of everyday life. These were to save Erica's father's life by saving money for his heart transplant and to avenge my nemesis. These thoughts seemed to transcend these goals to one day have a purpose for being myself. I wanted to achieve something with my life or be known for something that people would respect, like becoming a famous writer or artist.

Suddenly, I heard the sound of a motorboat far off in the distance, so I immediately fired off the flares and turned on my helmet light. I was so happy to hear the sound of the go-fast boat approaching. There are no words to describe it. I had never heard a more beautiful sound in my life! It got louder and louder as this boat roared toward me. I was laughing and screaming profanities like they were religious prayers sent to the lord while attending church on Sunday. A few minutes later, the boat pulled beside me with two friendly gentlemen inside.

"What's up, buddy?"

"I'm happy as hell to see you!" I replied.

"Yeah, I bet," the man responded with roaring laughter. "I've never actually sat in the middle of the ocean with a thousand pounds of coke tied to me before, but I bet it fucking sucks! Did you think you were going to get eaten by sharks?"

"Actually, yes!" I answered. "That was one of the many thoughts going through my mind out here."

"You got some balls, Buddy!" the man said. "I'm Victor, and my partner is Andrew. I was told that your name is Oliver."

"Yes, Oliver."

"Well, Oliver, let's get your ass in this boat," Victor said. "We have a beer, whiskey, weed, and a blanket for you... and I assume you have a shit ton of cocaine for us or the cartel. This boat ride back to Miami takes about an hour, so we will get you good and fucked up before we throw you back in the ocean. The next place you get dropped off isn't nearly as bad. You can see the lights from the city where we drop you off."

"Fucking awesome!" I replied, happy to see someone that wasn't an asshole and ecstatic to finally get out of the ocean to take off the stupid suit I was wearing.

It took a while to get all of the cocaine inside of the boat. Victor described the next hour very well. I drank whiskey and smoked weed while wrapped up in a blanket. I understood why this vessel was called a go-fast boat. It had four massive engines on the back of it, and it went fast as hell. It was safe to say that aside from airplanes, we traveled faster than I had ever traveled in my life. We were easily going over one hundred miles an hour. I wanted to talk with Victor because I had not had a good conversation with anyone since the weekend Fredrick and I went to the Warped Tour. Unfortunately, the roaring sound of the four engines was far too loud to hear anyone talk.

I was not looking forward to going back into the ocean with all this cocaine attached to me again. The hour I spent on the go-fast boat went by way too quickly. Just as we started to see the city's lights reflect off the night sky, the boat stopped, and it was time for me to put on that stupid suit again. I was assured that it wouldn't be long until the pleasure boat arrived and that I likely didn't need to shoot off any flares. Victor said the boat was likely already close enough to see the strobing light on my helmet.

He also pointed out that other boats in the area were chartered for night fishing or simply out for a pleasure cruise and that it would be wise not to draw attention. He said that if I fired off some flares, it may result in the Coast Guard thinking a vessel was in distress. Once I was dropped off, I just sat there in the Gulf of Mexico, two miles off the shore of Miami, with a blinking light on my helmet and six hundred kilos of cocaine tethered to my leg.

Victor was right about the pleasure boat. I was only in the water for twenty minutes before the large boat pulled beside me. As the crew got the coke out of the water, I got out of the crazy wet suit I was wearing. I was happy this boat also had amenities like beer, whiskey, and weed. I took several shots of whiskey to calm my nerves by the time we pulled into the Miami marina. After I was handed an envelope with money when I stepped off the boat, I thanked the people on the pleasure boat and called a cab to take me to the nearest Holiday Inn. I was super drunk and tired as hell by the time I made it to the hotel. This felt like the longest day of my life, and I slept like a baby that night.

I counted the money in the envelope I was given immediately after waking up the following morning. Just like the last two times the T6 Cartel paid me, it added up to precisely what the contract specified, which was fifty thousand dollars. I wandered down to the lobby after this to book another night in the hotel. After having coffee and eating some donuts, I explored Miami for the day. During the day, I just went down to the beach and ate some Mexican food for lunch. I also stopped in several bars later in the afternoon and had a good buzz when the sun went down. This is when I was told to go to South Beach to find some fabulous parties.

The cab I took from the city out to South Beach dropped me off in the middle of thousands of people partying their asses off right on the street. I hopped from bar to bar and club to club till I was drunk as hell that night. I ended up at this one particular club that was three stories tall and danced to techno music for a couple of hours. I wouldn't say I liked techno music, but I was so happy to have survived the T6 Cartel contract that techno music sounded incredible. It was three in the morning before I finally decided to get a cab to return to my hotel.

I remember standing out in the street trying to hail a cab when this black BMW pulled up along the curb. Then, I saw this gigantic, muscular man wearing a tank top get out of this car and start yelling at a couple of decked-out women walking down the street, "Get in the fucking car, Kristy, you stupid bitch!" this man yelled. "Get in the car right fucking now!"

These women were both incredibly attractive, wearing short skirts and high heels. One of these women started screaming back at this man, "I'm not going with you, Brad. We are over!" That is when I saw this massive man run up to this woman and grab her arm, with more screaming and yelling exchanged by both of them. This guy just picked this woman up and tossed her over his shoulder while he walked back to his BMW.

I made it a point to stand between him and his car as this woman was screaming her head off, "Put me down, you fucking asshole. I'm not going anywhere with you!" This man didn't know what was happening when he saw me standing in front of his car. He was 6'5" and had huge bulging muscles, so there was no way he was expecting me to stop him, but there I was, with folded arms and a mean look on my face.

"Put her down," I said. "She's not going with you!"

"Who the fuck are you?" the man asked with a puzzled look.

"I'm Kristy's boyfriend," I answered. This immediately resulted in this man setting down the screaming woman he had on his shoulder as he started to show aggression toward me.

"Did you say you are Kristy's boyfriend?" he asked, seeming dumbfounded with anger and confusion.

"Yep," I replied. "We were just headed back to my hotel room to fuck." That is when I looked at this woman, who was just as puzzled by me as this gigantic man was. "Tell him, Kristy," I said, looking at this woman with a wink. "We were just leaving to go fuck... right?"

"Yes, that's right," she said, not understanding what was happening. She couldn't figure out why a 5'10', 165-pound man was getting involved with a 6'5', 230-pound man. As I held out my arm while walking toward her, the look of bewilderment on her face rivaled that of the muscular man standing beside her.

"You are going to fucking die!" the muscular man said to me.

"Not tonight, Buddy," I responded. "You have two choices... one... get back in your car, and get the fuck out of here or... two... I knock your teeth out!" At this point, Kristy and this man stood there staring at me, not believing what they saw or heard. This was all pure comedy from my perspective.

"I warned you, little man, now you are going to fucking die!" the muscular man yelled. As he began to walk toward me, he was red in the face and had clenched teeth, while pounding his fist into his hand.

"You are about to make a big mistake, Dude!" I warned for the last time, but this didn't stop him. I was drunk and wasn't in the mood to be fighting. I also calculated how muscular this person was, so if he grabbed me, he might be able to put me in a situation I didn't want to be in. Rather than take my chances with a fistfight, I kicked his face with a roundhouse like Chuck Norris. This knocked him over, but it didn't end the fight.

He got right back up after this and then charged at me in a moment of rage. I jumped up and kicked him in his forehead to combat, but this didn't end the fight either. This guy had to have been high on coke or roid-raging because he was a total brute. When he charged at me again while trying to land a punch, I dodged his blow and ended the fight with a knockout punch to his upper cheek. If you hit a person just right and hard enough in the cheekbone, they are done. You have at least five minutes before they even realize who they are.

In the two minutes or so that this muscle freak and I were fighting, we attracted a crowd of over one hundred people. I looked around at all these people once this fight was over, and they all looked intensely bewildered. They couldn't believe that I just beat the living shit out of this guy considering our differences in size.

I remember Kristy looking at me with her mouth open and speechless. When I initially walked over to ask if she was okay, she just nodded her head and smiled. Moments later, when I whistled to hail a cab, Kristy ran up to me, "Wait, who are you?"

"My name is Oliver."

"That was amazing," she said. "Are you some sort of Karate expert or something?"

"Yeah, something like that," I replied.

"Where are you going?" she asked. "Can I come with you?"

"I'm sorry, but I have a girlfriend."

# Chapter XII

I WOKE UP THE following morning with a horrible hangover and needed to find my way around the Miami airport to fly back to Los Angeles. I don't know how engineers or architects came up with the design for the Miami International Airport, but they had to have been higher than Fredrick and the hippies. I'm amazed that I even got home. I bet some people never leave the Miami airport and get caught up in that maze for the rest of their lives.

I spent the next few days smoking joints with Fredrick. I also went over to see Anika and Jessica's apartment to pay the girls for helping me with the harvest. I told them to thank Tracy and Melissa for the work they did and made sure that they explained how grateful I was for driving the transport trucks. I didn't have an exact estimate on what I owed the four girls, but I thought Anika could figure it out if I gave her forty grand.

During our conversation, I explained that I was looking for an apartment, and Anika told me that one was available on the first floor of the building where she lived. One thing led to another, and I had keys to my first apartment by the afternoon of the next day. This place was about two miles away from Fredrick's house and the beach, but it all worked out because it had a nice parking garage for me to park my truck in.

I decided to contact Bile to get my next T6 Cartel contract within that same week. Surprisingly, I met with Bile at his house this time. He lived several miles south of Venice Beach near San Diego, and it took forever to get down there with traffic. However, his newfound trust was worth the drive.

I came to a few critical realizations during this meeting. The first one was that exploiting underage kids on the internet was just a hobby for Bile. The second realization was that Bile's career revolved around much higher levels of crime than I initially thought. The third realization was that the information contained in these contracts could potentially help law enforcement take down some T6 Cartel operations in the future. This particular realization became a crucial part of my reasoning for moving forward.

The first two contracts that I filled happened to be drug-related, which didn't stray too far away from my moral compass. I didn't support the idea of smuggling cocaine or Mexican pharmaceuticals into the United States, but it didn't bother me a whole hell of a lot. I didn't think that hallucinogenic drugs were even that bad, and I thought this to be particularly true for marijuana. I found cocaine, meth, and heroin to be on an entirely different level than acid or mushrooms, but not to the extent of actually being evil.

I got the impression that the other kingpins working for the T6 Cartel handled the vast majority of drug operations, while Bile was more into the weird shit. He had some exotic jobs that he had been describing, but these were not offered to me the first two times. It was obvious that I was still being groomed, and contracts involving drugs were the most straightforward.

There was little risk to Bile or T6 when it came to smuggling drugs. The FBI could know everything I did while fulfilling the terms of two contracts I had completed, but they still would have had nothing to secure a bust. At least not one they would be interested in pursuing. I was a tiny man in what were massive drug smuggling operations, so there would be no point in busting me. This would have likely not even been a possibility, out of an abundance of caution, to avoid interrupting massive international investigations. Because of this, realistically, drug smuggling was a relatively safe endeavor for myself and the T6 Cartel to be involved in.

My second contract is a fantastic example of this. I eventually learned that the cocaine plantation and processing facility that I visited in Columbia was the headquarters of a drug lord named El Loco. His real name was Daniel Barrera Barrera, and this man was far from a T6 Cartel employee. He was an essential member of the Revolutionary Armed Forces of Columbia guerrilla group right in the middle of his career as an international drug smuggler.

I learned that this plantation and processing facility was busted and seized in February of 2003, but El Loco avoided incarceration. He started an even bigger operation on the eastern plains of Colombia a year later and then became involved with members of the United Self-Defense Forces of Columbia. This was a paramilitary group who were members of Columbia Government Forces. This new drug operation would become even bigger than the one west of Bogota that had been seized. Eventually, this became a complex four-nation endeavor and eventually led to his 2012 arrest in Venezuela. This man was no Pablo Escobar, but he was still one of the biggest drug lords in history.

Despite my proximity to international cocaine kingpins and low-key involvement in massive drug smuggling operations, these contracts were not nearly as dangerous as one would imagine. Unfortunately, I was not offered any drug smuggling contracts at this meeting. I decided on a fifty thousand-dollar contract in Costa Rica for several reasons. The most important reason was that I was told that this assignment could be completed in a week or less, allowing plenty of time for me to make my court date back in Nebraska. It also didn't seem very hard to accomplish, nor did it sound anywhere near as frightening as my last contract.

"Do you want to go to Costa Rica?" Bile asked.

"Yeah, this seems like the contract I am most interested in," I replied. I like animals, and I have never been to Costa Rica." I said this without understanding what the contract actually entailed. I had no idea what was about to happen.

"Those are two excellent reasons to accept this contract," Bile responded with roaring laughter. "You'll love this place. The beaches and rainforests are beautiful. There are also plenty of exotic jungle animals to see. However, this contract requires you to drive a large truck. Are you able to drive trucks with a twelve-gear clutch?"

"Actually, yes," I answered. "I lived on a farm in Nebraska growing up, and I was taught how to drive a clutch at the age of twelve. My Dad also started a truck-driving business, and so he taught me how to drive semi-trucks. My Mom has always wanted me to go to college, but my Dad has secretly been trying to get me to drive trucks and take over his business someday."

"It sounds like you have a good family, which isn't common in this business," Bile said. "Almost everyone I have met in the T6 Cartel started with nothing to live for. Most of the members of this cartel don't have many friends or a family to go home to. I suppose there are a few exceptions to this, but not many. I'm curious now... why have you chosen to lead a life of crime?"

"I want to be rich," I answered. "Going to school and working hard for a living rarely makes anyone rich. I want to be like you!"

"You want to be like me?" Bile said, seeming to be taken back with fuel to become strangely arrogant. "Everyone wants to be like me, and no one wants to be like me. I am an evil man, Oliver. I'm not just going to hell someday. I assume that the devil himself will meet with me on my day of reckoning to give me an award in recognition of the highest honor of sin and evil."

"That would be quite an achievement," I replied.

"Why do you want to be like me anyway?" Bile asked. "Do you want to be an evil person, or is it just the money?"

"I want to drive fancy sports cars and own a mansion like you. I look through your windows and see three beautiful, topless women lying next to a pool in your giant backyard. You have fine art on your walls and nice furniture to sit on. How many bedrooms are there in this place?" I asked.

"Including my sex dungeon, all the bathrooms, living areas, and kitchen... there are thirty-five or so," Bile answered.

"That is what I am talking about... I will never live in a house with thirty-five bedrooms if I drive semi-trucks for my father. I need to drive them for you and the T6 Cartel," I explained. "And to answer your question about if I want to be an evil person... I don't think you are evil, and I don't think that what you do is evil. I think that this world is an evil place to live in. It wasn't the devil that created this world. It was God. I believe that he created you and me to carry out a higher purpose of being. What society has determined to be moral standards is only one perspective, which is jaded by religious freaks and stupid people. God needs people like you and me to carry out his wishes, his demands, and his quest to create a world full of evil. It is God that is evil, not the men that answer to him."

"That is fucking beautiful!" Bile said, while clapping his hands and turning to his three assailants. "Did you guys hear that shit? Oliver just explained that we live with a higher purpose of being and that we are crusaders of the lord. I have always thought that kidnapping and trafficking kids isn't just illegal, but that this was an absolutely evil thing to do to these little bastards. When I go down to my dungeon to fuck little kids, it isn't just about sexual pleasure to me... it's about finding pleasure in doing evil things. I love living the life of an evil person. These kids fear me more than anything else in the world, which puts a smile on my face. Well, hell... now I'm just confused."

"This is just what I think to myself," I said. "You can continue to think that you are evil. I don't think that it will make any difference." I was not expecting this response. I thought that I was raddling on about some bullshit to make Bile think that I wanted to be an evil person because I envied him.

"It might make a difference to Satan. I don't want to be an angel in heaven when I die. I want to become a demon in the inferno of hell," Bile replied, with a confused look on his face. "Now I don't even know if I want to be a goddamned criminal."

"Just forget what I said," I responded. "You are an evil man, and I am confident that you are destined to burn in hell. I'm sorry to have even told you this. Can I get the instructions for this contract in Costa Rica?

"Are you sure you don't want to stick around and watch me do evil things?" Bile asked. "I can teach you more about how I became so awesome."

"No, I'd like to just get going. I really have to take a shit, and kind of have this thing about shitting in someone's house if I respect the person that owns it. I know this may sound weird, but I only like to take dumps where I don't feel bad about rubbing shit on the walls. I have been seeing a therapist about this for years. It's just one of those things... you know."

"No, I don't know... but thank you for not rubbing shit on my walls," Bile replied. "Let's all just do a line of coke, and then I will discuss your contract in further detail."

"Cocaine just makes me need to take a shit even worse," I replied. "Is it possible to just get a quick overview and leave?"

"You will fly into San Jose, Costa Rica, to pick up a truck," Bile said. "You will then drive to a town called Quepos, which is just a little bit north of the Manuel Antonio Rainforest. You will meet a person named Juan there at a restaurant. He will load up your truck with a few exotic animals and reptiles to bring to Nicaragua. Juan will give you more instructions from there."

"Do the animals get hurt?" I asked, concerned that they were going to be eaten or something.

"No animals will get hurt. Everyone loves animals. I'm not even that evil, and I'm the evilest person I know," Bile explained. "I would tell you more, but that isn't how I like to handle this particular contract."

"That's good to know," I replied.

"Trust me, you'll love this contract. Easy money," Bile explained, as he reached for a pile of documents. "Here is a map of where to pick up the truck. Here is a map of where you will meet Juan and your voucher for American Airlines. You can still catch a flight to Costa Rica today if you are determined enough. Oh, and bring a large suitcase."

"Why do I need a large suitcase?" I asked. "I like to travel light."

"You will want to bring a few changes of clothes, I imagine, and some trunks if you want to take a swim in the ocean. Also, you will be paid with cordoba, so you're going to need a large suitcase."

"What the fuck is cordoba?" I asked. "I want to be paid in cash, not Costa Rican monkey shit."

"Cordoba is the currency used in Nicaragua," Bile explained. "Fifty thousand dollars is an awful lot of money to the residents of Nicaragua. People with fifty grand worth of Cordoba would be considered to be rich. This amount of cash will barely fit into a suitcase unless it is abnormally large... now that I think about it... maybe bring some clothes that you wouldn't mind throwing in the trash. Then a normal-sized suitcase may work. I'll let you decide that one."

"When do I get paid?" I asked.

"You'll meet a man named Rafiel in Managua. He will pay you immediately once you have dropped off the truck at his warehouse."

"Perfect," I remarked as I started walking toward the front door of Bile's house.

"Oh, and one more thing... tell Juan that his daughter's pussy is primo!"

I didn't know what Bile meant by this statement, but I knew that it was about something pure fucking evil. I left his house with a plan to document everything and eventually turn this information over to the authorities. I needed to continue thinking that my involvement with the T6 Cartel would eventually lead to its downfall to keep my conscience out of the weeds.

# Chapter XIII

I FLEW DIRECTLY OUT of Los Angeles International Airport later that same afternoon. It was a seven-hour flight to San Jose, Costa Rica, and I gained two hours going from Pacific Standard Time to Central Standard Time. I touched down just before midnight and felt pretty good about accomplishing the terms of this contract when I initially arrived at the airport. I wasn't scheduled to pick up the truck until 2 pm the following day, so this gave me plenty of time to explore the capital city. Unfortunately, I thought that San Jose was boring and wasn't worth the time I spent wandering around looking for something interesting to look at, so I went to pick up the truck about an hour before I was scheduled.

The truck that I asked to drive was rare to see in America. It was a huge fifty-foot container truck that didn't pivot, which was the biggest truck you could find in Costa Rica back in 2001. When I was initially shown this unusual automobile, I was informed that there was some added load weight from the modifications that were needed to keep the exotic animals alive during transport. Other than the fact that this truck was substantially larger than I expected, there were no significant concerns about the vehicle that jumped out at me. This country still had many characteristics of a third-world country in 2001, so there weren't any semi-trucks with long trailers due to its primitive system of highways and roads. This has since changed because of the incredible amount of advanced development and industrialization this country has seen over the years.

I was on the road by around three o'clock in the afternoon. At this point, I anticipated being able to make it to my destination before it got dark. I had a logical reason for thinking this. I looked at the map Bile gave me and calculated that San Jose was about one hundred and sixty kilometers from the town called Quepos. I thought it would only take me three hours to drive to my destination with good road conditions. Bile also explained that I needed to meet Juan at the restaurant just south of Quepos at four o'clock the following afternoon.

The man who arranged for my truck provided me with the rudimentary road conditions and basic vehicle information. He said that the road to Quepos was treacherous in several places, but I thought he was just telling me this out of an abundance of caution. I was also told that it was the beginning of summer in Costa Rica, so I thought the sun would set after 9 pm, like in America during summertime. Even though this person spoke perfect English, I never thought to ask him more questions. This was pretty stupid in hindsight.

I left San Jose confident that the drive to Quepos would be as easy as driving around in America. The roads were nice and easy to travel on for the first hour and a half, so everything was going great for the first fifty kilometers. However, it started to get dark a short while later, and it was completely dark out by the time I passed through a town called Orotina at around 6 pm. This caught me by surprise because I thought it would be another three or four hours till sunset. My lack of understanding regarding my proximity to the equator and how this affected time was just the beginning of a journey riddled with several misjudgments and honest mistakes. Knowing what I know now, I would have found a place to stay in Orotina.

If you were to travel in Costa Rica today, you'd find that Highway 34 is a pleasant drive. This is the road between Orotina, and a popular surf destination called Jaco Beach. Unfortunately, this nicely paved highway didn't exist when I made this trip. The road I had to travel on was very narrow and bumpy once it turned into gravel about five miles past Orotina. In many places, it winded around hills and miniature mountains, which exposed the edges of this road to several steep cliffs.

Driving on this road with a normal-sized vehicle during the day when the sun was shining would have been inconvenient, but driving on it during the night with a fifty-foot container truck was downright scary. It never really got dark out in southern California due to the light pollution. Even in rural Nebraska, the countryside always seemed illuminated by twinkling stars and moonlight. This was not what I experienced once I passed Orotina. Nighttime in Costa Rica seemed much darker than I was used to. About three hours into this driving expedition, I was convinced that no light existed in this country after sunset.

Not only was the darkness on another level, but I also discovered that my headlights didn't work very well once the road turned into gravel. Part of my problem was that I only had dim headlights. There wasn't even a bright headlight option on this truck. I also found that every time I hit a large bump, the headlights flickered, and they would turn completely off for a second or two if the bump was big enough. The extra dark darkness of Costa Rica and my stupid headlights were just the beginning of the problems I faced while traveling from Orotina to Jaco.

It started to rain shortly after nightfall, and I started to notice some weird shit immediately after the first raindrop hit my windshield. I didn't even think this drop of water was rain at all. I thought a small puddle of water had been collected in a tree or something, and it fell on my window as I was driving by. Even after ten more puddles of water hit my windshield a few seconds later, I still couldn't figure out where this water was coming from. It didn't take me much longer to realize that these water puddles were mutated tropical raindrops. These drops of water were so big that your hair would become completely soaked if just one of these drops fell on your head, and you'd probably fucking drown if these raindrops kept falling on your head, like how the song goes.

My introduction to tropical rainstorms and torrential downpours in Costa Rica that night was an experience I never thought was possible. Complex drainage systems typically mitigate the problems caused by rainstorms in America, so only the worst storms cause flooding. Conversely, everyone would probably have drowned years ago if America faced the same rainstorms as Central America. I bet that most states would be completely underwater right now, and that's only if the entire nation wasn't swept into the Gulf of Mexico by a biblical expansion of the Mississippi River.

Hundreds of rainstorms occur each year in Costa Rica. Some just cause small puddles and little streams to form on the roads, which are hazards that are not difficult to deal with. Unfortunately, the worst rainstorms would cause these small ponds to turn into lakes and the little streams into raging rivers.

It rained for only about twenty minutes initially, but the hazards created by this short rainstorm still caused some impressive delays. Once the rain started, it took me over an hour to travel five more miles, and then it took me another three hours to reach the top of the highest pass, which was only another ten miles down the road.

Costa Rica extends majestically from the Pacific Ocean to the Caribbean Sea with a width of well under two hundred miles at its furthest cross-section. This statistic helps you understand what makes this small mountain pass unique. On a clear day, you can stand on top of this pass and see the Atlantic and Pacific oceans simply by turning your head. It is the only location in this country where you can experience this. Thinking more about it, this is likely one of the only places in the world where this incredible phenomenon exists.

Unfortunately, it was nighttime when I went over this pass, so I wasn't able to observe this spectacular view. I only understood this part of the road as the pinnacle of treachery and the exact opposite of a splendid location to travel to. I reluctantly continued down this dangerous mountain in the dead of night for another three hours and only traveled another four miles during this time. That is just slightly over one mile per hour, which explains how far off my travel estimations were when I predicted an average speed of 55 mph.

I had to get out of the truck multiple times to figure out how to move past the obstacle in front of me, and that was before the second tropical rainstorm I experienced that night. This rainstorm started about halfway down this small mountain, and it rained for two hours straight. There were so many hazards to deal with the rest of the way to Jaco that I didn't think I would make it. There were two places where I honestly thought my truck would need to be abandoned. Both times, I stood outside my truck for nearly an hour while trying to find the answers I needed to move past these dreadful hazards. The first place was a tight switchback that caused my right rear tire and nearly the entire back end of my truck to hang off a cliff.

The other place was at a river that typically ran under the road through a large concrete culvert. Unfortunately, when I drove to this river, it was running over the road and caused my entire truck to experience a frightening horizontal drift that nearly sank the entire truck. Miraculously, I experienced a couple of low-key epiphanies that solved both of these problems, and I was able to continue onward. Thankfully, these were the worst road conditions and the most prolonged delays I experienced during my entire expedition while fulfilling the terms of this contract.

It took me roughly twelve hours to drive fifty-five miles from Orotina to Jaco Beach. My tank was completely empty when I finally made it into town. First and foremost, I had to stop for fuel, but I was also exhausted and hungry, so I grabbed a quick breakfast and took a short nap to combat my fatigue. The restaurant I ate at was across the road from the beach, so I could look out onto the Pacific Ocean while eating. I couldn't believe that this was the same ocean that created the West Coast of North America because this was nothing like I had ever seen before. What I saw that morning was absolutely incredible! The thoughts inspired by this insane observation fell nothing short of pure astonishment. I watched some of the most powerful waves in the world. These were likely the biggest waves I will ever see in my entire life.

The first set of waves crashed about two-thirds of a mile from the beach, and I was told that they were easily over fifty feet tall. When the sheer force from these waves crashed into the ocean, the impact caused a second set of waves that were roughly half the size of the first. These waves created a third set nearly fifteen feet tall, which caused a fourth and final set of waves that I estimated to be about six feet. This last set of waves was similar in size to the ones I tried to surf on in California. The enormous size of these waves was incredible, but that wasn't what I was so astonished by. I couldn't believe my eyes when I saw about thirty surfers riding the massive wall of water created by the first set of waves. This blew my mind. Over two decades later, I still have vivid memories of these gigantic waves and the surfers riding them.

Another thing that I saw while eating breakfast was a busload of kids dropped off at the beach. They mostly walked around in the sand and played in shallow water. However, I noticed one of these kids attempting to surf on the last set of waves about the time I was finished eating. He was struggling pretty hard and showed no sign that he would learn to surf anytime soon. Suddenly, this poor kid was desperately holding on to his surfboard while the undertow swept him a hundred yards or more into the ocean in a matter of a few seconds. I could hear him screaming in terror from where I sat at the restaurant. Thankfully, I didn't witness this boy drowning that day. By some miracle, the undertow quickly moved him parallel to the beach into some rocks on the south shore.

# Chapter XIV

After breakfast, I continued on my journey south and was happy that the rest of this drive was relatively mellow. Everything went so smoothly after this that I managed to arrive in Quepos with enough time to check into a cheap motel and rest for a few hours. I woke up from a pleasant dream around two o'clock in the afternoon feeling refreshed. I really needed this after the nightmare I experienced while driving from Orotina.

I was right on time to meet Juan at the meet-up location. This was a fascinating restaurant called El Tapatio Oceania that sat on a beautiful beach between Quepos and the Parque Nacional Manuel Antonio rainforest. It was built on top of giant wooden stilts that rose up from the sand of Playa La Macha. It was the only building on this entire beach.

When I walked into this restaurant, I was immediately greeted with a handshake by a very well-mannered Hispanic man named Juan. He spoke to me in broken English as we exchanged names and a polite introduction. Moments later, he started to explain that his brother was the chef at this restaurant. He repeated himself several times while trying to explain how good of a chef his brother was, and then he began to elaborate at great length about how he prepared every dish on the menu. I was told over and over how much he loved his brother during this conversation. My heart just melted from this man's admiration of his sibling.

Juan may have been the politest person that I ever met in my life. He was unbelievably pleasant to be around. From the moment I met him, I couldn't turn down anything he ever offered me, so I wholeheartedly decided to stay at the restaurant to have a meal prepared by his brother. This made both of us extremely happy. He was happy that I wanted to stay at the restaurant and have his brother cook for us. I was happy that this made Juan happy, and I was also starving.

We watched the sunset over the Pacific Ocean as we ate dinner, and Juan was not kidding about his brother's unique ability to prepare food. This man was an exceptional chef, and he went way out of his way to make sure that I absolutely understood this. I only ordered the Seafood Risotto and a single bottle of beer, but I was served so much more than this. Juan's brother spoiled me with ten small specially prepared appetizers before my Seafood Risotto entrée arrived, and I had a continuous refill of a Costa Rican-brewed beer called Imperial all night long. This was easily the best seafood meal I'd ever had in my life, and it didn't stop there!

This meal was followed by a dessert called Tres Leches Cake. Juan described this as Costa Rica's favorite dessert. Of course, he explained that no other chef in the entire country was better at preparing this dessert than his brother. This was a sponge cake baked from scratch with sugar, flour, eggs, and vanilla. Three types of milk were added... evaporated milk, heavy cream, and sweetened condensed milk. It was then topped with Chantilly cream to create its rich flavor. This dessert was incredible! I ate like a king that night and will never forget that meal.

After we finished eating dinner, I followed Juan with my giant fifty-foot truck to a little house on Costa Rica's Pacific coast. This unique home was built on a hill overlooking a beautiful beach and the official entrance to Parque Nacional Manuel Antonio. We sat on Juan's porch that night with two cases of beer, a big bag of weed, and a portable cassette stereo. Juan played all his favorite songs, which became a soundtrack for a perfect night. Remarkably, not a single word was mentioned during our many conversations regarding the T6 Cartel or our involvement in its animal and reptile smuggling operations. Instead, we engaged in numerous pleasantries, which resulted in several hours of swapping stories and kind words. Both of us had a fantastic time getting to know one another. Juan told me so many wonderful stories about Costa Rica that night that I thought that I might have arrived in paradise. It seemed that this man loved every single person on Earth and expressed admiration for his family, which seemed to be unrivaled by even the closest families. This initial experience would indicate that he was the happiest person alive.

I remember looking out into the ocean the following morning, and it was terrific. The beach was just down the hill from where Juan's house was built. After breakfast, Juan and I wandered down for a swim. Walking across this white sand beach, I noticed the grains of sand were similar to those in a sandbox, but the granules were just a smidgin smaller. There were sand dollars and small crabs everywhere. Except for the gigantic stingray I saw in the water right next to me, the ocean was a great place to swim and body surf.

We spent a couple of hours swimming in the Pacific Ocean and lying on the beach before putting on our clothes and shoes. Then we walked toward the rainforest and through the south shore entrance of Parque Nacional Manuel Antonio. I saw hundreds of animals and reptiles in the park that day. There were white-faced monkeys, squirrel monkeys, little monkeys, and big monkeys. I saw sloths in the trees that were moving around so slowly that they didn't even seem to move at all. There were dozens of lizards and snakes of all sorts. I saw birds everywhere when I looked up at the tree branches. I even saw a couple of toucans who appeared to be in love.

In 2001, this place was pristine and untouched by human development. No one was around for miles, and this meant something to Juan and me. My fifty-foot container truck and Juan's automobile were the only two vehicles on the road to get here, and we didn't see a single automobile or another person this entire day. This was a special place and a magical experience.

The next day, there would be a car full of people who came to this place and undoubtedly made the same observations as I did. I'm sure that this was a special place and a magical experience for them as well. They probably loved it so much that they took some pictures and told their friends about it. I bet their pictures were so beautiful that their friends couldn't believe their eyes. There would be no question that every person they showed their pictures to would want to come to Costa Rica.

However, as months passed and a few years went by, thousands of people did exactly what these folks did. They would come to this paradise, take pictures, and tell all their friends about this special place and the magical experience they had. Not a day passed by without people wandering around on the beach and through the park. Eventually, a tour bus showed up at the entrance of Parque Nacional Manuel Antonio. People of all ages and nationalities were on this bus, eager to explore the wonders of the rainforest. After this experience, everyone returned to the bus with a feeling that warmed their hearts.

Another year would pass, and then construction began. The first villa was built right next to a bar and grill just down the road from Juan's house. Juan was happy about this when these were the only two buildings besides his own home because the restaurant provided a place for him to eat and drink. He also enjoyed the small bar, where he could meet new people and have conversations. Despite this place being developed, I'm sure it was still a special place to visit... at least for the first few years.

*Erica and I came back to this place in 2019 with our three children. We sat in a traffic jam for over an hour between Quepos and the small destination city that had formed there. This was mostly caused by road construction, but it didn't help that hundreds of tourists were on their way to Parque Nacional Manuel Antonio, just like our family. Every square inch of land adjacent to the beach had been developed. There were people everywhere I looked, walking across the beach and through the rainforest. I still had a magical experience seeing all the animals in the park and watching my kids swim in the ocean, but it wasn't quite the special place that I remembered.*

*The magical time I experienced when I initially arrived in Costa Rica still has a special place in my heart. This led to a lifetime friendship I shared with Juan until the day he passed away in 2015. I was not able to attend his funeral, but I'll bet the overdevelopment of the paradise surrounding his house made him turn over in his grave.*

# Chapter XV

AFTER JUAN GUIDED ME through Parque Nacional Manuel Antonio Rainforest, we made the hike back up to Juan's house. Walking down to the beach toward the entrance of the park was much easier than walking back. It took two hours to walk across the entire beach, and then up the hill to Juan's little house. We made it back about a half hour before sunset. I would have normally spent more time admiring the horizon because it was gorgeous just like the night before. However, my enjoyment was allayed by exhaustion. I fell fast asleep on Juan's couch within minutes of our return.

I slept hard for about five hours before being suddenly awakened by someone shaking my shoulder. When I opened my eyes, I saw Juan standing above me. That was when he told me that we were leaving. For the life of me, I couldn't understand where we could possibly need to go at this time of night. I wasn't scheduled to leave Costa Rica until Saturday, and it was only Thursday night. When I asked Juan what was going on, all he told me was that I needed to meet some friends of his.

This seemed strange to me for several reasons, and I sensed a tremendous amount of anxiety because Juan was no longer the charming man that I had come to know over the past twenty-four hours. Juan wasn't being mean at all. It just seemed like something had gone terribly wrong. I tried my best to postpone this expedition until the following morning, but Juan demanded that we leave immediately.

We left just before eleven o'clock that night. I started to follow his tiny truck driving north in my fifty-foot container truck, hoping that Juan had a good reason for our untimely departure and that we didn't have far to drive. Incidentally, we only went down the road about two miles at the most before we turned off the gravel road onto a pathway through the jungle. I initially thought that this was our destination because the unkempt trail we turned into didn't seem conducive for large trucks to travel any further. Unfortunately, I was wrong about my assumption, and I soon realized this was just the beginning of a long drive cutting straight through the rainforest.

Thick foliage grew right next to this narrow pathway, so after a mile or so, there was no turning back. My truck was just far too large. I had no idea where I was or where I was going, and I continued to ponder this anomalous mystery for several more miles. I drove through murky fog and intense darkness for over an hour before I finally began to suspect that we were headed toward the smuggling operation. I knew at this point that a simple mission to meet some of Juan's friends no longer made sense.

As I continued onward, I stumbled upon another peculiar thought. I realized that Juan and I had some secrets we never told each other. The man I had become familiar with didn't seem like the criminal type. He seemed like a moral person who wouldn't ever do anything wrong. Our conversation was dominated by his profound love for everything, and there was no exception when it came to the exotic jungle creatures that lived in the rainforests of Costa Rica.

This left me feeling very puzzled about Juan's involvement with the T6 Cartel.

As I thought about this situation even further, I figured Juan might be thinking the same thing about me. He never asked me a single question about my involvement with the cartel either. I wasn't even sure I wanted to tell Juan anything about the illegal things I was involved in. This was mostly because I respected him and thought that he was nothing short of a saint. I honestly felt that his tainted judgment of me would burden my conscience. The irony in my reasoning was that he was also involved with the T6 Cartel. Something didn't feel right about any of this.

We finally arrived at our destination just past 2 am, and I was not surprised to learn that we had just ascended upon the animal and reptile smuggling operation. I had my windows rolled down and started to hear a low melody of spine-chilling misery echoing through the forest about a mile away from this hell. As this horrifying sound got louder and louder, I realized it was caused by the rainforest's imperious cry for help. This collective voice of terror was coming from the captive jungle creatures, and it reached a fever pitch where this unkept trail ended.

As I passed through the entrance of this evil place, I immediately saw hundreds of boxes and cages used to keep exotic creatures in captivity. These enclosures were mixed in with many bizarre trapping devices and appeared haphazardly scattered about in every direction I turned. I was surprised at how chaotic and disorderly this place was because T6 Cartel operations typically appeared to be systematic and tidy. It kind of looked like a junkyard. In addition to the unorganized assortment of weird gadgets used for animal and reptile captivity, there were all sorts of other random shit lying around. These things were mixed in with several giant piles of garbage and individual pieces of trash lying around everywhere I looked.

When I stepped out of the truck and saw Juan's face, it was painfully obvious that he hated this place. He looked like he wanted to cry. When he spoke to me, his emotional distress cultivated a level of embarrassment, sadness, and pain that cannot be described in words. What he felt when we arrived at this location was wicked and profound.

I partially empathized with his emotions simply by pondering the characteristics of this disgusting operation. When I typically look into a rainforest, day or night, I am usually greeted by an intriguing feeling of contentment. In contrast, the rainforest that surrounded us was disturbing as fuck! This place was horrific! Everything I looked at seemed to be pure evil. Unfortunately, this was as far as my blind empathy traveled, but this was nowhere close to all that was disturbing Juan that night. The massive pile of sins collected in this horrible place was something that I didn't understand just yet, and what I didn't understand was worse than I could have ever imagined... much worse.

I parked the truck on a long driveway that led up to a small house. This primitive dwelling appeared to have been built from lumber collected from a shipwreck or something. This strange residence wasn't just creepy, it was its own little version of hell. I was quickly brought into this house shortly after we arrived. Juan walked a few steps ahead of me, and as he opened the front door, I was immediately appalled by a terrible smell. A mixture of human bio waste, spilled booze, cigarettes, and an absurd amount of filth caused such a foul odor that it took all my remaining willpower not to add to the stench with my own vomit.

I realized moments later that this was all caused by the four wasted, drunk men we found inside. These four men were only a short step away from death by alcohol poisoning. Even if I could speak fluent Spanish, there would be no way to understand a single word that was said to me by any one of them. They couldn't even stand up, and yet they were still falling down. One of these men was completely covered in vomit, and I could see that all three men had pissed or shit themselves.

As petrifying as this was to look at and smell, I was about to hear something worse... much worse! When I asked Juan who these men were and why they were so drunk, he began to tell me a story that was beyond frightening. I was told that this operation was not in conjunction with T6 Cartel operations and that this was actually one of Bile's separate enterprises. He said that the only exposure these four men and himself had with the cartel was limited to genuine threats of torture and murder. Bile explained his evil involvement with the T6 Cartel in detail to Juan. He was specifically told about special teams of assassins who were experts at torturing people. Juan had no doubt that these members of the T6 Cartel would become involved in this operation if Bile ever needed their help. Fortunately, this hadn't happened yet.

Bile and his three assailants only occasionally visited this place since operations began a decade earlier. Three times a year, a man like myself came to transport the exotic jungle creatures from this remote Costa Rican rainforest to the largest city in Nicaragua. I was told that once my truck was loaded, I would need to drive 784 kilometers to a warehouse in Managua. When I arrived at this destination after two days of driving, my contract would be completed, and I was promised to be paid immediately.

I then asked if I would encounter treacherous or unstable roads on my journey to this city. Juan said that he had never actually driven to Managua, but he didn't recall the previous driver telling him about any treacherous or unstable roads. He didn't think my journey driving north would be anything like what I experienced on my drive from Orotina to Jaco.

When I asked Juan what happened to the previous driver, he told me something very disturbing. Despite the fact that this information related directly to me, it was still likely the least disturbing thing that he explained for the rest of the night. Juan told me that the previous driver who transported the exotic jungle creatures from Costa Rica to Nicaragua was the only person assigned to this particular contract since its inception. He went on to say that this man's name was Jeff, and he lived in the Los Angeles area just like me. Jeff was described as a very pleasant person who wore his heart on his sleeve. This person had become Juan's close friend despite his disapproval of this man's involvement with the jungle creature smuggling operation.

He said that Jeff worked for Bile as his personal truck driver for over fifteen years and completed assignments all over the world with no major incidents occurring. This particular information surprised me, but it also made me think that Bile's truck-driving contracts had to be relatively safe. He said that Jeff turned sixty-five years old roughly two months before I was given this contract, and that he just recently asked Bile if he could retire. Bile responded to this request by bringing him to this place in the jungle, only as a coincidence, as far as he could tell. Then he made Juan and the four drunk men inside this house watch his assailants brutally murder Jeff with hundreds of rounds of gunfire. I was told that this occurred only two weeks before my arrival in Costa Rica.

As disturbing as this was, I had to interrupt Juan briefly to ask why he was telling me this. I wondered why he trusted that I wouldn't use this information for future wrongdoing. I thought that this conversation could put myself, Juan, and the four drunk men in this house in grave danger. He didn't say much about this, and his explanation was short. He said that his ability to understand character was impeccable, which often gave him insight. This was in addition to something I said while we were drunk, which apparently assured him that his intuition was correct. He didn't elaborate or expand on this any further.

This was the point in this conversation where things seemed to take a hard turn further into the abyss. I was told that these four men were the hunters and trappers of all the exotic jungle creatures ever held captive at this evil place. They had lived in this house for the past ten years and were never allowed to leave for any reason. This hideous act of terror would follow them up into heaven and down into hell if Bile discovered any one of them to be missing. Even suicide would result in a punishment so horrific that it would transcend death and planet Earth.

They were told that no matter how their absence occurred, it would result in the missing person's entire family being brutally murdered, and that would only be the beginning. Costa Rica would experience a fucking genocide. This would begin with a team of T6 Cartel operatives looking for every family member related to all four of these men, and then everyone would be brought to this evil place in the jungle. They would then be placed in cages while Bile waited for the T6 Cartel's most skilled torture expert to arrive. It was promised that this person would spend a week torturing everyone and that he would eventually force these four men to kill each member of their own family... one by one, till they were all dead.

Juan paused here for a minute because his story caused me to start crying like a little baby. This is when I looked around the room at all four faces of these poor drunk men. What I saw at that moment was terrifying. Juan understood how this conversation was affecting me, but he didn't have any intentions of ending it here. He just politely asked me to get it together because there was a lot more that needed to be explained.

Once I regained a suitable composure to listen to the rest of Juan's story, he began to tell me a long-winded explanation of how much he hated this smuggling operation. He described how much he hated the place where we were standing and how much he hated participating in such an evil endeavor. He explained in great detail how much he hated Bile and his three thugs. He also told me how much he loved all the exotic jungle creatures. He then described the relationship he had with the four drunk men and the incredible sympathy he felt for them.

Then Juan finally began to tell me about his involvement with this smuggling operation and his personal interactions with Bile and his three assailants. He explained that Bile paid him one hundred thousand dollars a year to perform his job. Juan was essentially the manager of this operation and Bile's personal assistant for any contract found associated with Costa Rica.

He explained that Bile built his house, where we were just a few hours earlier, and it was built for a reason entirely different from what I had expected. It had nothing to do with its enchanting view of the Pacific Ocean, the short walking distance to the beach, or its proximity to the entrance of Parque Nacional Manuel Antonio Rainforest. This house was specifically built in that location because it was only two miles from the intersection of the road that led us through the jungle. It was built in that very spot because you could look north and south for over a mile in both directions.

Juan said he also owned a house in Quepos. This was where the rest of his family lived, except for his daughter. He said that he met Bile at a bar in Quepos in the early fall of 1997 and had no idea of his smuggling operations. Much like my initial conversation with Juan, he described how fantastic of a chef his brother was. Juan's kind nature and drunkenness eventually led to an invitation that he would regret for the rest of his life.

When Bile came over for dinner at his family's home in Quepos, he was promised the best meal he had ever eaten prepared by Juan's brother. This dinner was served precisely as was described. However, once Bile finished with his meal, he stood up from his chair at the dinner table and deplorably held everyone at gunpoint. He proceeded to make Juan tie up his family into one giant ball of human misery. This consisted of his brother, his brother's newlywedded wife, his own wife, two adolescent sons, and a one-year-old boy.

A beautiful little girl named Angel was spared from being tied to these six people. Angel was only twelve years old and had just started middle school. She was just a sweet, innocent child and the apple of her daddy's eye. Juan was so proud to be this little girl's father and described a love for her that could have gone on for days. Unfortunately, this description of love and admiration for Angel was cut short to describe something incredibly sinister. Juan and his daughter would experience a type of hell that night that was so evil that it transcended every description of hell that has ever been told.

Bile locked the frightened little girl in her bedroom that night and tied Juan to a chair pointed right in front of the bed. Then, he forced him to watch his daughter get brutally raped and sodomized for hours and hours. For the next six days, this family continued to sit all tied together in the living room, and Juan was never untied from this chair. He was forced to watch Bile and his three goons repeatedly rape Angel repeatedly.

These four demons finally left Juan's house with his daughter on the seventh day of this hell, and this was when the devil told Juan about his new job. He was told that if he was perfectly obedient, his family would never be bothered again, and Angel would be returned to him on her eighteenth birthday. Juan knew his daughter was still alive because Bile sent him a naked picture of Angel each year on her birthday. She was sixteen when this story was told.

When Juan finished deliberating this deplorable story of freakish misery, I immediately ran out the door crying. I tried to make it over to my truck, but I only made it about twenty feet before I fell to the ground, shaking and vomiting. Moments later, I passed out in a pile of puke and tears. I woke up fifty-three hours later on the couch back inside the house. I was passed out for so long that Juan thought I was in a coma and had suffered a life-threatening epiphany.

By the time I finally regained consciousness, Juan and the four drunk men had already loaded my truck with thousands of exotic jungle creatures. Despite having a horrible headache and cloudy vision from my lengthy slumber, I couldn't stand to stay another minute in that creepy place. I said goodbye to Juan and the four drunk men within the hour.

As I began to travel through the rainforest with my windows rolled down, I began to wonder why I didn't hear any sounds coming from reptiles or animals when the rainforest should have been full of them. When I stopped in Quepos to perform a vehicle inspection to ensure my truck was ready for my journey north to Nicaragua, I finally turned off the engine and stepped out of my truck. This was when I heard the faint sound of thousands of captive jungle creatures and made the disturbing realization that all the exotic jungle creatures that should have been in the rainforest were now in the back of my truck.

I had to bear the heavy burden of this terrifying captivity and the details of this haunting tale the whole way to Managua. For the next 784 kilometers, I contemplated Juan's story over and over, wishing to God I could think of something else, but this wasn't possible. I eventually realized that there was no way to break free. It was impossible to escape this nightmare. I was lucky enough to be able to leave the smuggling operation physically, but I was destined to spend the rest of my life mentally incarcerated by this freakish memory.

# Chapter XVI

Aside from the stress and trauma relating to the contract itself, I didn't experience any major problems throughout the remainder of my time in Central America. I only needed to stop once while on this journey. This occurred shortly after sunset when my headlights started to flicker again as they did in between Orotina and Jaco Beach. I no longer felt safe to drive. Fortunately, I had just driven past the coastal city of Puntarenas when I came to this realization, so I pulled into a truck stop on the outskirts of town. I managed to fix the problem with just a little electrical tape, but it was impossible to find the short in the dark, so I ended up spending the night at the truck stop.

Incidentally, the only other issue I experienced occurred only an hour after I left the following morning when I ran into heavy road construction. Thankfully, all this really amounted to was a forced two-hour detour through the Arenal region of northern Costa. I happened to drive right by Volcan Arenal while on this detour, which I found to be fortunate in hindsight. I remember seeing the smoke rising up from the chimney of this volcano from miles away. As I drove closer, I could see lava shooting up from the top and flowing down the side. I was able to stop at the official observation area, which was only a mile away from the base of the volcano.

The view from this advantage point was absolutely spectacular and ended up being the only pleasant experience I had while traveling through Costa Rica on my way to Nicaragua.

After crossing the border, I only needed to travel for another sixty miles to reach my final destination, which was a warehouse located only a few blocks from Managua's city center. I remember feeling incredibly relieved when the terms of this contract were finally completed. The obsessive thoughts I had been experiencing immediately began to fade into reflections much easier to deal with. It also felt like there was more for me to look forward to, like feeling happy again.

As relieved as I was to complete this contract, it didn't mean I left Nicaragua with a suitcase full of cordoba and a clear head. Unfortunately, my obsessive thoughts turned into permanent discernment and terrible memories that have refused to leave my head. I was so traumatized by Juan's story, and the burden of this assignment that it still causes symptoms of PTSD over two decades later. Half of the prescription pills that I take before going to bed are directly related to this specific experience.

It was well after dark by the time I dropped off the container truck full of exotic jungle animals in Managua. I left the warehouse carrying a suitcase containing 1,800,000 cordoba, and mixed feelings about my current situation. I was happy that my contract was completed, but I also felt very nervous about walking around with so much money. In America, fifty thousand dollars was slightly more than the average yearly salary in 2001, which was a lot of money, but it wasn't life-changing money for most Americans. This was in stark contrast to Nicaragua, where the average yearly salary was slightly less than 36,000 cordoba. My suitcase contained the equivalent of fifty yearly salaries in this country. This created several problems for me. The most obvious problem I faced was my safety. The other issue I had was figuring out how to exchange 1,800,000 cordoba for 50,000 American dollars.

Fortunately, I was able to hail a cab to the airport shortly after leaving the warehouse. This dramatically mitigated the issue of safety, but I still needed to check my suitcase full of cordoba and get through customs. The general vibe of airport security a month after the 9/11 terrorist attacks was downright bizarre. People were afraid that their flight would get hijacked by Al Queda. Everyone refused to take off their shoes, and George Bush Jr. was our president. It was awful. You just didn't want to be in an airport or in an airplane... period.

I only had three more days till I needed to be back in Ogallala, so I tried to get a direct flight to Denver, but this was not in the cards. Unfortunately, I didn't even have the option of flying through Houston. I only had two choices if I wanted to get to Denver. I could wait two days and fly through Los Angeles, or I could leave the following morning and fly through Miami. The element of time made it unrealistic to fly through Los Angeles because the connecting flight to Denver landed at 10 pm the day before my court date, and I had no way to arrange a ride from the airport back to Nebraska until I was stateside. Unfortunately, this meant I needed to fly through Miami International Airport. I was just in this airport, and it was a miserable experience. When considering the luggage I had to check, I would have been sweating bullets no matter where my flight connected, and now I had to add the chaos of Miami International Airport.

After suffering from alcoholism for a number years when I was younger, Erica made me quit drinking altogether shortly after our first child was born. However, at the age of eighteen, I still had no idea that I was an alcoholic. I just thought that I drank a lot because it was a fun thing to do. The first time I sat down at the bar in the Augusto Ceasar Sandino International Airport, I ordered a beer to kill time and think about my next move. This was before I figured out that I needed to fly through Miami.

Once I understood my flight schedule, I returned to the bar. This may have been the first time I ever experienced stress drinking. I drank all night long. There is no way to know how many beers I drank, but my best guess would be somewhere between twenty and thirty. It may have been closer to forty by the time I finally boarded my flight to Miami. I had already paid for my ticket to Denver and had this in my pocket when I sat down at the bar, but I had to wait till 5 am the following morning to check my luggage for my 9:36 flight to Miami. I was so drunk by 5 am that I left my suitcase full of 1,800,000 cordoba sitting under my bar stool when I went to go check my luggage.

When I realized my mistake, the airport was empty, so there was a good chance that all I needed to do to solve this problem was walk back to get the suitcase. Unfortunately, I didn't pay any attention on my way to the American Airlines check luggage station. All I could remember was that I got lost a few times trying to find it. I was so drunk that it took me two hours to find my way back to the bar. Thankfully, no one took off with my suitcase. Nevertheless, it was no longer at the bar at this point. I was told that it was brought to lost and found when the night shift bartender finished her shift.

This meant that I needed to find the lost and found area now. A sensible person would have immediately left the bar to go find the lost and found, but I was not sensible at all. I fully understood that drinking is how my drunk ass got into this ridiculous situation in the first place, but that didn't stop me from ordering a few more beers. When I got up from the bar, it was about 7:30, so I had two hours till my flight left for Miami. By the grace of God, I somehow found the lost and found area within twenty minutes or after giving a giant wad of cash to an airport disability electric cart driver. I should have asked him to stick around so he could have brought me to the check-luggage area after this. Unfortunately, he left with a smile on his face and a wad of cash equivalent to a months' salary with no intention of ever seeing me again.

After filling out my lost and found claim receipt, I carried around this stupid suitcase for another forty minutes. As stupid as this all sounds, you'd think that is where my problem ended. Unfortunately, my problems had just begun. When I went to check my luggage, I realized that I had now lost my passport. There wasn't a snowball chance in hell I was going to make my flight to Miami at this point, but that didn't stop me from checking my suitcase. Unfortunately, I wasn't thinking ahead, and American Airlines allowed me to use my airline ticket to check my luggage, so my suitcase boarded the plane without me.

Incidentally, I left my passport at the lost and found when I was filling out the claim for my suitcase. This didn't even occur to me. I went wandering around looking for the lost and found simply because I didn't know what else to do. Miraculously, I somehow found my way back to the lost and found within the hour. I tried to catch my flight to Miami at this point, but I didn't even come close.

The line to get through security was a total shit show because no one wanted to take off their shoes. I don't know if I would have made it to my gate on time before 9/11, but I definitely wasn't going to catch my flight after this tragic anomaly unfolded. Fortunately, I had sobered up enough at this point to navigate my way back to the American Airlines ticketing area rather quickly, and there were six flights leaving for Miami that day.

I don't know which one of the flights I took to Miami, but I do know that the stewardess couldn't keep up with my alcoholism, so I went through customs completely shitfaced. Despite being nearly blackout drunk, I still made it through rather easily because the only thing I was carrying with me at this point was twelve dollars, my passport, and my airline ticket.

This is when I started following around yellow arrows. I can't even make this kind of shit up. This airport is so fucked up that at some point, they needed to paint yellow arrows on the floor to help people navigate their way around this colossal pile of shit. The only saving grace I had was that all my money was spent by the time I arrived in Miami. This forced me to quit drinking. If I still had the giant wad of cash that I had when I first sat down at the bar in the Augusto Ceasar Sandino International Airport, I would have never made it to Ogallala in time for my court date, and I definitely would have never found my suitcase.

As horrible as my journey was getting back to Ogallala, it made my folks very happy that I made it to my court date on time. Everything went really well. The five grand of bail money was returned to my mom, and I only ended up with twenty hours of community service. I'm not sure what made me so motivated, but I knocked out my community service in only four days. My folks were ecstatic about all this, and they seemed really proud of me, but this didn't last very long.

I ended up flying back to Southern California only a week after my court date. This really pissed off my dad, and it broke my mother's heart when I told her that I had no intentions to start college the next semester. Erica wasn't very happy about my departure either, but she got over it pretty quickly after I explained my financial situation. I still hadn't collected all the money from the harvested weed yet, and even if I had, I still wouldn't have had enough money to pay for a heart transplant.

I never completely solved the problem of exchanging the 1,800,000 cordoba into American currency. This money was intended to help fund the heart transplant, so I gave it all to Erica before I left and asked her to call all the banks within a three-hundred-mile radius to get it exchanged. Unfortunately, this sounded much easier than it actually was to accomplish. Long story short, we still have about 500,000 cordoba in our bedroom closet. It's sitting in some shoeboxes next to some other shoe boxes.

Ironically, those shoe boxes are filled with receipts from all the shoes Erica has bought over the last twenty years. Once Amazon moved on from selling books, Erica developed quite the shoe buying problem. We are multi-millionares and so we can afford it, but I make her keep all her reciepts just in case she starts bitching at me for hunting and fishing more than I should. It's my insurance policy. I keep thinking to myself to someday exchange the cordoba for American currency, but I also plan to count up all the shoe reciepts as well. The fact is that neither one of these two goals are likely to ever get accomplished.

Despite having many reservations, I tried to go right back to work for Bile and the T6 Cartel immediately after returning from Nebraska. My heavy conscience and compromised moral compass made it incredibly challenging to continue assisting this man, especially after listening to Juan's story. Nevertheless, I marched onward believing my position with the lord and the world around me was righteous. This had largely to do with the two goals originating from my deep love for Erica, which were to save up enough money for her father's heart transplant and to seek revenge for her exploitation.

These two goals invigorated a passion I had never felt before, which only seemed to intensify as time pressed on. However, when I arrived back at Bile's house asking for my next contract, my elevated hatred for this person was no longer limited to my initial two goals. I now had a new goal that was as equally important to me as to the other two. This goal had nothing to do with Erica and very little to do with revenge. My new goal was to reunite Juan with his daughter and end Bile's reign of terror in the Costa Rican rainforest.

At this point in time, there was a lot that needed to be thought over regarding all three of my goals. I was making some serious headway on acquiring enough money for the heart transplant needed to save the life of Erica's father, but I still had no idea how the actual heart transplant would be accomplished. Unfortunately, it seemed that time was ticking faster than this man's heart because Erica told me that the heart surgery that was scheduled in America was not likely to be executed in time to save her father's life.

As far as this goal was away from being accomplished, out of my three goals in life, this was without question the closest to being achieved. There was only one thing that I had figured out regarding the other two goals. I knew that both of these goals would need to start by disabling or killing Bile's three assailants. In the goal pertaining to Juan and his daughter, I could also kill Bile. In fact, this goal would be accomplished much easier if he was dead. Unfortunately, this would profoundly affect my goal of revenge.

If all I wanted to do was remove Bile from the earth, I might have already completed this assignment. I already figured out when and how to disable Bile's assailants. I just needed to spend some more time watching their habits to ensure I didn't get murdered in the process. Nevertheless, I could end Bile's life at our next meeting if I really wanted to. However, this was not at all what I wanted to do. I may not have had any idea how I wanted to accomplish my goal of revenge just yet, but I knew it would need to be substantially more complicated than simply killing him. This man needed to suffer.

Unfortunately, Bile's existence was equal to that of law enforcement, terrorism, and war. He was a force that could not be fought against or destroyed without avenging the world for his creation. The devil lived inside this person, but his sins were not easy to explain. Bile's evil was incredibly complicated. He wasn't just looking forward to meeting Beelzebub at the gates of hell, he planned to burn for all eternity standing right beside him. To ensure this was accomplished, this man actually spent a great deal of time thinking about how to become more evil. So, if I wanted to make this man suffer, my plan for revenge needed to be as complicated as his existence.

This is the reason why I still had no idea how I planned to ac-complish my goal, and this was also the reason why I couldn't just kill this son of a bitch. All I knew at this point in time was that I needed to appear as a coke-fueled child fucker with absolutely no conscience when I asked Bile for my next contract. This was the next step, and it was as awful as it sounds. I had to describe factitious sexual desires for children in detail, and the content of these conversations resulted in some of the most atrocious experiences of my life.

Throughout the next month, Bile and I had several important conversations during six separate meetings at his house. The content of these discussions would allow me to approach my goals from a much better position. I gained a substantial amount of credibility and trust during these meetings, which was the most important thing that was accomplished. I also had time to observe the behavior of Bile and his three thugs.

In addition to the credibility I had gained, I also learned a lot about the T6 Cartel and Bile's involvement with this organization. I learned that the three contracts I completed were recurring and part of a large collection of contracts that Bile was in charge of. The smuggling of exotic jungle creatures from the Costa Rican rainforest was the only personal endeavor I was exposed to other than his weekend hobby of exploiting children on the internet. This meant that any future contracts I would be given would be provided to Bile from the T6 Cartel.

I never met the person or people Bile answered to, and I am very pleased about this in hindsight. I was incredibly fortunate and oddly protected by this limited exposure to other T6 Cartel members. I have thought a lot about this over the years, and all I have come up with is that the contracts I completed all occurred relatively quickly. Otherwise, my eventual introduction to other cartel members would have been imminent, and their revenge wouldn't be far behind.

The first contract I was given when I got back from Nebraska was identical to the first contract I was ever assigned to. This was a very easy assignment in comparison to smuggling cocaine from Colombia or exotic jungle animals from Costa Rica. All I had to do to complete the terms of this contract was take a train from San Diego to Tijuana, and pick up a large backpack filled with Mexican pharmaceuticals. Once I had this backpack in my possession, I just needed to cross the border again, go back to California, and return the bag full of drugs to Bile.

Bile told me that I would be closely watched by other cartel members while on this mission. He said that this watchful eye followed me around wherever I went. However, the surveillance level and other cartel members' actual involvement remain a mystery. I have many reasons to doubt the T6 Cartel surveillance that had been described to me. The most obvious reason was the fact that I am still alive after being threatened with death numerous times.

Fortunately, Bile only seemed to be aware of the fact that the terms of these contracts were completed and wasn't aware of how I managed to fucked things up along the way. I honestly do not believe to have been under close surveillance of the T6 Cartel as Bile described. However, I may have been under international surveillance by the CIA and INTERPOL as a result of their interests in the T6 Cartel operations. I had to have been a constant form of entertainment for these assholes.

My very next contract was a perfect example of all this. The terms of this contract were simple. I needed to fly from Los Angeles to Las Vegas, and then I needed to pick up a full-sized van at the airport. From there, I would drive across town to pick up a casket containing the dead body of an internationally known member of the T6 Cartel. Once this coffin was placed in the truck, I just needed to drive to Cincinnati and give this casket and the dead person to his family. That was it... then I'd fly back home.

This contract would seem that I was on the road to easy money. For the most part, this assignment didn't venture too far off from this assumption. However, this assignment didn't go exactly as planned either. I never thought to secure the casket containing the dead body and initially just haphazardly placed it in the back of my van. This lack of diligence caused the coffin to roll around, which made a loud banging sound when it hit the inside of the van.

When I realized my mistake, I stopped by the nearest hardware store to buy some straps, which happened to be a few blocks away from where I picked up the coffin. Unfortunately, this True Value was built on top of a hill, and its parking lot had a slight decline that extended to the road. This caused the coffin to fly out of the back of the truck when I opened the back door after buying the straps.

I don't know a whole lot about coffins, but there are some interesting ways to transport them from one place to another. This particular coffin had wheels with a spring-loaded hydraulic lift attached to it, so when it flew out of the van, it didn't just crash into the cement like I initially thought. Instead, it somehow popped out of the van and landed right on its wheels. As it started to roll across the parking lot, the hydraulic lift was also somehow activated, so now this casket was also beginning to elevate.

After the coffin was fully elevated, there was no stopping it. It rolled across the parking lot, down the curb, and out into the street. Then, it continued to roll down the street for nearly a block before it finally stopped in the middle of the intersection of West Twain Ave, and South Rainbow Blvd. This happened only three blocks from where I initially picked up the coffin. I hadn't even made it out of Las Vegas yet. I had no idea what to do at this point. When cars and trucks started to drive around this coffin containing the dead body of the T6 Cartel member, I just stood there, not believing what had just happened.

As much of a disaster as this was, you have to imagine what would have happened if it had just fallen out of the back of the van. There would have been a broken casket and an internationally known criminal's dead body lying in the True Value parking lot. The T6 Cartel would have murdered me in ten different ways if this had happened.

I was very lucky that all this nonsense never caused any significant damage to the casket or the dead body. I was also very fortunate that enough kindhearted people were inside the hardware store to help get the coffin back into my van without incident. I obviously never told anyone that there was a dead body inside. I just said that I worked for the local mortuary and was delivering an empty casket. After I told this bullshit story to everyone, and the casket was securely strapped down in the back of my van, I drove out to Cincinnati like nothing ever happened.

I completed one other short contract before being sent on a complicated international mission involving four separate contracts. This assignment started in Los Angeles when I met a man who made bombs. I picked up several car bombs from this person and drove them from Los Angeles to Philadelphia. This long drive sucked pretty hard, and the contract was only worth ten thousand dollars, but the connection I made with the bomb maker eventually made this all a very worthwhile endeavor.

Bile seemed to be working out the details of my next four contracts all month long despite this being an annual occurrence. Due to extreme weather cycles in East Asia, the terms of these contracts were impossible to complete outside of November, December, and January. The details of this $150,000 dollar assignment were so complicated that it took nearly two days to explain. Bile provided me with all sorts of information during this two-day conversation, which was never paused for any reason other than to take lines of cocaine. Interestingly enough, I was never told exactly what I would be doing on these assignments, or what would make these four missions around the globe illegal. My instructions, as complicated as they were, concentrated almost entirely on the logistics of these international crimes. I was told that I would be exchanging gold for obscure items of value that could only be obtained on the other side of the planet.

During this time, I had to listen to hours of horrific filth, and evil. What was worse was that I had to seem interested in these conversations. Moreover, I needed to appear to be a lunatic that liked to diddle little kids. This was the only way that I'd be allowed into the basement where the kids were, which I hoped would create an opportunity to find Juan's daughter. There were several times that I could have killed Bile and his assailants as the were letting there now letting their guard down. It took an enormous amount of restraint not to send Bile's ass on a one way ticket straight to hell.

Unfortunately, without a well thought out plan, there would be way too many things that could go wrong... like getting killed. I also was well short of having saved enough cash to pay for a heart transplant, so I was forced to play along with the miserable intentions of these four evil men. I was convinced that Bile may be the devil incarnated. There are no words to describe how horrible of a human being this man was, and I needed to walk in his footsteps if I wanted to find a way to free these children, and accomplish my goal of returning Angel to her family. After begging to see Bile's sex dungeon every time we stopped to take lines of coke, I was finally taken down into his basement. This dungeon was creepy as hell. Every room was built with the sole purpose of fulfilling underage sex crimes.

I had no idea how many little girls and boys lived down there because I stopped at the room where I found Angel. I told Bile that this was the girl for me, so he put us into a room by ourselves for about an hour, expecting me to fulfill a demented sexual fantasy. Regrettably, I couldn't explain anything to Angel regarding my plan to reunite her with Juan and her family. My reason for this was that I didn't want to trust the mouth of a scared sixteen-year-old to keep secrets, so we just stared at each other for an entire hour. This experience was as horrifying as it was necessary. Angel was naked when I walked into the room, which prompted me to immediately give her my shirt, which was large enough to cover most of her body.

I walked up from Bile's basement feeling traumatized and high as hell on cocaine. In addition to exercising a tremendous amount of restraint to not Karate chop Bile's head off, I kept asking myself some obvious questions about involving law enforcement. There were some personal reasons that I didn't want to contact the police, such as revenge, finances, and being high as fuck on cocaine. However, there were other reasons beyond these immoral and rather selfish endeavors.

The main reason was that I absolutely hated the police and was frightened to be in contact with them for any reason. I thought that I had definitely incriminated myself enough to go to prison while pursuing the few T6 Cartel assignments I had been on, and I figured Bile and his thugs would bring me down with them somehow. Also, I honestly thought that I had a better chance of bringing down this child sex trafficking operation than the police. My encounters with these dim-witted morons would suggest that there is no chance of claiming any justice in much of anything if the police get involved. I imagined them just dropping a bomb on Bile's house from a police helicopter rather than putting forth a serious effort to reunite these children with their families.

These haunting thoughts and peculiar questions were scattered amongst several others that would not be answered that day. As horrible of an experience as it was to encounter Bile's child sex dungeon and see Juan's daughter imprisoned, abused, and frightened, I thought that I had just made a huge step toward bringing down Bile and the unspeakable things his organization did to these children.

# Chapter XVII

A SHORT WHILE AFTER returning from the horrific misery I experienced in the basement of Bile's house, I was handed everything I needed to complete the next four contracts. I left LA on December 7th with a large backpack filled with documents, maps, and sixty grand worth of one-hundred-dollar bills. My international four-contract mission began with me flying around the United States to throw off any authorities that may have been following me.

Bile had planned for me to fly from Los Angeles to St. Louis, then to Charlotte, and next to Chicago before finally arriving in Seattle the next day. After a twelve-hour layover in Seattle, I had a fourteen-hour flight to Hong Kong and another four-hour flight to Jakarta, Indonesia's largest city. After an unusually long layover in this city, I would board my final flight to a tiny town called Mulia, which is located on the western coast of Indonesia's main island.

After several flights, layovers, and losing fifteen hours in flight from Pacific time to Western Indonesian time, I finally touched down at my final destination at 2 pm on December 11th. Mulia is the capital of the Mimika Regency, one of 412 Regencies on the island of New Guinea. When I looked out my motel room window, I could see a large mountain called Puncak Jaya, otherwise known as the Carstensz Pyramid. During my stay here, I learned that this is Indonesia's largest peak, with an elevation of 16,024 feet. It is part of the Sudirman Range of Central Papua and is ranked 5th by topographic isolation.

This information meant nothing to me other than that it led me to a peculiar realization. When I walked out the front door of my motel, I determined that I was standing in the middle of nowhere. There were many times in my life when I had loosely used this term, but those places were nowhere close to the middle of nowhere. They were all thousands of miles away from the actual middle of nowhere.

Interestingly enough, the reason why Bile arranged for me to fly around the world to Mulia had nothing to do with any of the interesting things I learned about while staying here. Bile didn't give a fly fuck about its remote location or the fact that it was the capital of Mimika Regency, and he definitely did not plan for me to look at a big ass mountain outside my window. Bile had planned for me to come to this place for one reason and one reason only. That was the price of gold.

An ounce of gold in Mulia, Indonesia, cost me just twenty-seven American dollars, nearly one-tenth of what it would cost in the United States. The day I landed in this town, an ounce of gold was going for $276 in America and almost everywhere else worldwide. Gold was incredibly cheap in Mulia back in 2001 due to its proximity to the Grasberg mine, which was and still is the third-largest producer of gold in the world.

My mission here was simple. I was expected to exchange fifty thousand dollars hidden in my backpack for 1850 ounces of gold, which is roughly equivalent to one hundred pounds. This could be accomplished at the local gold exchange building, which happened to be directly across the street from the hotel where I was staying.

Bile told me that the most challenging part of this contract would be carrying around a hundred-pound suitcase of gold. His plan would have likely worked out perfectly except for one major problem. This was no ordinary problem that could be thought through and eventually solved with a well-crafted alternative to the original plan. The only way to solve this problem was with a fucking miracle!

This problem originated back in Chicago. I had a layover at the O'Hare airport that was supposed to last only one hour, which would have been the shortest layover on this entire multi-destination, five-week expedition. Unfortunately, this layover lasted much longer than anticipated. My delayed departure was caused by an honest mistake I made immediately after landing in Chicago.

Back in 2001, phones didn't automatically sync to the time zone you were in. You actually had to physically set the time on your phone to match the time zone you were in. Unfortunately, I didn't think of this. I don't even know if I knew that this glitch existed. In any case, I never even came close to resetting the time on my phone to Central Standard Time. According to my phone, which was still set to Pacific Standard Time, I had three hours before my next fight departed.

I casually walked off the plane without a care in the world and then wandered over to the gate from which the plane headed to Seattle was scheduled to depart. Surprisingly, this gate was only three gates down from where I landed. Somewhere within the short journey between these two gates, I looked at the time on my phone and figured I had three hours to kill, so I naturally looked for the nearest bar. The bar that I found happened to be less than fifty feet from the gate I was supposed to depart from. I swear to God that this is how convenient all this was.

I continued to sit at this bar despite being fifty feet away from this gate and sitting in clear view of hundreds of people boarding a plane beneath a neon sign that read, "SEATTLE." I ended up sitting there getting shit-faced drunk for over two hours before finally walking over to the gate. This is when I looked around and saw no one. There wasn't a single person standing at this gate, and there also was no airline personnel to explain why there wasn't anyone standing there.

At this point, I wandered down the corridor, looking for some-one from American Airlines to explain to me what in the holy hell was going on. When I finally met this person, I was told something I never expected to hear in a million years, and this was the moment I realized the mistake I had made. I initially thought that my mistake appeared to have a simple solution, which was to simply board another plane destined for Seattle later that night. Problem solved... right? Fucking wrong.... wait for it.

At this time, I was scheduled to leave in one hour from a gate in corridor C. I was currently in corridor A. The O'Hare airport happens to contain an enigma that is completely fucked! Much like the Miami airport, this airport was built by idiots. It has these incredibly long corridors with gates that go on for miles, and this was before they installed horizontal escalators, so I needed to run over a mile to make it over to corridor C in time to board my flight.

Fortunately, I had youth on my side to combat fatigue, but my shoes slowed me down. Since I was headed to a tropical country, I decided to wear sandals, or what were called "thongs or flip flops." These were the exact opposite of running shoes. This sandal was attached to my feet by a single piece of fabric between my big toe and the one next to it, so I made this loud clapping sound all the way to my connecting flight.

Nevertheless, I managed to board this flight to Seattle. When I walked onto that plane, I thought all my problems were solved. Unfortunately, my problems had just begun. It was illegal to carry over ten thousand dollars on you in 2001, and I think it still is. This meant I needed to check the large backpack containing sixty grand and all the information Bile had given me. Since I never made it on my original flight, this bag ended its journey at the American Airlines luggage exchange in Seattle. It then sat there for three days before anyone realized what had happened.

This resulted in me becoming a religious person real quick. I suddenly felt the profound urge to pray for a miracle and to ask God for this bag to somehow arrive in the middle of nowhere... AKA... Mulia, Indonesia. I stayed in this bumblefuck town for another six days with only a remote possibility and a shitty promise. To make matters even worse, this promise needed to be interpreted by two different people. I can't even make this kind of shit up... there are 700 hundred languages native to Indonesia, and this airport employee spoke just one of them. Only by the grace of God did I find someone who spoke English and whatever the hell language was spoken by the employee at the Mulia airport.

For the next six days, I woke up each morning and wandered down to the airport to see if my backpack had arrived. I would then stop by a church to pray for a miracle, and my day always seemed to get worse from there. I ate shitty Indonesian food at the same restaurant and got drunk as fuck at the same shitty bar for six days straight. No matter how much weird Indonesian booze I drank, my problems always seemed to get worse.

I had no idea where I was and had no idea how to get home. I only had a thousand dollars in American money in my wallet, which wouldn't even come close to paying for plane tickets back to America. I was in the middle of nowhere. When I woke up on the seventh day, I thought that there was a better chance of me dying in Mulia than my bag showing up at the airport.

After leaving the airport with a profound sense of disappointment that morning, I thought hard about committing suicide but ended up deciding to give it one more day. I stopped by the church once again to pray my ass off and spent over an hour asking God for a miracle. I asked over and over again for my backpack to be returned to me.

After leaving my religion back at the church, I headed straight for the bar, intending to get drunker than I had ever been before. However, I never followed through with these intentions to get drunk.  I was strangely interrupted by the bartender as he reached down for something other than a glass of booze that morning. When he pulled up my backpack, I fell backward right the fuck off my bar stool. My prayers were answered. I witnessed a miracle that day.

There was no way to explain how my backpack ended up at the bar, and I didn't care. I just walked down to the gold exchange and purchased 1800 ounces of gold. I then went straight to the airport, dragging around a hundred-pound backpack filled with gold. Remarkably, I was able to catch the next flight to Jakarta later that same morning and never looked back.

I landed at the Seokarno-Hatt International Airport in the afternoon and went straight to the baggage carousel, feeling paranoid and nervous about everything. My experience in Mulia was rivaled getting caught or losing the one hundred pounds of gold in my checked luggage. I didn't take long for my camping backpack full of gold to arrive at the baggage carousel, but it felt like an eternity. With the assistance of a good Samaritan, I somehow managed to get it put on my back.

I left the airport with one hundred pounds of gold and took a cab over to a very tall apartment building, which could be described as seventy stories of disenchanting poverty. Bile rented a shitty apartment in this building for the past four years. This was the inception of the contracts I agreed to. The reason Bile rented this apartment was to have a place to stash gold while T6 Cartel members and people like myself traveled around East Asia committing crimes.

It was originally planned for me to spend an extra four days in Jakarta. Bile wanted me to become familiar with the slummy neighborhood where this apartment was located. He didn't want me getting robbed with a hundred pounds of gold and hoped that this extra time would help.  As much as I hated this man, I appreciated not being too far behind schedule. Unfortunately, after my prolonged stay in Mulia, I flew back to Jakarta with my backpack full of gold. Unfortunately, I had no time to rest. Since I was already four days behind schedule, I needed to leave for Thailand only six hours after landing in Jakarta.

Unfortunately, the time I spent in Indonesia and the gold I had attained in Mulia was just a form of currency, which didn't complete the terms of any contract existing on its own. This gold would be used to make three separate purchases while completing the terms of the four contracts given to me. The items Bile expected me to attain from these three purchases were known internationally as criminal for anyone to possess or transport. These items were considered so illegal that they inspired millions of activists to create laws and animal sanctuaries all around the globe. I never understood the majority of this information when I boarded the plane headed for Thailand.

I arrived at the Suvarnabhumi International Airport in Bangkok just before midnight that same day. Bile arranged for me to stay at Hotel Thanabumi, which was within walking distance of Khao San Road, the Grand Palace, and the Temple of Emerald Buddha. Interestingly enough, I realized the following day that Bile must have thought of me as a friend by the time he sent me on this five-week mission. I came to this surprising conclusion because he expected me to stay two days in Bangkok for no other reason than to enjoy myself.

In addition to a list of essential tourist destinations, Bile had written down two places where I could find underage girls to have sex with. I obviously didn't go to these places, but I followed up on his strong recommendation to attend a Ping Pong show. He never told me what this was because he wanted it to be a surprise. I remember Bile laughing his ass off when he wrote this down in his notebook of instructions.

After doing some sightseeing during the day, I ended up going to several bars on Khao San Road that night and got wasted while drinking an estimated thirty beers. While stumbling back to my hotel room that night, I was asked by a tuk-tuk driver if I wanted to see a Ping Pong show, which was an offer my drunk ass couldn't refuse.

A tuk-tuk is essentially a three-wheeled modified motorcycle with a carriage on the back, which is large enough to transport three normal-sized people from Thailand or two normal-sized Americans. Even though the population of this metropolis was only six million people in 2001, which is only half of what it is today, there were never-ending traffic jams on every single road. This made tuk-tuks a far more reasonable form of transportation when compared to taxicab because it was small enough to scoot through all the obstacles and hazards you'd encounter while traveling around on the chaotic city streets of Bangkok.

A Ping Pong show consists of several strange sexual acts being performed on an elevated circle stage, which was about eye level with the people sitting in the audience. The whole time this show was being performed, the fifty or so attendees would be continuously accosted by waitresses. I'm not sure what they offered the women attendees, but they made all the men abundantly aware that they were ready and willing to suck dick for twenty dollars.

I sat three rows back from the stage, where I regrettably watched several horrific sex acts being performed. Most of these acts were nothing different than what you'd see in a shady strip joint on the wrong side of town in large metropolitan areas across America. However, some more intense acts involved performances that would be considered illegal in most stateside cabarets. One of these acts consisted of two attractive people having sexual intercourse in positions you would have never thought to be possible.

The show ended with a bizarre grand finale, which you'd have to see to believe. This entailed a woman stuffing several ping-pong balls in her unusually large pussy. I thought it was strange that she actually demonstrated how many ping-pong balls she could fit. The show actually started when she walked around shooting these ping pong balls out at the people sitting in the front row. As terrifying as this sounds, this woman had an incredibly talented vagina, which caused everyone to obnoxiously applaud every time a ping-pong ball came shooting out of it.

I left this ping pong show drunk, disgusted, and terrified, with no intention of ever attending another one. Since I spent the majority of this night borderline blackout drunk, it's surprising that I remember so many details from this show. What's even more surprising is that I somehow made it back to my hotel room that night.

My second day in Bangkok didn't amount to much. Aside from walking fifty feet to the 7-11 to eat breakfast, lunch, and dinner, I spent the next day in my hotel room sleeping off one epic hangover. At four in the morning the following day, I walked out the front door of Hotel Thanabumi and caught a cab back to Seokarno-Hatt International Airport.

By noon, I had already traveled 584 kilometers north to Chiang Mai, which is the largest city in northern Thailand. The city limits are less than 50 kilometers away from the eastern border of Burma and less than 100 kilometers away from the southwestern border of Laos. I was instructed to go to a specific location in the middle of Chiang Mai, where Bile planned for me to pick up a 26-foot box truck. I was then instructed to drive this vehicle twenty-five kilometers west to a remote village called Samoeng. This tiny village was uniquely located in the middle of a tropical forest known to inhabit the very last population of free-roaming Asian elephants on planet Earth.

There are three species of elephants. Two are native to Africa, and the other is native to India and Southeast Asia. Ironically, the species native to Southeast Asia is classified as an Indian elephant. A male Indian elephant can stand nearly twelve feet tall and weigh up to 12,000 pounds. It has been estimated that in the early 1900s, over 300,000 Indian elephants roamed freely throughout a massive tropical forest in northwestern Thailand, and 100,000 more existed in captivity throughout the rest of the country.

Ninety percent of Thailand was covered by dense tropical forest going into the 20$^{th}$ century, and the northwestern regions of this country were the perfect habitat for elephants. However, robust industrialization reduced the cover of this vast forest land to less than 40 percent of its original size by the early 1980s. This has killed the Thai elephant and resulted in the IUCN adding Indian elephants to the endangered list in 1986.

When I came to Thailand to embark on this mission in late 2001, it was estimated that less than 4000 elephants remained in this country, and only a fraction of these animals still roamed freely. Sadly, no one out of the seventy or so residents living in the tiny village of Samoeng seemed to give a rat's ass about elephants... or anything else for that matter. It took only thirty pounds of Indonesian gold to fill my 26-foot box truck full of elephant tusks.

About ten people loaded my truck up with 8000 pounds of unprocessed ivory, and not a single person spoke a word of English. This limited me to gesturing when I tried to communicate because I couldn't ask them any questions in my language or theirs. At the time, these things didn't look familiar to me, and no elephants were standing around with their tusks missing, so I ended up driving away without any damn clue what I was hauling.

Bile's instructions only included rudimentary details about where to pick up the truck and where I needed to drive it to... this sort of thing. He never said a word about elephants or how illegal it was to be driving a truck around with four tons of poached ivory in my possession. I wasn't even aware that elephants lived in Thailand, so I drove 584 kilometers back to Bangkok without any goddamn clue as to what the fuck was actually happening.

My contract ended when I drove my truck into a warehouse at a large shipping port south of Bangkok. All I had to do was hand my keys over to an Asian man and walk away. When I left the warehouse, I looked up at a gigantic ship docked at this port and was suddenly filled with curiosity. I asked my taxicab driver where he thought this container ship was going. He said it was headed out into the South China Sea, and its destination was likely Hong Kong.

This information meant nothing to me at the time, but I would eventually learn several strange and frightening details about this contract. Ironically, a lifetime prison sentence was imposed for possessing elephant tusks in Thailand, but it wasn't illegal in Bangkok to have processed ivory in your possession. This made for a very sought-after commodity because a kilo was worth about $800 USD in Southeast Asia and up to $1600 USD in East Asia.

Ivory was used to make artwork in cities such as Shanghai, Tokyo, and Hong Kong, where some artists could turn one kilo of ivory into $10,000 worth of artwork. I have no idea what happened to the four tons of elephant tusks that I transported to Bangkok, but they were hypothetically turned into artwork worth about $30,000,000 USD. It is incredible that I purchased thirty pounds of gold for $13000 and exchanged this for ivory, which could have eventually generated thirty million dollars.

# Chapter XVIII

I COMPLETED THE FIRST contract of this four-contract mission on Christmas Eve and flew back to Indonesia the next morning to grab another thirty ounces of gold. On Christmas Day, I spent all afternoon looking for a place to call my family and Erica to wish them a merry Christmas. Today, your cell phone works in any major metropolitan area on planet Earth. However, in 2002, you had to find a phone and internet store to connect with someone across the globe.

I finally found one of these places and made the first call to my folks at four in the afternoon without thinking of the fifteen-hour time difference. My Mom picked up the phone at 11 pm on Christmas Eve. We were both very confused by the time difference, leading to a very weird conversation. I decided to wait nine hours to call Erica. By this time, I was already at Soekarno–Hatta International Airport. This was also a very weird conversation. These conversations didn't amount to much. I attempted to placate the strange vibe and misunderstanding with a series of lies, excuses, and words that more or less amounted to, "I love you."

I flew out of Jakarta at 10 am the day after Christmas and touched down at Ninoy Aquino International Airport in Manila three hours later. Unfortunately, I was stuck in Philippine customs for a half hour or so before finally being allowed to grab my bag from the baggage carousel. After checking to make sure it still contained thirty ounces of gold, I left the airport and took a taxicab to a hotel next to Manila Bay. That airport experience could have gone in a much worse direction. I felt rather fortunate to walk out with myself, my loot, and good intentions intact.

The next day, I followed Bile's detailed instructions. This led me to a large boat docked in Manila Bay with five people aboard. I noticed that this boat had a lot of scuba gear and a crane on the back of it. At this point, I exchanged the thirty pounds of gold in my backpack for an adventure loosely interpreted by the captain, who spoke broken English at best. In 2001, thirty pounds of gold converted to about $135,000 stateside, which converted to $8,000,000 Philippine Pasos, or one hundred average yearly salaries in the Philippines.

We left Manila Bay on December 27th and spent three days in the South China Sea, traveling straight south for just over 300 kilometers. We finally arrived at our destination on December 30th, a small village named Coron, located on the western shore of the Palawan Island of Busuanga. At the time of our arrival, slightly less than 5,000 residents populated the entire island.

Conversely, if you were to read about this place today, you'd learn that people from all around the world come to this unique Philippine destination for a multitude of reasons. The typical tourist comes to the village of Coron because it is within fifty kilometers of dozens of small islands that can be accessed by various boats and tours. These islands have beautiful beaches, amazing lagoons, and incredible cliffs that stick right out of the ocean. The exquisite natural beauty of this destination is often seen on the internet listed under the most gorgeous places in the world.

Coron Bay is also considered the fourth-best diving location in the world for three unique reasons. The first reason is that the entire Busuanga island is surrounded by a massive coral reef that is home to a wide range of marine biology and tropical fish. The second reason is that there are twelve sunken wartime ships from the Imperial Japanese Navy lying in the ocean less than fifty feet deep. These battleships were bombed by US Navy aircraft during the Second World War in September 1944. The third reason is that the water in the lagoon around Coron Island are often argued to have the clearest water on planet Earth.

Today, tourism is the primary source of income for Busuanga Island residents. This is followed by exporting tuna, grouper, and snapper to other parts of the Philippines. However, there is a secret export that nobody wants to tell you about, which comes and goes during slow economic times. This secret is the Giant Clam. The shells from this marine animal are harvested for the same reason as elephant tusks and can be turned into artwork that looks identical to ivory.

While on this mission, I regrettably swam around for three days with the four men the T6 Cartel employed to poach these fantastic creatures. During this time, I saw several Giant Clams living happily in the coral reef surrounding Busuanga Island. It was amazing to see these beautiful creatures. They sat with their mouth open until something swam by, and then they would clamp their big mouth shut, hoping to capture something to eat. Even though these marine animals couldn't swim and were stationary, it scared to shit out of me every time I saw one close its mouth.

A giant clam can weigh as much as 500 pounds and was worth as much as USD $100,000 on the city streets of East Asia at the turn of the 21st century. The terms of this particular contract were to poach 40 Giant Clams and partially process them at sea. We would then put them in cardboard boxes and wrap them in plastic just before returning to the port in Manila Bay. At this point, they were transferred onto a truck, and that is when my second contract of the series of four ended.

I have to keep repeating this because I know this all sounds evil and wrong, but my thoughts on this expedition were innocent at the time. I was eighteen years old and clueless when these contracts were handed to me. Bile provided me with incredibly detailed instructions on completing the terms of these contracts but always stopped short of explaining why they were illegal.

I had never even heard of a Giant Clam before going on this mission, so I didn't know this marine animal was endangered. I lacked life experience, a college education, and reliable internet at this point in my life. You couldn't just push some buttons on your phone to come up with the answers to your questions in 2001, so nobody seemed to know jack shit about anything outside of the plethora of useless information we learned in school.

The entire internet was a giant pile of shit back then. Other than checking e-mails on Yahoo accounts, it was primarily used to download free music from a website called Napster. Search engines were primitive and barely contained the framework to answer your questions with accurate information. This meant that you actually had to go to the library to search for the answers to a lot of your questions, and so most of us never learned a damn thing because we all said, "fuck that!"

I arrived at the Félix-Houphouët-Boigny International Airport in West Africa three days after completing the terms of my second contract in the Philippines. My third contract began on January 9th, 2002, when my plane touched down in Abidjan, Côte d'Ivoire...AKA... the Ivory Coast of West Africa. I was nervous about my backpack when I arrived in this city because of all the airplanes and layovers it took to get there.

My journey began when I flew from Manila back to Jakarta to fill my backpack with the remaining 40 pounds of Indonesian gold. I checked my backpack at the Seokarno-Hatt International Airport in Jakarta the following day and flew six hours to Guangzhou, China. After a four-hour layover in Guangzhou, I flew nine hours to Dubai, United Arab Emirates. After a seven-hour layover in Dubai, I flew another nine hours to Accra, Ghana, where I boarded my final flight to Abidjan, Côte d'Ivoire.

After all this, I was incredibly happy to see my backpack fall onto the baggage carousel. At this point, my contract instructed me to meet with a T6 Cartel member from the Liberian Rebel Group. Bile explained that this man was my guide and that he would stay with me during my entire mission in Abidjan. The specific terms of this contract were to exchange forty pounds of gold for five-hundred diamonds. My contract would be completed once I returned to the airport with these diamonds.

In May 2000, representatives of the diamond industry and leaders of African governments convened in Kimberley, South Africa, to develop a certification process intended to assure that export shipments of rough diamonds that were free of conflict. The United Nations General Assembly formally supported this certification process in early 2001. The Kimberley Process Certification Scheme was finally ratified and signed in April 2002.

Diamonds from conflict on the Ivory Coast before April 2002 were considered Blood Diamonds. There were two reasons these diamonds were given this label. The first reason was that they were mined in war zones and were sold to finance bloody wars against legitimate West African governments. The second reason was that thousands of people have been found dead and bloody while in possession of these diamonds.

I didn't know any of this information when I arrived in Africa. The terms of this contract planned for me to leave the Ivory Coast of West Africa with hundreds of blood diamonds in my possession. Ironically, this mission sounded simple and relatively safe when I first read the instructions. My loose interpretation was that I needed to follow some guy around Abidjan for a couple of days until I exchanged the gold in my backpack for a bunch of diamonds. At this point, I just needed to check my bag at the airport and fly away.

Unfortunately, this mission didn't go as planned. My guide wasn't the person Bile expected him to be. This man guided me through the exchange, but vanished as I was putting the diamonds into my backpack. When I looked up, I found myself alone in a whole new world. I was suddenly stranded and lost in the middle of Abidjan with five-hundred diamonds in my possession.

At this point, I knew something had gone terribly wrong and was nearly certain that my reality was going to get worse from that point forward. This creepy prediction manifested itself in a real-life nightmare within minutes. The man described as my guide returned with the four men I exchanged my gold with. I immediately knew that these men planned to kill me over the diamonds in my back-pack.

When I first saw these five men, I anticipated being shot and killed within a few seconds. Surprisingly, this didn't happen, which meant that they were not carrying firearms. They intended to kill me using knives and baseball bats, which wouldn't have been so bad if I wasn't outnumbered five-to-one. I realized very quickly that my death was certain if I didn't execute my six years of martial arts and boxing training to absolute perfection.

Fortunately, all five of these men walked up and stopped in front of me rather than surrounding me. This allowed me to attack them before they attacked me. Two of the men were carrying knives and stood beside each other, holding these weapons in front of them. I kicked each their hands holding the knives, and punched one guy in the right temple, which knocked him right the fuck out. I'm not great at physics, but i'm pretty sure Einstein would have been impressed at how hard this guy's head hit the ground. I don't know what hit this guy harder, my kick, or the Abidjan, Côte d'Ivoire's best attempt to pave a road. Then, I did a Chuck Norris roundhouse kick smashing the other thug's nose hard enough that he wasn't go-ing to see anything for a solid hour or so. The third man, I punched his throat so hard that he fell to the ground and eventually died from suffocation. This all happened in a matter of seconds.

The other two men were not prepared to see me disarm three of their comrades so quickly, which left them dazed and confused. While I was kicking, and Karate chopping their buddies, it would have been a great opportunity to walk away from this fight, but that wasn't going to happen. Not only was I in possession of over a thousand yearly salaries for residents in West Africa, these men's dim-witted pride was on the line.

They were armed with baseball bats, which would normally give these men a huge upper hand against your average person. However, this was not the case when fighting an expert in Martial Arts. The thing about bats is you need to swing them hard to cause a damaging blow, which requires an untimely backswing and then a forward swing. This ensemble takes at least a second or two, which is an extremely long time for a world-class fighter. I could have dodged these men and their swinging bats all afternoon unless they walked down the street and came back with some sort of strategy. These two men had no strategy, so I Karate-chopped the nose of one of these men into his brain, and punched the other one so hard in his cheekbone that he likely forgot who he was for a day or two.

The last man I punched posed no real threat to my life, so he lived to tell this story without significant injury. His four buddies were not as fortunate. Abidjan's version of 911 needed to be called very quickly to avoid suffering from permanent injury or death. I didn't enjoy any of this. My training focused heavily on discipline. I could explain what this entails, but it is the least exciting part of Martial Arts training.

This was the first time I intended to seriously hurt anyone by fighting. Unfortunately for these men, I needed to apply death kicks and punches, or else I would have been the one who ended up dead. Since my ethical discretion was already severely compromised by the necessity to potentially murder these men, I decided that stealing their loot wouldn't be out of line in this particular situation. Their fatal mistake led to me walking away with fifty more diamonds and ten pounds of gold. This was obviously not planned for and left me with much to ponder as I spent the rest of the day trying to find my way back to the airport.

My third contract ended later that afternoon when I checked my bag containing all five-hundred blood diamonds and ten pounds of gold at the Félix-Houphouët-Boigny International Airport. I flew from Abidjan in northwestern Africa to Botswana in South Africa, which was known as one of the poorest countries in the world in 2001. Ironically, this country was also known to have the most expensive diamonds in the world based on clarity, carat weight, and color.

My fourth and final contract instructed me to exchange the blood diamonds in Botswana for ten diamonds worth roughly five million dollars stateside. This contract was executed to perfection. Actually, it was executed better than perfection because I exchanged the additional loot gathered from the five thugs in Abidjan for an additional diamond.

I left Africa on January 9th, 2002, and three days later, handed ten diamonds to Bile in exchange for $150,000. He had no idea that I had purchased eleven diamonds instead of ten. The eleventh diamond was only 1.63 carats but was worth $550,000 stateside in 2002. Today, this diamond is worth well over a million dollars and is, without question... among the most expensive diamonds by carat weight on planet Earth.

When I finally returned to Venice Beach, Fredrick had the rest of the money he owed me from the weed we harvested in Nebraska. All told, my portion of the profits was $475,000. This was added to the $280,000 I had made from T6 contracts and the $200,000 found in

Billy's basement. Erica also informed me of an additional $100,000 that mysteriously ended up in our joint account on January 2nd, 2002, which was the day Billy's estate was transferred into my name. This unexpected payment was generated from Billy leasing out land and farm equipment.

I didn't understand this at the time, but this was all tinker toys compared to the assets I had just attained. All told, Billy's estate was worth roughly four million dollars. After adding this to the cash I had been saving for the heart transplant and the diamond I acquired in Africa, my net worth was well over five million dollars. Although I understood that I officially became a millionaire when Fredrick handed me the rest of the money he owed me, I thought this was close to all I was worth at the time. After collecting this money, my next move was to return to Nebraska to figure out how to turn my million dollars into a new heart for her father.

I was so eager to see Erica at this point that I drove for sixteen hours straight through from Venice Beach to Ogallala, only stopping twice for gas. When I arrived on Erica's doorstep, she stepped out onto the front porch and closed the door so her Dad wouldn't catch us making out. I remember how gorgeous she looked that morning, wearing a furry purple bathrobe and giant slippers with Garfield's face on them. It was below freezing that cold winter morning, so there was steam rising up from an unfiltered sensation of love. Knowing that she was completely naked under this ensemble was the sexiest thing in the whole fucking world.

After several minutes of making out, the cold air and excitement finally caught up with us. Our lips had turned numb, and our tongues were tired from kissing. Erica's hair was now completely frozen, her nipples were next level rock hard, and her robe only covered her backside. At the same time, my pants were at my knees, and Erica had her hand wrapped around my cock, with soft love, tender passion, and a filthy desire to be stuffed in every position imaginable. When we finally realized that we were standing in proximity to our neighbors, our untamed libidos had been metaphorically standing on third base for at least five minutes. Thankfully, our public display of affection seemed to go unnoticed, or so we thought.

At this point, Erica and I just looked at each other for a few crazy seconds before running toward my truck. I'm not sure how we shed our clothes so fast, but I remember us being completely naked by the time I put the truck into first gear. As we drove toward the edge of town, Erica proceeded to give me a wet, sloppy roadhead, which turned into wild truck sex just past the city limit sign. After satisfying our immediate sexual desires, we drove out to our new house... where we fucked for hours. We finally made love just after sunset and fell asleep in each other's arms, exhausted from the heat of passion.

# Chapter XIX

Erica and I spent the next two weeks on the internet researching alternative ways to accomplish her father's heart transplant. This research didn't seem to amount to a lot of valuable information in general, but we came up with one promising lead in Prague, Czech Republic. There was a surgeon named Dr. Tomas Davork, who worked out of Hospital Na Františku Prague. The information on the internet claimed that he had performed several successful heart transplants for $800,000, about $300,000 less than what this procedure costs in America. This was enough information to convince Erica and I to go to Europe. We were very hopeful that our meeting with Dr. Davork would go well and that it would lead to a successful heart transplant.

Our original plan was to only go to Prague for a few days, but our plans seemed to change after having several discussions about this trip. Every time we talked about going to Europe, Erica seemed to get increasingly excited about spending time there as a tourist. We didn't officially make plans beyond going to Prague, but we discussed traveling around Europe for a while if our meeting with the heart surgeon went well.

Our journey began on Thursday, February 1st when Sherly gave us a ride to Denver International Airport. We flew out to JFK in

New York City early that morning and then boarded a direct flight to Prague at 11 am EST. Our flight was nine hours long, and we lost five hours in the air, so we touched down at the Václav Havel Airport Prague at 3 pm DST that same day.

After gathering our luggage, we took a train into downtown Prague. I remember the moment we stepped off the train because we were immediately approached by several people wanting to rent us their apartments. One woman was very persuasive and had a brochure with pictures of her two-bedroom apartment. She told us that her place was a couple of blocks away and only wanted $14 per night. We thought this was a fantastic deal, so we handed her the money, and she handed us the keys along with a handful of city brochures.

We discovered rather quickly that our apartment was located a block from the subway station and only two stops away from a place called Old Town Square. This was where Praugue was initially built over a thousand years ago and seemed to be where the majority of the city's tourist attractions were. Our apartment was also nine blocks from Hospital Na Františku Prague, where Dr. Tomas Davork performed his heart surgeries.

Before leaving Nebraska, Erica dedicated a substantial amount of her time and effort to secure a meeting with Dr. Tomas Davork. Her dedication was admirable, effective, and essential if we wanted to meet with the doctor in a timely manner. We realized quickly that this was an accomplished heart surgeon with a full schedule stretching out weeks in advance. She was actually lucky to arrange a meeting at all. We were scheduled to meet Dr. Tomas Davork at 10 am on Monday, February 5th. This meant that we had all weekend to explore the city of Prague.

After spending a couple of hours having marathon sex in our apartment, Erica and I decided to go do some sightseeing in Old Town Square. Neither one of us had ever been on a subway train, nor did we speak Czech, so it took a bit of an effort to arrive at our destination. We initially boarded a train going the wrong way because we couldn't wrap our heads around the fact that this train also needed to bring people back from wherever they were going. I know this sounds elementary, but we were both from a town of three thousand people, and the only big city Erica had ever been to was Denver. Not being able to speak Czech was also an issue which wasn't at all important once we reached Old Town Square.

In contrast to the modern architecture surrounding the subway station and our apartment, this part of the city was riddled with buildings constructed as early as the 9th century. We had plenty of time that morning to do some random exploration, and by early afternoon, we found a unique series of five gorgeous buildings, which all bunched up together. We spent the rest of the afternoon touring the Prague Castle, St. Vitus Cathedral, Power Tower, St. George's Basilica, and the Rosenberg Palace. This was a wonderful way to spend our day. The only times we weren't smiling from ear to ear was when our mouths were saying things like, "Oh my God... look at that, or can you believe what we are looking at?"

We had no idea where we were until the very last tour when we found out that this was the oldest castle complex in the world! After leaving this vast fortress, we watched the sunset from the St. Charles bridge walkway. This medieval stone arch bridge was constructed in 1357 to provide a pathway over the Vltava River and was a venue of profound beauty that evening.

After observing all the romantic feels of St. Charles Bridge, Erica and I walked over to the Pilsner Urquell Brewery to eat dinner. I couldn't believe how inexpensive the beer was in this city. A pint only costs five Czech koruna, equivalent to just twenty cents in America. Pilsner Urquell was pretty much the same price everywhere we went in Prague, and it was the only beer I found to drink in this city. There may have been other types of beer, but I couldn't find one. After eating dinner and drinking a few pints of beer, Erica and I walked back across the square to a four-story nightclub called Karlovy Lazne. We wandered around this four-story club without any goal, ambition, or plan. I remember the top three floors of this nightclub playing different styles of EDM and having unique scenery themes.

Erica seemed to be particularly fond of the fourth floor, which was designed to look like a giant ice cave, and so that is where we spent most of the night. Sometime around midnight, I remember walking down to the bottom level, where a beer waterfall was flowing down the stairs. You had to walk on your tippy toes if didn't want to get your shoes soaked. This gives you an idea of how much beer was being served and, furthermore, spilled in that club. What brings this more into focus is the fact that there were substantially fewer people drinking excessively on the top three floors

There were a few hundred people who were profoundly drunk on the bottom level. When I took a gaze across the room, every single person appeared to be giving zero fucks about holding it down. I have a terrifying memory of seeing several naked people dancing around the bar, with an unprecedented level of blackout drunkenness. I witnessed more than just a few people experiencing near-death experiences that night. These were the drunkest bunch of people I have ever seen in my life, and I'm not just saying this to make this story sound shocking. These people were literally, by far, the drunkest people I have ever seen.

About twenty bartenders were serving these crazy ass, drunk people from behind a gigantic bar that stretched across the entire room. The only drinks served on the bottom floor besides gargantuan oversized draws of Pilsner Urquell beer, were shots of rum, whiskey, and vodka. This enormous bar was the only thing besides people, booze, and regrets on this entire floor. It had no tables, no music, and nothing on the walls besides two signs. One was a giant neon sign hanging over the bar that simply said "bar." Apparently, this word means the same thing in English and Czech. The other sign was hung over the restrooms, which said, "umývárna."

I was pretty happy when I figured out what "umývárna" meant because I was ready to shit my pants hard by this point in the night. I walked into this club at level 6 or 7, and I was now at 81/2 or 9. I had to take a shit so bad that if I sneezed, I would have joined the zero fuck crowd that wasn't holding it down.

Unfortunately, this restroom only had two stalls, and each of them had shit piled up almost to the ceiling. I'm not in the least bit exaggerating about these piles of shit, either. I know this all sounds far-fetched, but I swear to God, and all that is right with the world that I'm describing this club exactly as I remember it. I have no idea how shit got stacked up over seven feet tall or why these were the only two shitters I could find in this huge four-story nightclub. I still imagine some drunken gymnast, with his pants at his ankles, doing an iron cross with his arms spanning the stall. All I know is my memory of these two giant piles of shit is just as terrifying as the night I saw them.

Erica and I stumbled out the front door of the nightclub when it finally closed at 4 am. It took about five minutes to walk over to the subway station, where the train had dropped us off earlier in the night. This was when we discovered that the Old Town Square subway station closed at midnight. Once we figured out that boarding a train back to our apartment was a hopeless endeavor, we stumbled back to the nightclub, thinking an answer to our transport problem would come to us along the way, and it almost did!

There appeared to be hundreds of taxicabs lined up on the road in front of the club. We jumped in the back of one of the cabs with renewed hope that our problems were solved. Unfortunately, I left the apartment with an equivalent of one hundred dollars in my pocket and decided to leave my credit card behind so it wouldn't get lost or stolen. Despite beer only costing equivalent to twenty cents, Erica and I spent every Czech koruna in our pockets. It was as if math didn't exist in the Karlovy Lazne Nightclub.

This heartbreaking realization meant we had to walk back to our apartment. Thankfully, Erica had a crumpled-up map of Prague stuffed in her pocket, and we were only about three miles from our apartment. The entire city of Prague seemed to be asleep when we embarked on this journey, but we soon encountered an exception. Our early morning solitude was interrupted by a prostitute who could barely speak a word of English.

Incidentally, this language barrier didn't stop me from engaging in an off-the-wall conversation about sex and butt stuff. This woman appeared to know only a few English words. She could say five-dollar, ten-dollar, and twenty-dollar in English, but this seemed to be about it. She would gesture the sex acts she was willing to perform while she poorly communicated the amount of money she was expecting. If I remember right, she expected five dollars for a hand job, ten dollars for a blow job, and twenty dollars for sex.

Despite her advertised rock-bottom prices, I was not interested in having any sort of sexual encounter with this woman. I just needed a place to take a shit, so after watching the prostitute's weird sexual animations, I pointed at my ass with an expression of pain on my face. What happened next was just pure comedy and is the only reason this story isn't as bad as the actual experience. She answered, and I quote… "Oooo… naughty boy… thirty dollars."

It took some time for the humor in this conversation to be realized. The only thing I remembered for a solid year was the epic dump I took that night when Erica and I finally got back to our apartment. However, looking back on all this, it paints a different picture of entertainment and once-in-a-lifetime experiences. Incidentally, most of these experiences I would not want to relive.

We returned to Old Town Square the next day, feeling invigorated to see more tourist attractions and not make the same mistakes as the day before. I don't specifically remember what we did during the day. I vaguely remember going to a museum, but I could be thinking of a different trip and a different city altogether.

In any case, I do remember returning to Karlovy Lazne Nightclub again. I thought I was much older and significantly smarter than I was the night before because I used the restroom before going in and stuffed my pockets with an equivalent of $300 of Czech koruna. I figured there would be no way Erica and I could spend this much money. This was way more than what we had spent the night before.

Unfortunately, I was thrown one massive curve ball. Almost immediately after walking into the nightclub, someone asked Erica if she wanted to roll, and surprisingly, she said yes. This was the first time Erica ever wanted to do drugs beyond smoking weed, and so I had no plans to stand in the way of this whimsical endeavor. I just handed over an equivalent of forty dollars for a couple of pills, and thought to myself, "I got to see this."

I remember Erica's glowing happiness and astounding beauty being radiant that night. Excitement, deep bass techno music, true love, and this pill of ecstasy caused a rosy glow on her face that I thought was an expression exclusively reserved for times of intense sexual pleasure. I watched her dance and shed sweat-soaked clothing all night. It seemed that every twenty minutes, she handed me another piece of clothing that she didn't feel was necessary to wear anymore. By midnight, she was wearing only a tank top, pink lace panties, and tennis shoes.

This lack of clothing would not typically be something I'd approve of in public, but hundreds of women walked around this nightclub wearing almost nothing. If you looked into the dark corners, you'd see silhouettes of people fucking just about everywhere. Taking all this into consideration, Erica's exposed skin seemed to just fall in line with this nightclub's unusual dress code.

Erica's body was a bit petite when she first moved to Ogallala, but this was no longer the way I would describe her. She was now a full-figured woman, and this was on full display that night. Occasionally, she'd look over at me with a sexy grin just to make sure I was watching her dance. Around two in the morning, she came over to sit on my lap for a little while. I could smell her heated pheromones mixed with a subtle scent of CK1 perfume and Herbal Essence shampoo. She had me full-tilt, craving sex within a matter of seconds.

When Erica felt my erection, she looked into my eyes and said, "Follow me." Then she grabbed my hand and led me to a darker ice cave, where another couple sat at a table with a big pile of molly in front of them. "Will you buy me some of that?" Erica asked, as she pointed at the pile of white powder.

"It's almost two in the morning," I replied. "Aren't you getting tired?"

"Yeah, kind of... and well... that's why I want to do more drugs."

"I don't know about that, Erica," I responded hesitantly. "You took only one pill, and you have nearly taken all your clothes off. What's going to happen when you take more drugs?"

"Good things," she replied.

"Good things... like what?" I asked, which was a question that led to a very provocative experience.

"I'd like for my boyfriend to buy me some of your drugs," Erica told the couple sitting at the table. "But it seems that he needs a little incentive. Would you mind if we sat in that corner next to you for a few minutes while I incentivized my boyfriend?"

"Not at all, but I think that you should take a little sample before you start incentivizing?" the girl answered, as she carded out a couple of little lines for us to take.

After powdering her nose, Erica pushed me into the corner and immediately went down on me. I couldn't believe what was happening. It was as if MDMA unleased a turbo trollop hiding deep down inside my girlfriend. After a minute or so of giving me sloppy head, Erica crawled on top of me and pulled her pink lace panties to the side. Then she proceeded to ride my cock like an eight-second bull rider.

I had some serious inhibitions about this sexual experience, but I was not in a position to stop it. Erica pulled her shirt up and pushed my face in between her tits while she bounced up and down like a mad woman. It took only a few minutes for Erica to reach a climax, which set a new record for our collective lovemaking. Her pussy was as wet as a swimming pool after this. She finished me off with an aggressive hand job that made a big sticky mess.

I remember cleaning the cum off of Erica with a napkin and looking over at the couple sitting with a pile of molly in front of them. Their eyes were as big as saucers. I'm sure this was partially because of the drugs, but mostly because they were thoroughly impressed with the show. When Erica crawled off me, she held out her hand and said, "Money, please!" So, I reached into my pocket and handed her a wad of cash. This wasn't something I could debate. At this point, that money was rightfully hers.

The couple with the pile of molly in front of them seemed to be so entertained by all this that not only did they dish out a huge line for Erica, but they also stood up and started clapping when I handed her the money for drugs. Then I watched Erica put her head down to take a massive line of molly straight to the dome. I didn't know what the fuck to expect after this. I just watched in awe as the powder hit the back of her head.

Moments later, Erica handed me her sweaty tank top and headed straight to the dance floor. For the next two hours, I watched the love of my life dance her ass off, wearing only tennis shoes and a pair of pink-laced panties. I never even got up off of my chair. I just sat there watching Erica smiling and dancing with her tits jiggling everywhere.

There were a couple of times I wanted to get up to punch a few guys in the face for staring a little too long at my sweaty, naked girlfriend, but I digressed in the fact that I really couldn't blame them. Erica had turned into a drug-fueled, crazy naked dancer and didn't appear to care about much of anything, particularly her compromised moral compass. As much as my conscience morally disapproved of all this, the rest of my brain approved slightly more. This was the first time I ever seen her act like this, and it was also the last. Erica and I did some drugs here and there as we navigated through the rest of our teens and twenties, but she didn't ever lose her sexual inhibitions like this in a crowd of people ever again. This experience was unique, fantastic, and strangely beautiful.

The following day didn't amount to much. Erica and I occasionally made love between meals and long naps, so we were well-rested when we went to our meeting on Monday morning. I remember Erica smiling from ear to ear as she walked through the front doors of Hospital Na Františku Prague. She was so hopeful that this meeting would secure a heart transplant for her father that I thought nothing could stand in the way of her glowing smile... with the exception of just one thing. Only a few minutes into the conversation, Dr. Tomas Davork explained that the $800,000 price tag for a heart transplant was accurate, but then he went on to say that the wait list for this procedure was at least fourteen months long, which was three months longer than the waiting list her father was currently on in the United States.

At that moment, I watched Erica's giant smile instantly turn into an expression of pure sadness. This was incredibly heartbreaking. Her father's life expectancy was calculated to be only three to nine months at this point. Her high hopes were destroyed. I listened to Erica tell Dr. Tomas Davork about her father's life expectancy with tears running down her face.

"Isn't there anything you can do?" Erica asked in desperation.

"I'm sorry," Dr. Tomas replied. "I cannot change the order of the waitlist."

"Please, you got to do something!" Erica demanded as her slow trickle of tears increased in tempo. "Please, I don't know what else to do... please... please... please... I'll do anything!"

"I'm sorry that there is nothing I can personally do for your father," the doctor explained. However, after listening to Erica cry for nearly a minute, he regressed, "I can give you the name of another heart surgeon in Denmark who may be able to help."

"Really?"

"Yes... really," Dr. Thomas answered. Just wait here while I go get his information." A few minutes later, Dr. Thomas returned with a piece of paper torn from a notebook, "This is the contact info for a heart surgeon named Dr. Valdemar Moller. He has spent the last two decades performing heart surgeries for the Cardiothoracic Department at Rigshospitalet University Hospital in Copenhagen. He is now hired freelance. Hopefully, he can help you."

# Chapter XX

ERICA DIDN'T WANT TO waste any time going to Copenhagen, so within a couple of hours, we packed our bags and were on a train headed north into Germany. I remember Erica being so excited that we could purchase Euro rail passes for only $70 since we were under the age of 26. This allowed us to travel anywhere in Europe. She talked about this like Kmart talked about blue light specials. Thinking back on this, that was a good deal.

We made it to Berlin by nightfall and found a hotel near the train station. It took a bit of convincing, but I talked Erica into sightseeing a little bit traveling onward. I couldn't believe how WWII affected this city. It looked like the majority of the buildings were built with a weird type of cardboard, and the tallest building wasn't over twenty stories. I'm sure this city is much different these days, but this was both sad and unexpected. Anyway, the only thing Erica and I accomplished here was eating a couple of Bratwursts and seeing where the Berlin Wall was before it was torn down.

We were back on the train headed north by noon. Remarkably, we arrived in Hamburg by nightfall and were able to take the last ferry ride out of Port Lubecker Bucht that same night. Our oversight was that we would arrive in Copenhagen so late at night that it was impossible to find a hotel room. This was partly due to our arrival time and partly because we had no idea where we were. Younger folk have it easy with smartphones these days... back then, you were just fucked if you didn't have a map. Thankfully, after sleeping on the pavement near the pier that night, we managed to find a hotel early the following morning.

Erica seemed enthusiastic about the meeting with the heart surgeon in Copenhagen, but also more grounded in her expectations than she was in Prague. Luckily, Dr. Valdemar was very down-to-earth because he had a lot to explain. "I spoke with Dr. Tomas Davork for a little bit about the urgency regarding your father's surgery," Dr. Valdemar said. "He told me that your father's life expectancy is hovering between three to six months, which is very unfortunate because this leaves very few options. He also told me that you were likely going to cry a lot if I told you that I couldn't perform this operation, so I'm going approach this from a different angle."

"Thank you," Erica replied.

"Yes, thank you," I repeated.

"I know of a couple of options that may work out for you so long as you are brave and up for an adventure," Dr. Valdemar explained. "The slang term for the transplant that you are looking for is a "death row transplant," which essentially means that your father's heart donor would be someone that is currently in prison somewhere waiting for execution. The good news is that these organ transplants occur in several places around the world, but I only know of two of them."

"So, what is the bad news?" Erica asked.

"Well, the bad news is that there is nowhere in the world where these organ transplants are technically legal... at least that I know of, anyways."

"Okay," Erica said. "I was somewhat prepared for this, and I'm more familiar with these types of heart transplants than you'd probably think."

"Oh yeah... how is that?" Dr. Valdemar asked.

"Please don't ask this question," I interrupted, "and Erica, I don't want you to answer it. Let's just move on... okay?"

"Okay," Erica replied. "So why can't you perform the surgery?"

"I can perform the surgery, but it's much more complicated than just being able to," Dr. Valdemar explained I get hired to fly around the world to perform heart transplants when the scheduled heart surgeon isn't available. This means if you were to hire me, you'd not only need to come up with a beating heart, but you'd also have somehow secured an operating room for the procedure. Before you even ask, I'll tell you this would be nearly impossible, if not completely impossible."

"So, what are our options?" Erica asked.

"One option I have for you is in Thailand, and the other option I have is in Brazil. Now, before you start asking me a million questions about which one is the best option, I will tell you that they are both very unique. You'll need to meet with each of these doctors to discuss their practice to see which one will work out best for you. They each have different pay arrangements and unusual puzzles to solve before you'd be able to secure a heart transplant."

"But both of these two options are possible?" Erica asked.

"Yes, they are each viable options," Dr. Valdemar answered.

"Oh, thank God," Erica replied. "So, what do we need to do to get started?"

"Well, I will let both doctors know that you are on your way and give you their contact information," Dr. Valdemar responded. "The rest is up to you."

"Oh my God," Erica responded. "Thank you so much! You don't have any idea how happy this makes me".

"You are very welcome. I hope your father gets his heart transplant," Dr. Valdemar replied.

"I guess this means we are on our way to Thailand," Erica said, with excitement, "Right, babe?"

"Thailand, here we come…"

Erica and I left this meeting feeling fantastic. It finally seemed that there may be light at the end of a very dark tunnel. Arranging our flights to Thailand took all day, so we decided to stay another night at the Marriot Hotel before beginning our journey to the Far East. Erica had no idea I was just in Thailand a couple of months earlier, but the fact that I was already familiar with Bangkok came in handy because I knew exactly where to book a hotel.

We woke up early the next morning and caught a taxicab to Copenhagen Airport, Kastrup International Airport. It was impossible to prepare our minds and asses for the travel that stood in front of us because it was going to be one hell of a long trip to Bangkok. Our initial flight boarded at 7:15 am on February 10th. We had a two-hour flight to Malpensa Airport in Milan, with had a four-hour layover. We then had a six-hour flight to Bahrain International Airport, a country just north of Qatar and west of Saudi Arabia. After a two-hour layover at this airport, we had another eight-hour flight to Singapore Changi Airport and then a two-hour flight to Bangkok. We finally arrived at the Suvarnabhumi International Airport at 4:40 am on February 12th.

Erica and I slept until late afternoon that day after finding our way over to Hotel Thanabumi. Once we got ready to explore Bangkok, I found myself in an interesting situation because I wanted to bring Erica straight over to Khao San Road, but I had to act as if I knew nothing about the place. However, after thinking about this a bit more, I didn't figure Erica would ever know the wiser, so we headed to Khao San Road.

Erica ended up loving this place just as much as I did. It was chaotic, creepy, and strange, which was the perfect dynamic for experiencing an epic time. We went from bar to bar and club to club, drinking beer and taking shots. After we were good and drunk, we started to dare each other to eat the street food, which had an enormous contrast in flavor. I watched Erica eat a fried tarantula, and she watched me eat a fried scorpion. We probably ate a rat, which was fucking disgusting, and we both ate giant roaches, which was also fucking disgusting.

We were so drunk by ten o'clock that nothing mattered. This was when I thought about Tuk Tuk's and decided that Erica needed to experience this awesome form of transportation. We walked down the street and hopped in the back of a Tuk Tuk. I handed the driver USD $100 and told him to take us somewhere interesting. This driver understood the assignment as he began to weave in between traffic, over sidewalks, over bridges, and through alleyways. We ate more street food in Chinatown, smoked a joint outside a Buddhist temple, and yelled at the fish in the Chao Phraya River. At some point, we stopped by a bar to take a few more shots, and that was when things started to get interesting.

I remember taking off our clothes and streaking through a ping pong show. Then, we stole a giant snake from a street performer and ran around the block before giving it back to him with a weird little hat on its head. By two in the morning, Erica and I had caused so much mayhem in Bangkok that Khao San Road wasn't even strange anymore. We finally ended the night speeding through the city while making love in the back of a Tuk Tuk. That night was perfect, radical, and Far East!

We woke up the next morning hungover as hell but still managed to score some continental breakfast. After filling our bellies full of hotel food, we started to sightsee the living shit out of Bangkok. We visited the Grand Palace, the Emerald Buddha, Wat Pho, Wat Arun, and the Ayutthaya Temples.  Later, we bought a bunch of useless shit at the Damnoen Saduak Market, Maeklong Railway Market, and the Temple floating market.

Late in the afternoon, we traded everything we bought at these markets for a joint and two shots of snake blood. We were told this would make things more interesting, and it did. It was like a mellow form of LSD mixed with an upper or downer, but never both. The sensation seemed to depend on which direction we were walking. When this strange drug really kicked in, the world turned sideways, so we asked a Tuk Tuk to turn the world back to normal.

That was when he brought us to Wat Paknam, □□□□□□□□□□□□□□□□□, which was a massive Buddha located in district. We saw an awful lot of golden, fat-ass Buddhas that day because Bangkok is filled with these statues, but this thing was gigantic! Our Tuk Tuk driver told us that we needed to become Buddhists if we wanted the world to turn back to normal. I'm not sure if either one of us became Buddhist that day, but we both meditated and tried our best to achieve enlightenment. Oddly enough, the world turned right back to normal after this.

Erica and I had so much fun in Bangkok that we almost forgot what we came here for, but we eventually had to sort out a plan to meet the heart surgeon. We were mulling over our next move later that night as we ate dinner on the outer edge of Khao San Road. Dr. Valdemar Moller gave us some interesting instructions on how to go about meeting the heart surgeon in Thailand. We first had to meet up with someone named in Phuket City. This man would guide us to a remote island in the Strait of Malacca, where the surgeon lived and worked.

We didn't have any timeframe to follow, but time was ticking like the failing heart of Erica's father. However, just as we started to make plans to travel down to Phuket City, a young couple from New York happened to sit down next to us in the restaurant and unintentionally interrupted our conversation. These were very polite people named Ben and Jamie.

They had also just spent the last couple of days in Bangkok and were now on their way to an island called Ko Pha-Ngan to attend a monthly event called the full moon party. They explained this as a massive beach party with DJs and bands playing music all night under the full moon. Erica and I ended up talking with this couple for over an hour, and by the end of our conversation, we had decided that we were going to go with them to the full moon party.

The next morning, Erica and I wandered down to our hotel lobby to eat breakfast. A short while later, we met up with Ben and Jamie to go to the full moon festival. We all climbed into a van around noon and headed south to a city called Surat Thani. The ride to this city was horrible for a couple of reasons. The van had no air conditioning, and the road wasn't paved, but when we arrived in Surat Thani, everything suddenly took a turn for the better.

This city was adjacent to the ocean and was incredibly beautiful. It was surrounded by white sandy beaches, palm trees, and thick tropical forests spread out over rolling hills. We ended up spending the night here, which allowed us more time to get to know Ben and Jamie. I couldn't believe how pleasant these people were. It was as if their life was perfect in some mysterious way.

The next morning, we all boarded a ferry to the island of Ko Pha-Ngan. When we arrived, it appeared to be a tropical paradise full of people wanting to party, and that is exactly what we all did. Everyone gathered on the beach as the sun began to set, and that is when the music started. There were several stages playing all sorts of different types of music. Erica and I wandered around and danced all night long.

This party certainly met our expectations, but we didn't stay long because Erica was very eager to continue the mission that brought us to Thailand. We ended up saying goodbye to Ben and Jamie the next day before boarding a fairy back to Surat Thani. We really weren't paying attention to the specific location of this city because a twenty-dollar plane ride would connect us to anywhere in Thailand within a couple of hours. Incidentally, this city happened to be only an hour away from Phuket City using ground transportation, so air travel wasn't necessary.

The ferry ride from Ko Pha-Ngan back to Surat Thani took a couple of hours, and several van shuttles were waiting by the port when we arrived. We made it to Phuket city in the late afternoon, and wasted no time trying to contact Duangkamol Adulyadej. Unfortunately, this man of mystery didn't answer his phone the first time we called, and there was no one at the address Dr. Valdemar Moller gave us. This made me, and particularly Erica, pretty nervous.

Thankfully, he was just out fishing all day, so we were able to meet up with him in the early evening while we were eating at an Indian restaurant for dinner. I was finishing my last bite of shrimp masala when Duangkamol walked through the door. Having a name with that many vowels in it, I made a shallow judgment that he likely wouldn't be able to speak English, but I was wrong about this. To compensate for my silent poor judgment, I commented on how good Duangkamol's English was. That is when he told me that he also spoke Thai, Los, Chinese, Arabic, French, Portuguese, Spanish, German, and Mandarin. This blew my mind, and I didn't inquire further.

This was when Duangkamol began to tell us about the information we came for. He explained that we needed to go to a remote island called Ko Lanta to meet a heart surgeon named Dr. Chakrii Anurak. Unfortunately, he couldn't personally leave Phuket until Monday the 18th, which was two days away, so he gave us a couple of options. We could stay in Phuket and go with him to Ko Lanta, or we could go ahead and meet up with him on Monday at an island called Ko Phi Phi.

When we inquired about Ko Phi Phi, he asked if we had ever seen the movie <u>The Beach</u> with Leonardo Dicaprio, which came out a couple years earlier. Incidentally, Erica and I had gone to see this movie in the theater, and both of us remembered it quite well. He went on to explain that the movie was filmed on the island of Ko Phi Phi and that even though the movie described this island differently than what the island was like in reality, there were still a lot of similarities.

Erica and I talked it over and decided that we had no invested interest in staying in Phuket City. This was partially pursued by Erica's massive crush on Leo. I think she just wanted to stand in the same place as he did and think dreamy thoughts about him. At this point, Duangkamol gave us some insider information about where to stay since we were going ahead of him.

The following morning, we boarded the earliest ferry to the island of Ko Phi Phi. For the first two hours of this boat ride, there wasn't much to look at except for water, but about thirty minutes before we arrived at the port, the scenery started to drastically change. There were giant, gorgeous cliffs surrounding all sorts of little islands that came right out of the ocean, and there appeared to be a very small tropical forest on the top of each one. These same cliffs surrounded much of the island of Ko Phi Phi, and white sandy beaches surrounded the rest of the island.

The Ko Phi Phi village island appeared to be in the middle of only flat land on this island. The rest of the island was covered with rolling hills and tropical forests. Duangkamol drew a rudimentary map of the island on a napkin while we were at the Indian restaurant so Erica and I would know where to look for the hostels and villas. He said we should try to find a room in one of these places as soon as possible because there probably weren't even 200 rooms for nightly rental on the entire island.

We were able to locate the places that Duangkamol told us about after walking through the village for about a half hour. He was not lying about the situation either. Several people were in the same situation as us. When you think about it... <u>The Beach</u> came out exactly two years before we came to this island, which wouldn't allow much time to get the plans and infrastructure in place to accommodate Hollywood's inadvertent advertising campaign for the island. That and we were in the middle of nowhere. It wasn't quite like Mulia in Indonesia, kind of nowhere, but we sure as hell were not on the beaten path of the millions of tourists that came to this country each year.

This place was truly unique, as most remote islands are. Everything about this place was fun and surreal. *(Erica and I dropped our kids off with my folks for a couple of weeks during Christmas break one year, and we returned to this island. I still had the same feelings about the place as the first time we came here. The only difference was that we were much older than most of the people we saw on the island a this point in our lives. There were also more people and more development, but this is true about everywhere in the world I have ever returned to.)*

I wish my description of this place was a little better than what I will leave you with, but if you ever go to Thailand, I would make it a point to stop here, at least for a night. I don't particularly remember there being all sorts of bars in this village back in 2002, but Erica and I found a way to get good and drunk anyway. In fact, at one point in the night, we thought it would be cool to get tattoos, and I don't think either of us even thought about getting inked before this. In any case, Erica got an orangutan tattoo on her hip, and I got an elephant tattoo on my back.

The tattoo artist told me a lot about elephants while I was getting this tattoo. I saw an advertisement somewhere along the way for elephant rides and told him I wanted to go on one before leaving the country. This was what inspired his wealth of elephant information. He explained that elephants are the most intelligent animals on the planet and have a very high integrity for kin, so much so that families of elephants would stay together for centuries. He then explained that in order for an elephant to reach a point where they allow people to ride on them, their spirits must be completely broken. He said that this was accomplished by separating the mother elephant from its child around the time that the incredible bond between a baby and its mother is fully understood. This information is still crystal clear in my memory, and so is the tattoo on my back.

# Chapter XXI

Erica and I met up with Duangkamol just before noon the next day. We had two hours before the ferryboat departed for Ko Lanta, so we found somewhere to eat lunch. Duangkamol knew of a unique little Indian restaurant on the other side of the village. You wouldn't probably expect this but, the food in Thailand is excellent. The types of food that impressed me the most was the Italian, Indian, and Chinese food. The meal I had at this restaurant was a perfect example of this.

After lunch, we casually walked across the island and were right on time to board the ferryboat. It was about a two-hour boat ride to Ko Lanta. This island seemed to be even more isolated that Ko Phi Phi and it happened to become a tourist destination for those seeking more solitude a couple of decades later. All I can say is that they should have shown up when Erica and I initially came to this island because they would have had all the solitude they could handle. This place seemed to be asleep or something. I think this had a lot to do with the fact that there were very few vehicles here. I bet there were fewer than thirty cars and trucks on the entire island. The main form of transportation was motor scooters that were rented out at the pier for five dollars a day.

Neither Erica nor I had ridden a motorscooter before, but there wasn't much of a learning curve. We just put on our funny little helmets and followed Duangkamol around for about thirty minutes until we reached the other side of the island. Then, we rode up a short gravel road until we reached a massive fence made of rock and concrete. This was where the heart surgeon lived.

I was a little surprised when we finally met Dr. Chakrii Anurak because he didn't look like the person I imagined. This man had to be 6' 5" or taller, which was the tallest person I had seen in Thailand the whole time I was there. Not only was this man's height surprising, but his voice was also not in line with what I envisioned when I met him. Being such a large man, I didn't predict the weird, high-pitched, squeaky voice he had. Aside from these superficial characteristics, he had a pleasant composure and was very polite.

We all sat in a nook in the living room that seemed like a nice place to read a book during a thunderstorm or something. Dr. Chakrii began the conversation by telling us that he spoke with Dr. Valdemar Moller briefly about the life expectancy of Erica's father, but he didn't know many details so he asked Erica for more information.

"My father's heart has been failing for almost two years now," Erica said, "and he didn't get put on a list for a transplant until February 2001, which was too late to save his life according to his recent check-ups. Also, until just recently, we couldn't afford to pay for a heart transplant. They are expecting us to pay about 1.3 million dollars, and very little of this appears eligible for government assistance, so that is why we are here. We have been flying around the world looking for answers."

"Well, hopefully, I can help answer some of your questions," Dr. Chakrii responded. "As you probably already know, my practice is far from standard, but how I perform the procedure is identical to the best heart surgeons in the world. With this said, since my practice is rouge, my waiting list is extremely short compared to almost everywhere in the world. I typically see between two and six donors per month, which is sometimes more than the people that are currently waiting in line for a transplant."

"Dr. Valdemar told us that your donors come from people awaiting execution on death row and that it's not technically legal," Erica responded. "Is this true, and how would we know that we wouldn't get caught?" Erica asked.

"Indeed, what we would be doing is not technically a legal practice," Dr. Chakrii replied, "but death row inmates are released from incarceration all around the country of Thailand and brought here by government-employed prison officers. The average yearly salary for prison officers is 326,617 Thai Baht or an equivalent of 8900 American dollars, and there are 423 prison officers employed in Thailand. I pay all of these prison workers a matched yearly salary. I also pay a matched annual salary to all local and state government officials connected to Thailand's prison system. This provides a guaranteed safe haven for everyone involved with my practice."

"Isn't that a lot of money?" Erica asked. "How do you afford to pay all of these people?"

It costs me the equivalent of about six million dollars a year," Dr. Chakrii replied. "However, I charge eight hundred thousand dollars per heart transplant, so this expense is easily covered by the income generated from these procedures."

"How do I know that all these people are waiting on death row and are not just some common criminals?" Erica asked.

"Unfortunately, I have no way to prove this to you. However, I can offer an alternative to death row hearts and a fifty-thousand-dollar discount to my typical rate," Dr. Chakrii answered.

"Like what?" I asked. "What is this alternative?"

"About two years ago, there was a man named Henry Lee from Australia whose father got a heart transplant from me, and the heart donor was Henry's brother-in-law. Henry explained to me that his daughter was sexually abused by his brother-in-law and that he was arrested. Unfortunately, this evil man was able to post bond and immediately went over to Henry's house to kidnap his daughter. Long story short... Henry took the law into his own hands at this point and found this sick fucker before the police did. Then he somehow found a way to bring him here with his hands and feet ducked taped together when his father was scheduled for his transplant."

"Wow," Erica replied. "That is pretty extreme!"

"Yeah, but that man probably deserved to die as much as anyone waiting on dead row," Dr. Chakrii replied, "and he technically saved someone's life."

"I guess that is a good way to look at it," Erica said. "Unfortunately, I don't have an evil brother-in-law wrapped in duct tape to bring here. I wish I did, though, because that would make this surgery a little easier on my conscience."

"Then, you'll just have to be comfortable with the assumption that your father's heart donor came from an evil person who deserved to die, Dr. Chakrii stated.

"How do you want us to pay you the nine hundred thousand dollars?" I asked.

"You'll need to open an account in Zurich, Switzerland, and deposit nine hundred thousand dollars at the same bank as where I have an account. Then, you'll need to transfer half of the money to me thirty days in advance and the other half the day before the procedure is scheduled," Dr. Chakrii answered.

"How long would it take for my father to recover from a heart transplant, and where would he do this?" Erica asked.

"It takes approximately a month to recover from a heart transplant, and it is expected for my patients to recover here at my home. This house you are in has sixty-seven rooms and a fully functioning hospital inside it."

"Holy shit," Erica shouted. "I didn't know that your house was that big!"

"It needs to be," Dr. Chakrii replied. "I have a hospital staff of twenty-three and a maintenance staff of five, and all of these people have rooms here. Then there are typically between three to eight people here in recovery, in addition to several of their family members, who all need rooms as well. I also have two children and a wife, so all the bedrooms in this house are necessary to accommodate everyone living and staying here."

"Wow," Erica replied. "That's a lot of people."

"Yes, it is," Dr. Chakrii replied. Do you have any more questions that I can answer quickly? I have an important meeting that starts in five minutes, so I unfortunately need to wrap this conversation up."

"I can't think of anything else," Erica replied. "Oliver, can you think of anything else to ask the doctor?"

"No, I think that pretty much covers it," I replied.

"Great, well, here is my contact information," Dr. Chakrii said, handing Erica his business card. You will need to e-mail me at least two months in advance to schedule your father's heart transplant."

"Thank you," Erica replied.

"Yes, thank you," I said.

"You are welcome," Dr. Chakrii responded. "I will see to it that Duangkamol escorts you back to Phuket."

As we were leaving, Erica mentioned that she really didn't like the idea that she didn't know where these hearts were coming from. She pointed out that Billy and Adam were in prison, and they didn't even mean to break the law. She said that Billy was a good person and my best friend. I was asked how I would feel if Billy was randomly selected to donate his heart to a stranger. I didn't think about this perspective at all and just blindly trusted that heart donors who came into Dr Chakrii's office were all evil. Erica continued to explain that she really wished that she could somehow know for sure that her father's heart donor was actually an evil person. This type of thinking was one of the many reasons that made me fall in love with Erica. There is usually more than meets the eye in most of life's most important decisions, and she had a way of pointing these things out.

After leaving the office, Duangkamol explained some options for us to return to Bangkok. He said we could follow him back to Phuket and then fly to Bangkok. He planned to catch the last Ko Lanta Pier Ferry at 7 pm and he told us that if we came with him then we would get to Ko Phi Phi just in time to catch the last Phuket Ratsada ferry to Phuket City. However, we would then need to find a hotel in Phuket City because only three planes departed for Bangkok daily, and the last one was scheduled at 6 pm.

He also recommended following him back to Ko Phi Phi and taking the last Rai Le ferry to Hat Noppharat Thara National Park and flying out of Krabi instead of Phuket. He explained that Rai Le Beach had a bustling modern village with many hotels. He said that this is where people with families visit and that it would be easy to find a hotel room when we arrived.

Duangkamol went on to strongly recommended this option and for us to take a longtail boat ride over to Rai Le Island in the morning to explore for a few hours. He said that once we returned, we would have plenty of time to make it to the airport and fly back to Bangkok that same afternoon. He also mentioned that if we had time to stay for an extra day in Mu Ko Phi Phi National Park, it would be beautiful and well worth seeing.

Erica and I decided we would get a hotel at Rai Le Beach that night and decide what we wanted to do the following morning. Rai Le Beach was precisely as Duangkamol described. The port of Hat Noppharat was only a short walk to Rai Le Beach, and the village was about eight city blocks of bustling commerce, which looked like it was built entirely to accommodate tourism. The place was still crawling with tourists when we arrived, and we saw hotels everywhere we went, so it was pretty easy to find a room.

After getting a hotel room, we explored the village and conservatively drank beers at local bars that evening. Early the following morning, we woke up and caught the first longtail boat ride over to Rai Le Beach. Longtail boats are primitive-looking vessels in structure with a motor attached to a long shaft and propellor. The top speed of these boats was only about fifteen miles per hour. I couldn't believe that longtail and large ferry boats were the only type of vessels we saw in the Bay of Hat Noppharat.

Rei Le Island was beautiful and well worth the time we spent there. This was the only place in Thailand where Erica and I saw monkeys. We were dropped off at the north shore beach and wandered through the island village for an hour or so. This was a very unique village surrounded by rocks that created a maze that led down to the south shore beach.

The south shore beach was opposite of the north shore beach where we were dropped off. The north shore was a large, rocky, black sand beach, while the south shore was a small brown sand beach with no rocks except for two gigantic boulders that enclosed the area. You wouldn't want to swim at the north shore beach, but the south shore beach was gorgeous and inspired all types of water recreation.

After exploring the island village and swimming at the south shore beach for a few hours, we returned to the mainland for lunch. After eating, we caught a cab to the airport in Krabi just in time to catch the 2 pm flight to Bangkok. This was only an hour-long flight, so we arrived at the Suvarnabhumi International Airport at 3 pm and were able to make arrangements to depart for Rio de Janeiro that same afternoon.

We boarded our plane at 8 pm Tuesday, February 20th, and flew nine hours to Bole International Airport in Addis Ababa, Ethiopia, where we had a four-hour layover. Then, we had a twelve-hour flight to Guarhlhos International Airport in Sao Paulo, Brazil. After another two-hour layover, we boarded a final one-hour flight to Rio de Janeiro International Airport. Despite the total trip time of twenty-eight hours, we gained twenty hours flying west, so we landed at 4 am on Tuesday, February 20th.

When we arrived in Rio de Janeiro, we needed to meet a man named Fransico Oliveira. He wanted to meet us at a nearby restaurant to provide us with further resources to contact the heart surgeon. Since it was so early in the morning, Erica and I decided to get a room at the hotel airport and call this person when we woke up. After a few hours of sleep, we called Fransico and were lucky enough to get a hold of him. He said he would meet us at the Marine Restô restaurant at 1 pm. We took a taxi from the airport to this restaurant that morning and wandered around the neighborhood for a few hours while waiting for Fransico to meet us.

This restaurant was in the Copacabana neighborhood, on the beach, looking out into the South Atlantic Ocean. It was also only about three miles from Christ the Redeemer, a colossal statue of Jesus Christ at the summit of Mount Corcovado. Our conversation with Fransico was quickly completed during our meal.

He told us that we were not allowed to meet the actual heart surgeon and that he would provide us with the information we needed to make our decision. He said that the doctor operated out of an underground operating room located in a favela, which was described as a massive shantytown in the poorest neighborhood in the city. We were told that the doctor's operating room was located here because there were no formal addresses in this neighborhood, making it nearly impossible for anyone to find.

Fransico explained that the cost of the heart transplant would be $600,000, which was expected to be paid in cash the day before the procedure. He said that once the procedure was completed, patients would be shuttled to Hospital São Lucas Copacabana, which was coincidentally only three blocks from the Marine Restô restaurant we were eating at. It would be up to us to secure a room for recovery. Toward the end of our conversation, Fransico gave us contact information and told us how scheduling worked.

Fransico left immediately after lunch in a quick hurry and didn't even ask about paying his tab. After paying for his tab and ours, Erica and I wandered around the block to look for a bar to discuss our next move. We decided not to stay in Rio de Janeiro that night because we were exhausted from travel, so we just caught a taxicab back to the airport after having a few beers at the bar.

We were lucky to get a direct twelve-hour flight to Houston late that afternoon. After a short one-hour layover, we flew directly into Denver. We called Sherly from the airport in Houston to arrange to come get us the following day, so we ended up staying at the Hilton in downtown Denver that night. I remember having a conversation in our hotel room before we went to bed, discussing the pros and cons of the two places where Erica's father would potentially be getting his heart transplant.

We thought the most significant benefit of getting the procedure done in Thailand was that it was all-inclusive, and we wouldn't need to secure a place for Erica's Dad to recover. We also liked the pleasant demeanor and personality of Dr. Chakrii Anurak, in contrast to the doctor in Brazil, whom we didn't even meet. We also liked the fact that we had seen the place in Thailand and that it seemed to be much more pleasant than what was described to us by Fransico Oliveira in Rio.

Conversely, the only reason we could think of that opposed getting the transplant done in Thailand was the intense amount of travel it takes to get to the remote island of Ko Lanta, especially considering her father's failing health. It was also three hundred thousand dollars more expensive. However, we figured there would also be a significant expense to pay the recovery hospital in Brazil, so this factor was determined to be a wash. After discussing the contrasting differences between the two places, we decided it would come down to where Erica's father felt the most comfortable.

This conversation ended because Erica fell asleep mid-sentence, and I fell asleep shortly after she did. We slept until check-out time and then waited an hour or so for Sherly to meet us. I finally entered my parents' house just before dinner on Thursday, February 22nd. Erica and I had touched down in four different countries and had been on seven flights since Tuesday morning, so I was ready to eat a home-cooked meal and go to sleep the moment I walked through the front door.

# Chapter XXII

"How was your trip with Erica, Oliver?" My mom asked after our family had all sat down for dinner.

"It was pretty awesome," I answered, "I'll tell you all about it sometime when I'm not so tired."

"Will you at least tell me if you found a place to get your girlfriend's dad a heart transplant," my mom asked.

"Yes, I think that we did," I answered.

"That is good," my mother replied. "Heart surgeries must be way less expensive in Europe with their socialized healthcare and all."

"Communist bastards," my dad said.

"We all missed you," my mom replied.

"I didn't miss him," Angela, my thirteen-year-old sister blurted out.

"I didn't miss him either," my sixteen-year-old sister Lesley said with a sigh.

"Yeah, you did."

"No, I didn't."

"Did too."

"Did not."

"Did too."

"Enough!" Mom shouted. "We all missed you, Oliver. That includes your dad... right, Dad?"

"Yep," Dad responded.

"Why do you always make stuff with peas in it?" Angela asked. "I hate peas!"

"Well, just pick them out and give them to your Dad," my Mom responded. "He loves peas... Jim, tell your daughter how much you love peas."

"I love peas," Dad replied.

"Did you and Erica hump on vacation?" Angela asked.

"Angela!" Mom shouted. "Don't talk like that at the dinner table."

"Hump isn't a bad word," Angela replied. "I know that they do because I heard them."

"How would you even know what sex sounds like?" Lesley asked.

"Lesley... Angela... quit!" Mom shouted. "You are both too young to talk like this."

"Thanks, Mom," I replied. "I don't want to listen to that shit anymore, either.

"Oliver!" Mom shouted. "Watch your mouth."

"What is for dessert?" Angela asked.

"You haven't even touched your dinner, and you are asking what's for dessert?"

"I can't get these stupid peas out," Angela responded. "What is this anyways... some sort of baked meat pie with peas in it?"

"It's hotdish," Mom answered. "Your dad loves hotdish... Jim, tell your daughter how much you love hotdish."

"I love hotdish," Dad replied, with food falling out of his mouth.

"Dad can eat mine if he loves it so much," Angela said, as my dad reached across the table for her plate."

"Oh my God," Lesley said. "Dad is so gross!"

"By the way, Mom… what did you make for dessert?" I asked.

"I made apple pie this morning, but there is none left?"

"What do you mean there is none left?" I asked. "Did the dog eat it or something?"

"No, your dad saw it sitting on the stove when he got back from the hardware store this morning and thought that's what I made him for lunch."

"Dad ate a whole freaking pie for lunch?" Angela asked.

"I was downstairs sewing when he came home, so he didn't know any better," Mom replied.

"Normal people don't eat entire pies for lunch, for God's sake," I responded. "I would have loved to have a slice of apple pie for dessert!"

"If you want some apple pie, I will just make another one to-morrow," Mom said.

"I'm just going to go downstairs to play video games," I replied, standing up from the dinner table. "Let me know of you make another pie."

"Oliver, you are going to help with the dishes, or I'm going to stop making apple pies," Mom responded.

"I haven't even been home in three weeks," I responded. "How the hell is it my turn to help with dishes?"

"I helped last night, so it is your turn," Lesley said.

"Yeah," Angela said. "I helped too."

"You are all going to help clear the table and put the dishes in the dishwasher," Mom said. "Jim, tell these kids what will happen if they don't help with dishes."

"If you don't help your mom, I'm going to whoop your ass," Dad said, as he walked into the living room.

I probably heard my dad tell my sisters and me that he was going to whoop our asses a million times over the years. The irony in this threat is that my father never laid a finger on us. My mom was the one who did all the spanking when we were kids. With this said, my dad was an extremely intimidating man when he was mad, and that alone was an underlining threat that no one wanted to encounter. In any case, my sisters and I helped my mom like usual, and then I went downstairs to play a few video games before going to my room and passing the hell out.

I spent the next couple of days sleeping and playing video games. Erica stopped by daily to watch a movie or tell me about the gossip she heard. She also told me about the conversations she had with her father and his reservations about traveling to another country for his heart transplant. This finally stopped on the third day when she came over to tell me that her father wouldn't agree to leave the country unless he knew that he could pay for the transplant. She explained that she had hit a brick wall and didn't know what to do or how to convince her father that she could pay for the procedure.

This was when we went to Billy's house, which was technically my new house. I had every dollar I had in legal tender stuffed into suitcases, shoe boxes, desk drawers, and grocery bags, but I never put the effort into counting it all. Honestly, the primary reason that kept me from putting the effort into this endeavor was the increments that it was in. There were as many one-dollar bills as fives, as many fives as tens, as many tens as twenties, as many twenties as fifties, and as fifties as hundred-dollar bills.

In other words, I had avoided the daunting task of counting my money because I knew it would be a shitty process that would take forever. Unfortunately, you can only put off important things for so long before a good reason comes along to end procrastination. I guess this was a good reason, so I spent the next three days counting money.

Erica started work at the supermarket the day after we returned from our heart transplant expedition, so she would come over for a few hours to help, either before or after her shift. The minimum wage in 2002 was $4.75 an hour, and Erica had spent the last two years working her way up to $5.50 an hour, which would generate about two hundred dollars a week if she worked full-time. Incidentally, this was plenty to live on in rural Nebraska in 2002. Nevertheless, I found profound irony when I saw her sitting beside a pile of cash estimated to be over a million dollars.

Once this money was counted and organized with rubber bands, Erica and I went to her house with a big suitcase full of cash. The total was more than I anticipated. I counted out $1,130,043. We had devised an elaborate story to tell her father about how I acquired the cash. This story was that it was partially acquired from a treasure hole of sorts that was left over from Billy's Dad's meth organization. Back when Billy first inherited his farm, this was a massive drug bust, which still holds the unrivaled title as being the biggest meth bust in Nebraska state history.

We also told him about how I had acquired all of Billy's assets. This story was believable because the crimes that Billy and his Dad committed received substantial news coverage, so everyone in town knew plenty of details about these matters. There were some reservations about accepting this cash from me, but he eventually gave in to the constant begging and pleading he received from Erica.

Erica's father quickly decided that he wanted the procedure done in Thailand. Erica and I were both very happy about his decision. One added benefit to all this was that I won Erica's father's approval when he realized that I was the one who would be paying for it. This was a good feeling because his approval of me had been on shaky ground for some time now. This was one of my first encounters with him after he heard Erica and I having sex. I was still traumatized and haunted by that horrific encounter, so it was nice to move on and not relive those sentiments again.

After squaring away everything with Erica's father, I decided to bail Adam out of jail. I felt this was the noble thing to do, and he certainly appreciated it. I would have bailed him out sooner, but I didn't want to be short on money for the heart transplant. It was much easier to make this decision once all the cash was collected and counted. Particularly when I realized my cash on hand was evaluated to be a hundred grand over my estimates, which was well over what was needed to save the life of Erica's father.

After all these small goals in Ogallala were wrapped up, I felt ready to tie up the loose ends back in California. After all the traveling I had done over the past several months, I wasn't excited about this. Unfortunately, the tasks at hand were critical to accomplish, so

I made love to Erica, hugged my mom, and left for California on March 4<sup>th</sup>. The twenty-two-hour drive to the West Coast seemed to go quickly because I spent the whole time thinking about accomplishing the three goals that stood before me. Most of these thoughts were about how dangerous and complicated they were.

I thought that my goal of reuniting Juan with his daughter would likely be the most complicated and dangerous goal of the three to achieve. This was due to a couple of interesting factors. The first factor was that Angel wouldn't have the credentials to travel by airplane, meaning I would need to drive from southern California to Costa Rica. The second factor was that although it was a noble intention to unite Juan with his daughter, international law enforcement would likely consider what I was doing to be child trafficking. The ironic thing about this is that I predicted myself putting an end to Bile's entire child trafficking ring before this drive began.

This thirty-six-hundred-mile journey would involve traveling through Mexico, Guatemala, Honduras, Nicaragua, Costa Rica, and potentially El Salvador. Aside from Costa Rica and Guatemala, I knew nothing about these countries, which made me very nervous about crossing their borders. This anxious feeling organized a plan to avoid all major entry points along the way, hoping to increase my chances of avoiding government authorities.

My goal to inform the FBI of the crimes being committed by the T6 Cartel would be an interesting one to achieve because I committed many crimes while completing the terms outlined in the contracts that Bile had given me. This made it difficult to expose the bigger picture of how the T6 Cartel was involved in these crimes without incriminating myself.

I felt that the crimes involving children and sex trafficking were the most important to resolve. Fortunately, I figured Bile's sex trafficking ring to be the easiest to inform authorities about. I planned to make a anonymous call to inform them of the sex dungeon in Bile's basement once everything I needed to do in southern California was accomplished.

My goal to seek revenge on my nemesis would also be complicated and dangerous. Unfortunately, I needed to move on this very soon to accomplish my other two goals before leaving southern California. My initial plan was to disable and capture Bile, which meant I would also need to disable his assailants. I realized that there was a very high chance that Bile's three assailants would be killed in this process and that there was a very real possibility that I may get killed as well.

I had been watching and analyzing Bile and his thugs for a long time, anticipating that this day would come. What I came up with was the fact that Bile's assailants became preoccupied and let their guard down when Bile dished out lines of cocaine. Unfortunately, I had never seen them without automatic weapons around their necks, so my plan to disable them would need to be accomplished very quickly. My observations and best estimates were that I had between three to six seconds to disable all three of them if I planned not to get killed myself.

Thankfully, I had never seen Bile carry a weapon and was fairly certain he had not been concealing one either. After I disabled and captured Bile, I planned to bring him to Costa Rica with me and Juan's daughter. This was mostly because I hadn't figured out how to properly execute my plan for revenge. I figured Juan and the three drunk men I met in the tropical jungle of Costa Rica would like to seek some personal revenge of their own while I thought about this some more.

I planned to accomplish one other thing in southern California while I was there. I brought the diamond I acquired in Botswana with me and planned to have it turned into a wedding ring. I spent some time researching the best jewelers in America to get a custom diamond ring made, and coincidentally, one of the top-rated jewelers in the world happened to work out of a store in downtown Los Angeles.

After I made it back to my apartment in Venice Beach and got all caught up with sleep, I started to make a list of the items I needed to achieve my three goals. My finalized list included several miscellaneous items that were easily attained. These things were a friendly-looking mask, a sledge hammer, a regular hammer, a crowbar, a small backpack with lot of pockets, gray primer paint, black primer paint, rope, a Leatherman multitool, a box of rubber gloves, three roles of duct tape, pillows, blankets, a big tarp, eight pairs of quality handcuffs, two cans of mace spray, a gigantic bottle of KY jelly, two electric dog collars, thirty pizzas, one hundred bottles of water, a large pile of various types of junk food, a big cooler, forty pairs of sweatpants, and forty tee shirts in varying sizes.

The other items on my list were not store-bought, so they were more challenging to acquire. This list included a well-maintained older model, extended cab Toyota truck with knobby tires. It also included three bombs with remote detonators, two inches in diameter and six inches long. In addition to this, I needed to find an ounce of supreme quality 100% pure cocaine. Finally, I needed to acquire all the road maps and information I could for Mexico, Guatemala, Honduras, Nicaragua, Costa Rica, and El Salvador.

The three bombs were easier to acquire than I expected. I kept the contact information for the bomb maker I met while on assignment with the T6 Cartel, and he had no problem creating the bombs I needed. Fredrick was able to find the ounce of cocaine for me, so that wasn't much of a problem either. The maps and information about the countries in Central America weren't so hard to attain as it was time-consuming.

I ended up finding the Toyota truck on Craigslist. I brought it into an auto shop once it was purchased to get the suspension raised and to get brand new, big, knobby tires. Then, I took it to Fredrick's house and parked it in his garage for a night. At this point, Fredrick and I got drunk and beat the shit out of the truck with the hammers and crowbar that I purchased. Afterwards, we covered it in gray and black primer paint. By the night's end, we thoroughly accomplished making this truck look like a pile of junk and had fun doing it.

Acquiring all these items took three weeks, one week longer than I had anticipated. This meant that I would need to execute the tasks required to accomplish my three goals to perfection without delay. Erica booked plane tickets for her and me to fly to Zurich on April 4th to deposit the nine hundred thousand dollars in cash into a Swiss bank account. She made regular trips to Denver to turn this money into smaller increments.

I went over to Bile's house early on March 24th to finally carry out my plans. Bile thought I was coming to his house to review my next contract, so it was just business as usual when I arrived. I came into his home wearing a backpack filled with duct tape, handcuffs, rope, my Leatherman tool, and an ounce of cocaine, which I offered to Bile and his assailants as soon as we sat down to discuss my next assignment.

Once everyone, including myself, was high as hell, I dished out the last lines of cocaine these four men would ever see. I watched with crossed fingers as Bile and his three assailants were doing these lines, hoping to see the opportunity I was looking for. I purposely stood up and put these lines on the opposite side of the table from where Bile was sitting. Fortunately, this caused the thugs and Bile to do precisely what I hoped.

Bile stood up and walked over as the three thugs gathered around the lines of cocaine. I watched Bile take the first line, and the next two lines were dished out to his thugs. Just as the third assailant bent over with the hard plastic straw in his nose, I slammed his head into the table, causing the straw to shoot through his nostril and into his head. Then, I immediately administered a death blow punch to the face of the second thug standing to my left and slammed my elbow into the nose of the third assailant, which caused him to die within a minute or two.

Finally, I maneuvered around to the back of Bile and performed a move called a neck throw pile driver. This move starts with you and your opponent standing back-to-back, and then you reach your arm back to wrap it around your opponent's neck. Next, you lean over while bending your opponent's back over yours and then toss him to the ground. If administered correctly, this causes your opponent to flip over and leaves you face-to-face with your arm across their neck.

I slapped Bile across his face as hard as I could right after making this move to temporarily disable him so I could look around to see where his three assailants were and assess the condition they were in. Fortunately, all three men had been disabled enough to allow me to take a pair of handcuffs out of my bag and put them on Bile. Then I went around to the three thugs with handcuffs and duct tape, planning to go overboard with the duct tape. I loved using duct tape for projects like this. If it were possible to find a full-time job wrapping up evil people with duct tape, I probably would have made a career out of it.

After tying up Bile and his three assailants, I tried to go downstairs to his sex dungeon and carry out my initial plans to reunite Angel with her family in Costa Rica. Unfortunately, I realized pretty quickly that I didn't have the keys or lock codes I needed to open any doors. So, I had to go back upstairs to get the keys from Bile. By this time, two of his assailants were dead, and the last was still unconscious. Fortunately, Bile was still conscious and fully aware of what was going on. This was nice to see because I had no idea where to find the key and lock codes to the basement. I also really wanted him to watch as I began to destroy his life. It wasn't easy getting the keys from Bile, but I put a sharp lid from a tuna can inside his mouth between his upper and lower lip and threatened to punch him in the chin.

Once I had access to the basement, I went to my truck to get the rest of the things needed to keep the children in the basement healthy. Walking around with dark sunglasses to conceal my identity, I told them that I had killed Bile and his assailants so they would not be abused anymore. I also explained that law enforcement would come to the house to rescue them within the next twenty-four hours if everything went as planned. Since Bile took me on a short tour of this dungeon, I knew these kids didn't have much if any, access to clothing, so I brought them all sweatpants and a T-shirt. Once I had visited each of them, I returned to my truck to get the pizzas and junk food so they would have something to eat. Since there were no windows in the basement, and the door was secured from being opened without the lock code, I could let them all out of their rooms once I went back downstairs. This allowed them to walk around, watch movies, and interact with each other until the police arrived. Some of these kids were as young as ten years old, and most of them were trafficked into America from other countries, so I didn't want to just let them free before the police arrived. I figured that they may never find their way home or see their families again without the assistance of the proper authorities.

After bringing all the food and water in my truck to the basement, I left with Angel and drove straight toward San Diego. This drive didn't take long since Bile's house was in a San Diego suburb northeast of the city and only a few miles from the metro train station. Angel and I had a conversation while on this drive. I explained that her father was my good friend and that I planned to bring her home to Costa Rica.

I told her that she would have to trust me and remain very calm if we ever needed to interact with law enforcement. Then I explained that we would get on a train just north of San Diego, bringing us down to the Mexican border. I said we needed to take the train because this would allow us to walk across the border without contacting authorities. I told her that I would get a room at the nearest hotel once we made it to Tijuana and that she would have to wait for me to return. I planned to return that same night if all went as planned. I needed to make it to Costa Rica as soon as possible because Erica and I were scheduled to leave for Switzerland in less than a week, and I anticipated that the drive would take two or three days.

We made it to the train station and boarded the train at 10:30 am. It was an hour-and-a-half train ride to the border, so we were in line to get into Mexico by noon. It took about a half hour to get through the corral and over the bridge where kids try to sell you Chiclets gum. I was fortunate enough to get a room in a hotel only a couple blocks from this bridge. I put the ounce of cocaine in the motel room safe. Not only did I plan for Bile and his assailants to take lines just before I beat the hell of them, but I also needed it as fuel to drive straight to Costa Rica without sleeping.

It took a little longer than I had anticipated to take the train back into America. After picking up my truck at the train station, I drove to my apartment in Venice Beach to park my new Dodge Ram in the garage and then drove my beat-up Toyota back to Bile's house. This is when I had to do the most disgusting thing in my life, which was to shove the two bombs I had into the ass of Bile and the dead assailant. The fact that an unusual amount of lube and a rubber mallet was needed to accomplish this task made it that much worse.

After taking the shit and KY jelly-covered rubber gloves off my hands, I dragged one of the two dead assailants over to Bile's giant living room, where I sat him in a recliner. Then I made Bile sit down in a table chair about thirty feet away, facing toward the dead guy, and finally detonated the bomb in the thug's ass. This blew the man up. I saw bones and flesh everywhere, and it sent the recliner flying across while busting into a million pieces.

This was horrifying to watch and definitely something I didn't want to do, but it needed to be done for three reasons. The first was to show Bile what would happen to him if I detonated the bomb in his ass. The second was to keep Bile in line and under my thumb wherever we went. The third reason was to test the bomb to understand its impact and how it worked. Bile made no hesitation to help me obtain his passport after watching this bloody explosion. I put the house keys and lock codes into the mailbox just before leaving for Mexico.

I made it back to the hotel in Tijuana at 10:30 pm. At this point, I called the Los Angeles Police Department to tell them that I was an anonymous witness to Bile's sex dungeon. I explained where his house was and that they would find exploited children in the basement. I didn't elaborate on this much further. Once we made it past the border into Mexico, I pulled over to tie up Bile in the truck bed away from Angela. I told him that if I heard him say anything before we arrived in Costa Rica, I'd shove the bomb up his ass even further and that I would detonate it if he pissed me off for any reason. This was the last time Angel ever saw Bile.

# Chapter XXIII

I DROVE LIKE HELL headed down Highway 3 and started taking a line of cocaine once every hour or so to stay awake from this point on. I couldn't afford to fall asleep for many reasons and it was 6,636 miles from Los Angeles to my destination in Costa Rica. I followed this road past the Baja Peninsula until it intersected with a long series of thoroughfares adjacent to the Gulf of California and the Pacific Ocean. I started driving inland when I was about one hundred miles from Mexico City. This was the first and only major delay on the entire drive. This was a result of traffic and getting lost in the labyrinth of roads surrounding the city. That place is nuts! I didn't plan to drive in Mexico City again after this six-hour departure from an otherwise uneventful road trip to Costa Rica.

Although there were no more delays, and everything went as planned, I took some roads less traveled on when I reached the borders of Guatemala, El Salvador, Honduras, and Nicaragua. When we finally made it to Costa Rica, I drove down the same road that I had taken to Nicaragua some months earlier. The drive south to the rainforest of Manuel Antonio wasn't nearly as bad as when I was hauling the captive exotic jungle creators in a fifty-foot box truck, but it wasn't exactly pleasant either. I hoped to find Juan at his house because I was exhausted after three days of traveling without any sleep.

Fortunately, Juan opened his front door almost immediately after I knocked on it. This was a very memorable moment in my life. I watched Juan and Angel rejoice in utter happiness for several minutes before explaining the circumstances leading up to this incredible reunion. Juan was so mind-blown by my story that he could barely cook us lunch. Especially as I began to explain that Bile was tied up in the back of my truck, and I planned to bring him to the exotic jungle creature captivity compound. I told him I planned to leave Bile there for a month or two until I figured out what I wanted to do with him.

I continued to explain to Juan that I had been awake for three days and was exhausted. I hoped he could lead me to the compound as soon as possible so I could wrap up business. When I told Juan that I wanted to find a hotel room as quickly as possible, he strongly encouraged me to stay at his house instead, which would mean that I'd get to sleep a little sooner. After hearing Juan repeatedly say thank you, it was obvious that he wanted to show his gratitude and thought this to be a small but necessary gesture to express his convictions.

Despite my explanation of a larger perspective that resulted in Bile's captivity, he initially seemed to think that I had done all this specifically for him. My goal of returning his daughter to him didn't come without challenges, but this reunion was something I needed to do for myself in many ways. After listening to Juan's story, I couldn't have lived with myself if this noble goal wasn't pursued, especially knowing it was something within my reach to accomplish.

After explaining all this to Juan, his eagerness to bring me to the compound extended far beyond my convictions. The three men that Bile imprisoned to work at this operation for over the past decade were going to be set free, which meant a lot more to Juan than it did to me. Not to undermine my own convictions or the peculiar empathy I felt for these men, it is that Juan understood these people to be close friends. With my limited interactions, I only understood them to be humans through a rather terrifying perception and the unfortunate fate of being three drunk men.

When we arrived at the compound, these three men were just as drunk as the night when I first met them. While in this state of obliteration, they didn't understand a word that Juan or I said to them. Their drunken demeanor didn't change even when I got Bile out of the back of the truck and put half his body mummified with duct tape in front of them. It was as if they were looking at something in the back of their mind and not what their eyes were seeing.

Unfortunately, I needed them to sober up so I could explain what was happening and how they were involved. After about an hour or so of Juan and I preventing them from drinking any more booze, they started to sober up enough to where they seemed to understand a portion of what we were saying to them. That is when I took out the secret weapon of instant sobriety, hoping to figure out how to get them to each ingest a small pile of cocaine.

My efforts began with setting out three gigantic lines on the table inside the shack where these men lived, and eventually, my persistence paid off. Over an hour or so, I somehow managed to get all three of them to ingest a fairly substantial amount of cocaine. Thankfully, this rendered all three of them sober as a priest on Sunday within a couple of hours.

Once they were sober enough to understand what I had to say. I explained the circumstances that led to Bile's captivity and what their involvement with this situation would look like moving forward. I told them that they were free from the operation of collecting exotic jungle creatures and that they could release the animals currently in captivity. I also acknowledged their intense feelings of hatred for Bile and told them that they were welcome to seek their own revenge as they saw fit.

My only request was to keep him healthy, able to walk, and free from visible flesh wounds where his skin would need to be exposed to society. I said that he would be held captive here for the next month or two until I figured out what my plans for revenge would be. Then, I asked that at least one of the three men at least check on him every couple of days. I continued to explain that when I eventually came up with a plan for my revenge, I'd return for him, and at that point, they would be free from this hellhole forever. The gratitude of these men was enough to ensure that my requests and guidelines would be reciprocated with a sense of responsibility.

Once I finished my conversation and felt satisfied with the loose list of instructions I had provided, we started working diligently to prepare for our departure. Unfortunately, I was stuck with the task of digging the bomb out of Bile's ass with the anticipation that I may need to use its force of intimidation in the future. Everyone else just went around to all the cages to let the exotic jungle creatures free. Once we finished these tasks, we threw Bile in a cage with enough food and water to survive for a few days.

I handed the three sober men the keys to my truck and told them they could use it as needed. Quickly, they got in the truck together and drove away from their decade-long nightmare, eager to return to a normal life. I then got in Juan's truck with Angel sitting between us, and we began to drive back to Juan's house in Quepos.

There isn't much I remember about the rest of the night because I was so exhausted that it was incredibly difficult to keep my eyes open. I remember the shrieks and gasps when Angel's family saw her walk through the door and her mom's monumental hug. However, beyond this, I only have a hazy memory of hearing happy crying and laughter while drifting into sleep.

I passed out on Juan's couch in his living room and slept soundly until early evening the following day. I probably could have continued to sleep for several more hours, but Juan woke me up to join his family for dinner. His brother came over with his family and cooked the meal for us. He and his wife had two younger daughters. Juan and his wife had a six-year-old son and two teenage sons, and, of course, the glowing star at the dinner table was Angel.

When we all sat at the table for dinner, I saw nothing but smiles and joyful expressions of love. Juan's brother had cooked a fabulous seafood pasta, so it wasn't surprising that much of the dinner conversation was filled with Juan explaining how wonderful of a chef his brother was. The rest of the conversation seemed to revolve around a long-winded description of the profound love he had for his family. Other family members added a few mindful sentiments of their own, but for the most part, everyone seemed content listening to Juan carry on about how much love he felt for everyone at the dinner table.

Juan's description of his brother's unrivaled cooking skills and love for his family had only one meaningful interruption, which caused a butterfly moment and low-key tears to form in the pit of my eyes. This was when Angel spoke up and told everyone how happy she was, followed up with a sincere expression of gratitude for my efforts to reunite her with her family.

Sometimes in life, you don't know if you are doing the right thing because of the risk of it not turning out as you imagined. However, the reward you get if you're lucky enough to realize that everything turned out better than anticipated gets stored in your heart right next to the things you love the most. This moment was one of those realizations, and it created a metaphorical trophy to sit on the shelf alongside the most noble endeavors of my life.

Juan gave me a ride to the airport the following morning and sent me off with his deepest expression of gratitude, which I found to be just as meaningful as what his daughter said to me during dinner the night before. The feeling I had when my plane departed Costa Rica was left in the sky over the Atlantic Ocean. Sometimes, I look up into the clouds and pray that the sky never falls on Juan's family ever again.

# Chapter XXIV

WHILE ON MY WAY back to Ogallala, I had a seven-hour flight to Houston and another short flight to Denver. I made a few interesting realizations during my two-hour layover at the Houston airport. One occurred while watching the nightly news with Tom Brokaw on the TV near my departure gate. I saw that the raid at Bile's made national news. Incidentally, this investigation turned into a month-long national news story with plenty of tear-jerking reports of the abused children being returned to their families and other children who were still hoping for their moment to arrive.

A less impressive realization was made when I contacted Erica to ask her to come get me at the airport when I landed in Denver. I had to come up with an explanation on the spot as to why I didn't drive my truck back to Nebraska. With everything going on with Bile, his sex trafficking ring, and everything that my recent trip to Costa Rica entailed, I simply forgot that I left my truck back in Venice Beach. Thankfully, I was able to come up with somewhat of a believable story explaining how much I missed Erica and couldn't bear the lonely drive back. I was happy she believed me but was disappointed with the reminder that I would need to return to southern California at some point to get my truck. With this said,

I also needed to pick up the wedding ring I had custom-made for Erica.

The last realization was by far the most pleasant of the three. It made me incredibly happy to accomplish my goal of reuniting Angel with her family, and the fact that this happened sooner than I expected was an added bonus. This gave me three solid days of rest before Erica and I left for Switzerland. Unfortunately, this time flew by way too fast because I spent all three days sleeping, eating, and playing video games.

I was so exhausted from travel at this point that I wasn't even excited to travel with Erica to Switzerland, and usually, I was excited to do anything with her. She planned to spend four days in Europe with an abundance of caution that our financial endeavors would be achieved. It wasn't the amount of time Erica had allotted for us to spend in Switzerland that was creating a moot point of excitement, so much as just being tired of layovers in airports and sitting on a plane during long fights.

In any case, this trip was almost a mirror image of when we flew to Prague because it started with Sherly giving us a ride to the airport in the early morning, and then we flew into JFK in New York again, where we had a two-hour layover. The only difference was that instead of having a direct nine-hour flight from New York to Prague, we flew to Zurich instead. We ended up leaving New York at 4:25 pm, and after losing six hours in the air, our nine-hour flight landed in Zurich at 10:40 am on April 5th.

I was a little nervous about this trip to Zurich because of the money in my checked luggage. I had flown around the world with gold, cash, and diamonds in my checked luggage during my T6 Cartel experiences and encountered no problems. However, that loot wasn't mine, even though it carried a similar risk to my future. However, this experience seemed to be influenced by an elevated feeling of paranoia that I wasn't familiar with. Fortunately, this paranoia ended with an epic sigh of relief when my suitcase fell onto the baggage carousel at the Flughafen Zurich Airport.

Even though Erica and I didn't sleep much on the plane, we both felt rested enough to go to a bank called Zürcher Kantonalbank to open an account. We chose this bank because it was where Dr. Chakrii Anurak had an account, which made money transfer seamless. It would take forever to legally deposit nine hundred thousand dollars of cash into an American bank account, and there would be no question that the IRS would get involved somewhere along the way.

My experience with banking in Switzerland was the exact opposite of banking in America. This was partially due to the zero fucks Swiss banks seem to give about depositing money, but mostly because the people who worked at Zürcher Kantonalbank all seemed to share the same carefree attitude. The moment, Erica and I walked into the front door,  we were greeted by a female receptionist who appeared to be strung out on good-time vibes and drank Vodka. When this woman asked what type of business we intended to conduct at the bank, we told her that we planned to open an account to deposit money. "Okay, whatever," she said, pointing toward a long desk of bank clerks, "Go over there."

The female banking associate standing at the teller desk also asked what business we intended to conduct at the bank. However, this interaction was slightly different because I thought it was important to be more descriptive. I explained that I intended to open an account, deposit money, and make a large sum money transfer. She responded to this information by handing me an envelope with a piece of paper inside, "When you are finished filling this out, bring it back to me or any of the other tellers, and we can open an account for you."

"Okay, do you have a pen I can borrow?" I asked.

"I'm sorry, but this is the only pen that I have," she replied, holding up the pen in her hand. "I'm sure there is someone around here with an extra one." She wasn't wrong about this because the next teller over had a whole bucket of pens at her station, so I grabbed one and began to fill out the paperwork.

Even this information form fell in line with the peculiar collection of zero fucks this bank seemed to give. It simply said in bold lettering "Information" at the top of the page, and then it asked to provide a name, address, phone number, and e-mail address. The email address was optional. This was all the information needed to open a bank account in Switzerland. After spending thirty seconds or so writing down this information, I walked back to the bank teller, wondering why I wasn't offered the option of filling this form out at her teller station.

"Here you go," I said, handing the piece of paper over to the teller.

"Are you sure this information is correct?" the bank clerk asked.

"Yes, I am sure."

"Okay, well, you need a minimum of ten Swiss francs to open an account. Do you have ten Swiss francs or a check to deposit today?"

"I only have American dollars with me," I replied.

"Okay, you'll need twelve American dollars to open an account with us today. Do you have this money with you?" The teller asked.

"Yes, I have plenty of money to open an account," I answered.

"Alrighty then, just give me a second to enter this information into the computer," the teller replied. Even though she sounded very proficient as she typed, it still took a couple of two minutes for her to say, "Everything looks good here, so all we need now is at least twelve American dollars to deposit, and you will be all set."

"Okay, well, I actually have an awful lot of money to deposit today," I replied, reaching for the two shoeboxes full of cash in my suitcase.

"How much money are you planning to deposit?"

"Nine hundred thousand dollars," I replied.

"Is it all USD legal tender, or are there checks to deposit as well?" the teller asked.

"I don't understand."

"You don't understand what?"

"What you just said," I replied.

"What did I say that you don't understand?"

"You said something about legal tender," I responded.

"Is all the money you have USD legal tender?"

"What is USD legal tender?" I asked while setting the shoe boxes in front of the teller.

"American dollars, cheddar, bread, clams, greenbacks, dead presidents... you know, money," the clerk replied with an annoyed look on her face.

"Oh, okay, I just wasn't familiar with that term is all."

"Wow, really?" the teller said, while rolling her eyes. "So, how many American dollars do you want to deposit today?"

"Nine hundred thousand dollars," I said while opening one of the shoe boxes.

"Is it safe to assume that these two shoeboxes contain the nine hundred thousand dollars you plan to deposit?" the teller asked.

"Yes, that is correct."

"Okay, wait here while I get this counted for you," the teller said, as she grabbed the two shoe boxes full of cash. She then walked into a room behind the teller's desk and returned less than a minute later.

"Is everything okay," I asked, expecting it to take several hours to count all the money.

"Yep," the teller replied.

"Is this going to take a while?"

"Nope."

"Can I get an ETA?" I asked. "Because if it's going to be a little while, I'd like to find somewhere to eat breakfast.

"Go eat breakfast if you are hungry," the teller replied.

"Well, how long will it take to count the money," I asked, "and when would be a good time to return?"

"I'll have the money all counted in a couple of minutes," the teller replied, as she began to paint her nails. She didn't look up from her nails for almost twenty minutes after this response, so I eventually asked her how much longer it was going to take. This is when she finally looked over to her computer, "Okay, it looks like there was $900,650 in the boxes you gave me... Is this what you want to deposit today?"

"Yeah, I guess so," I replied.

"Is there anything else I can do for you today?" the bank teller asked.

"Yes, I need to transfer $450,000 into someone's bank account."

"Then, I will need their routing and bank account number."

"I have that information right here," I said, reaching into my pocket for Dr. Chakrii Anurak's banking information. "Here you are, and the name of the person I need to transfer money to is Dr. Chakrii Anurak. He also has an account at this bank, if that helps at all."

"It doesn't matter, really," she replied. "It just takes a little longer to transfer money to another bank."

"How much longer?" I asked.

"Up to fourteen days," the teller replied.

"And how long will it take for the money to transfer if we both have an account at this bank?"

"Just give me a minute," the teller answered, while typing something on her computer, "Okay, here is your account number, routing information, and your total balance. Is there anything else I can do for you?"

"Yeah, what about my money transfer?"

"The money has already been transferred."

"How do I know this?" I asked. "Can I get a receipt or something?"

"Oh my God," she responded. "I've already provided a verbal confirmation. Do you really need a receipt?"

"It sure would be nice," I said.

"Yes or no?"

"Yes, I want a receipt."

After a serious eye roll and a few seconds of angry typing, the teller handed me a small piece of paper. "Here is a receipt for your money transfer. Is there anything else I can help you with?"

"Nope, I think that is it." I joyfully replied.

"Great! Zürcher Kantonalbank appreciates your business," the teller said, looking relieved to see another customer leave the bank. "You can leave the same way you came in."

Erica and I planned to stay in Switzerland for five days out of an abundance of caution to ensure that Dr. Chakrii Anurak was sent the initial payment for the surgery. This left us four full days to go sightseeing. I found the city of Zurich to be a wonderful place to visit. It was potentially the nicest city I had ever been to, which I didn't expect or at least knew nothing about before spending time in this city. Lake Zurich, Rhine Falls, and the Limmat River were stunning water features. Much like Prague, the city also had a place called Old Town, where nearly all the buildings and architecture were built during the 17$^{\text{th}}$ century.

We made it easy on ourselves when it came to sightseeing by booking tours to places like Grossmunster, Lindenhof, the Swiss National Museum, Fraumunster Church, the Zurich Opera House, Rietberg Museum, and Uetiberg. We even booked a tour through the Swiss Alps to see Interlaken and Grindelwald. Considering how small this country is, I couldn't believe how much there was to see. I wasn't very excited to be traveling when we initially left for Switzerland, but after seeing how beautiful this country was, I didn't want to leave.

# ChapterXXV

Our flight departed International Airport Switzerland at 8 am on April 9th. We ended up flying back to America exactly the same way we came. The only difference was that instead of losing six hours on the flight from Zurich to New York, we gained six hours flying in the opposite direction, so we arrived at JFK just before noon with time on our hands. Because of some airline bullshit, our one-hour scheduled layover was now expected to last eight hours.

Erica and I had never been outside of JFK Airport in New York City, so we decided to spend the afternoon sightseeing. After buying some day passes for the subway, it only took us about ten minutes to get from the airport to Grand Central Station in downtown Manhattan. This subway station was only a few blocks from the Empire State Building, so Erica and I decided to start walking in that direction. This was really neat to see because it was the second tallest building in America when I was growing up, and for some reason, kids love to talk about it.

We walked all around Manhattan that afternoon and were having so much fun that we almost forgot about the 9/11 terrorist attacks. Unfortunately, we were reminded pretty hard while walking through the Financial District. When the Twin Towers initially crumbled, I didn't think about how this affected the people living in

New York City. I was mostly just pissed off that the nonstop 9/11 news coverage was on TV rather than the Simpsons or South Park.

This day quickly changed my juvenile perspective about the terrorist bombings, leaving me with a memory I will never forget. I saw all sorts of awesome things in New York City during our layover, which was a fantastic experience. However, what I remember the most about that day was the colossal piles of concrete rubble where the Twin Towers majestically stood. What I learned from that experience helped me understand what it meant to be human. From that day forward, I was able to empathize with people all around the globe experiencing terrorism, war, and poverty.

I realized sometime on our flight between New York and Denver that I needed to go back to southern California sooner rather than later. This thought gained a lot of traction when we touched down at the Denver International Airport. At this point, the last thing I wanted to do was continue to travel but flying directly from Denver to Los Angeles would save me a round trip from Denver to Ogallala and back. After an intense internal debate spanning several hours, I ended up deciding to take the Redeye flight from DIA to LAX that same night.

I only had a few things to accomplish during my stay in southern California. In addition to picking up my truck, I needed to pick up Erica's wedding ring, clean my apartment, and say some goodbyes. I planned to spend only three days in greater Los Angeles. I planned to spend one of these days with Fredrick and another with Anika and Jessica. My goal was to arrive back in Nebraska by April 16th.

I finally arrived at my Venice Beach apartment around three in the morning and slept like a baby despite my blow-up mattress having no air in it. When I woke up the following morning, I initially thought about walking up the stairs to smoke a joint with Anika and Jessica. But as much as I wanted to get high and see what the girls were up to, I was far more eager to see what Erica's wedding ring looked like.

When I arrived at the diamond store, the actual jeweler who built and designed the ring came out from her office to talk to me. "I finished this ring about a week ago," the jeweler said while she opened a small blue velvet box containing Erica's wedding ring. We both stood admiring the exquisite beauty of this diamond ring for a moment before the jeweler continued, "I have to tell you that the diamond you brought me is absolutely incredible. The clarity rivals that of any diamond I have ever seen and the stone was cut with such precision that it has to rank amongst the rarest diamonds in the world. I cannot believe what I'm about to tell you, but I estimate the value of this 1.63-carat diamond to be upwards of two or three hundred thousand dollars."

"I think that it is worth more than that," I replied.

"Really," the jeweler responded. "Why do you say that?"

"I know where it originally came from and what it was worth when I acquired it."

"Would you mind if I asked where it came from?"

"I acquired it in Botswana, Africa," I replied. "I traded a pile of over five hundred blood diamonds from the Ivory Coast and ten pounds of gold from the Mt Muro Gold mine in Indonesia for eleven diamonds of impeccable quality. Since I plan to ask my girlfriend to marry me soon, I kept the nicest one out of the eleven for her wedding ring. I know that this particular diamond is worth a little over half a million dollars, give or take, because the value of the other ten diamonds was estimated to be close to five million dollars."

"That's unbelievable," she said with a look of bewilderment. "Well, the diamond that you acquired was turned into an Emerson Cathedral Engagement Ring. I placed twelve .35-carat accent diamonds on a 24-karat white gold band, and your 1.63-karat diamond from Botswana was carefully placed right in the middle of them. Do you like it?"

"It's absolutely stunning! I love it," I replied, "and I'm sure my girlfriend will love it as much as I do, if not more."

"I'm sure she will, too," the jeweler said. "Especially if she likes to make other women jealous."

"My beloved has no interest in making anyone jealous," I replied. "Aside from what my love means to her, I seriously doubt that she will ever know what makes this ring so special."

"So you don't plan to tell her how much this ring is actually worth," the jeweler asked with another puzzling expression.

"Nope, I intend to leave this can of worms closed. Besides myself, you will most likely be the only person who will ever know how valuable the diamond is."

"Well, you better not let anyone else make adjustments to the ring or schedule routine maintenance at another jewelry store because other diamond experts will notice the same qualities as I have. Speaking of which, I usually suggest that people, especially women, bring in their wedding rings once a year for routine maintenance, but in your case, I wouldn't ever go longer than three or four months out of an abundance of caution.

I left the jeweler around noon and drove all the way to Venice Beach in gridlock traffic. I thought about what the jeweler said about routine maintenance, which I didn't even know needed to be done, let alone every four months. Incidentally, this created an ongoing challenge for me moving forward through the future. Not only did I need to get the ring maintained more than usual, but I also needed to come up with some creative stories to tell Erica regarding the frequency of maintenance and why I always chose to do this myself. Luckily, I found a jeweler in Denver and didn't need to return to California for this.

About fifteen years after Erica and I married, my curiosity got the best of me, so I decided to get this ring appraised. When the jewelry appraiser initially saw the ring, he instantly turned white as a ghost. "Where did this diamond come from?" he asked. After I told him my story, jewelers from all around the world came to look at it. Their best guess was that Erica's wedding ring was worth nearly two million dollars in 2022. There are hundreds of wedding rings spread out around the globe worth more than Erica's, but every one of the centerpiece diamonds on these rings are north of three karats. As far as the six jewelers were aware of, the diamond on Erica's wedding ring was one of only six in the world with the same unique characteristics. These six diamonds all weigh less than two karats and are worth nearly two million dollars, making them some of the rarest stones on planet Earth.

It took me four hours to get back to my apartment. My intentions were to smoke a joint with Anika and Jessica that afternoon, but when I finally made it back to my crib, a strange feeling of nostalgia swept over me. With a tear in my eye, I looked around at the minimal belongings I had acquired, and I decided to spend the rest of the night reminiscing about the first and only apartment I had ever rented.

This was when I sat down in my living room on the only piece of furniture I owned. This was a lawn chair I set in front of a small 20-inch television with tin foil wrapped around the antennas. My PlayStation 2 sat on the floor right next to the TV. This was my most prized possession, so I sat and played the original Tony Hawk video game for several hours while nursing the last three beers in my fridge.

When I finally got around to cleaning out my apartment, I found a hodgepodge collection of plates, bowls, glasses, and silverware that I bought at a thrift store. There was a single towel hanging over the shower curtain in the bathroom, along with a few rolls of toilet paper, a toothbrush, and some toothpaste placed on the vanity. The only things found in my bedroom were a deflated blow-up mattress, a blanket, and a hard feather pillow. Last but not least, I found a pizza in the freezer that I ate for dinner that night and a green pepper in the bottom drawer of my refrigerator from the only time I went grocery shopping. The rotting smell of this thing created a stench that I will never forget.

I woke up the following morning around 9 am, which was when Anika usually made breakfast. The stench from the rotting pepper, my hunger pains, and Anika's cooking skills were perfect reasons to finally wander up to Anika and Jessica's apartment to smoke a joint. Before I even knocked on the door, I smelled the aroma of bacon frying in a cast iron pan. When I walked inside their apartment, I saw pancakes, breakfast potatoes, scrambled eggs, fresh fruit, and a giant pile of bacon sitting on the kitchen table, along with Anika's invitation to grab a plate of food.

I spent the entire day with Anika and Jessica, lounging around their apartment, smoking joints, and watching movies. When I told them this would likely be the last time they would see me for a while, they called up Melissa and Tracy to see if they wanted to go out for dinner. This was their best effort at creating a farewell party for me. I had a great time hanging out with the girls that night. When I left southern California, I anticipated that all of us would be friends forever because that is just how young people think. I didn't have enough life experience to know how easy it is to lose contact with friends and lovers.

Unfortunately, this was the last time I saw Anika and her friends. A few years later, Myspace hit the internet, and I became friends with Anika and eventually became Facebook friends with both her and Jessica. We are still friends on social media platforms, but we have never put forth the effort to see each other again. I guess that is the way it goes with some people. You create a close friendship that lasts for a year or two, and then they are gone... maybe not completely gone... but gone enough that they are not a part of your life anymore. If you are lucky, you'll see a few pictures pop up on Instagram or see an occasional status update on Facebook, but that's about it. I'm still not old enough to know what happens when our kids are all grown up or when we retire, but I hope that time is special, and all our old friendships come back to us like a boomerang.

I called Fredrick after I left Anika and Jessica's apartment and was happy to hear that he had no plans for the day. I went over to his house shortly after eating breakfast, and we sat around smoking joints for an hour or so. Once the munchies started to kick in, we wandered down the street to a Mexican restaurant for tacos and a margarita.

The tacos at this place were excellent, and the margaritas were gigantic. Fredrick and I had only two of these colossal drinks and were already feeling a tequila buzz, which only led to more drinking. We spent all afternoon walking around to various bars near the ocean. By early evening, we were so trashed that we both had double vision. As entertaining as it was to see two Fredricks sitting at the bar beside me, I thought it was time to go home and pass the fuck out.

This is when Fredrick asked if I wanted a line of cocaine to sober up. The thing about cocaine is the drunker you are, the more appealing it sounds, so with little reluctance, I gave in to his peer pressure and took a line. The other thing about cocaine is that if you take one line, eventually you want another one, and then several more after that. These two things about cocaine are what kept the party going.

After walking a fine line between overboard drunkenness and cocaine sobriety for a couple of hours, we went back to Fredricks's place with a handle of whiskey and a sizable bag of cocaine. That is when Fredrick turned on the music. After sifting through his vast record collection for several minutes, he stopped to ask if I ever heard "Morning Dew" by the Grateful Dead. When I told Fredrick that I never heard this song before, he got all excited and put a record on the turntable. This was an obscure Grateful Dead bootleg EP. Fredrick told me stories about how his Dad attended the concert in the late seventies. He said that after almost a decade of touring with the Dead, his father had never seen Jerry Garcia so high on LSD as the night this EP was recorded. Fredrick turned up the volume to level eleven and laid two more giant lines of cocaine on the table.

We listened to "Morning Dew" repeatedly all night long while taking shots of whiskey and blowing line after line. Fredrick got so high that around 10 pm, he started organizing his baseball cards. Fredrick was always surprising me. Aside from frisbee golf, I have never met a hippy who was into sports... except for Fredrick, anyway. Fredrick loved baseball, and his card collection was extensive, to say the very least. It nearly filled the entire walk-in closet in his bedroom from top to bottom.

This left me in la la land without anything to do for a while, but then I asked for a pen and piece of paper, and all my problems seemed solved. I worked on one picture and one single poem until late afternoon the following day. By the time we finally ran out of cocaine, Fredrick had organized his entire baseball card collection, and I completed both of my art projects. I had written the longest poems of my life in addition to drawing one of my favorite pictures. What may be even more remarkable than my artwork and Fredrick's card collection is that when I put my pen down for the last time that afternoon, I had listened to Fredrick play "Morning Dew" only eight times.

I left for Nebraska around noon the following day with a horrible headache that lasted nearly the entire drive. Unfortunately, I didn't see much of Fredrick after that day—at least not for a couple of decades anyway. We saw each other about a year later during a special occasion, and that was it. We made tentative plans to see each other many times, but Fredrick's life as a wandering hippy made him hard to track down. It also didn't help that Erica and I spent nearly all our time raising three kids on our farm in Nebraska.

Fortunately, the power of social media kept us in touch as my kids were growing up, so we were able to reconnect about five years back. Since this connection was made, we have attended dozens of concerts together. I don't know how much I've changed since leaving southern California, but I assume family life has made some profound adjustments, for better or worse. Conversely, Fredrick hasn't changed one bit. He still has dreadlocks, a big goofy smile, and smells like patchouli oil. Most importantly, he is still one of the nicest people that I have ever met. I had to ask a burning question when we met up at our first concert. I was incredibly surprised when Fredrick told me that he never once got busted for drugs, not even with misdemeanor charges. That man travels through life with God's speed.

*Picture drawn at Fredrick's house*

# Chapter XXVI

Shortly after arriving back in Ogallala, my horrible headache finally went away. This moment of clarity finally inspired a thought I had been waiting months for... a solid plan to avenge my nemesis. I thought back to the conversation Erica and I had with Dr. Chakrii Anurak when he said that there was a man who brought his evil brother-in-law to Ko Lanta island to remove his heart and donate it to his father.

When we were leaving his office that day, Erica mentioned that she was feeling uncomfortable with the authenticity of Dr. Chakrii's heart donors. She explained that just because the donors were locked up in prison and put on death row, it didn't necessarily make them evil people. She said that Billy and Adam were put in prison for a crime they didn't even mean to commit and were far from being evil people. We had a few other conversations about this, and it was brought up that some people go to prison for a lifetime in Thailand for selling way less weed than what was harvested from Billy's farm. She really wished that there could be a way to know for sure that her father's heart donor was truly an evil person.

This didn't initially weigh as heavily on my own conscience as it did for Erica, but this changed when I imagined Billy's life ending tragically after all the horrible things he has experienced in his life.

I thought a lot about these conversations. It made me feel horrible when I imagined my best friend sitting in an electric chair based on the decisions of a corrupt national prison system and the deplorable moral values of local law enforcement. In America, at least we have a justice system and jury trials where the people ultimately decide who gets sent to death row. In Thailand, there is no such thing as a jury trial. The entire decision as to whether or not someone committed a crime evil enough to be sent to death is made by people employed by Thailand's government.

Erica understood this almost immediately and expressed several times that she wanted to be sure that a good person wasn't going to die to save her father's life. She tried hard to come up with someone evil enough to die by heart donation against their will, and she couldn't think of anyone, even when she thought about some of the nation's worst criminals. I think the only reason she was able to go through with an illegal heart transplant was that it would be easier to accept the death of someone she didn't know than seeing her own father die.

This was it... the plan that I had been waiting for. Not only would I save the life of Erica's father and grant Erica's wishes to find an evil person as a heart donor, but it would also force Bile to do something noble with his life. He hated noble endeavors more than anything else in the world, and nothing would be more noble than saving someone's life with his own beating heart. I finally figured out my final plan for revenge. I wrote Dr. Chakrii an e-mail immediately after realizing how I planned to avenge my nemesis.

April 18<sup>th</sup> 2002

Dear Dr. Chakrii Anurak,

I met a very sinister and disturbing person about a year ago. I'm not the law or God, but I can say with certainty that this evil person has committed nearly every sin known to man. I don't think there are any laws created by the good in humanity or by a righteous system of government that his man hasn't broken. The worst of these crimes is that he ran a sex trafficking ring for several years and kidnapped my friend's daughter at the age of twelve. My friend spent his life looking for this man and finally found him. He is currently being held in captivity in Costa Rica.

You said that it is possible to remove the heart from someone whose moral compass rivaled the criminals on death row waiting for execution. What I am specifically asking is if I brought this man to Thailand, would you agree to use this man's heart for the transplant we discussed? I'd love to know that this man's death caused some good in this world because the only thing that his life has brought forth is pure evil. If you agree to allow this man to be the heart donor for Erica's father, I will need to keep this a secret from my girlfriend just because I don't know what her reaction to this would be.

Please get back to me with your answer as soon as possible so I can.

Thank you,
Oliver

Dear Oliver,

It is not my place in the world to determine God's will or if a person's journey through life has been righteous. My only job is to transfer hearts from evil people who have nothing left to give to the world into people whose lives are better off saved. I'd think the burden of truth and the sanctity of these secrets would live inside your conscience, not mine. With this said, you may bring this person to me if you wish, but come with a decision of unwavering certainty because you are determining the fate of two men. As for keeping this a secret from Erica, I cannot see her asking the necessary questions for me to have to lie about anything. I will not stand in the way of your particular goal, but you need to make sure that the donor has the same blood type as the person receiving the heart. Also, be aware that there may be a delay in the procedure if you realize somewhere along the way that you cannot transport this person to Ko Lanta in time for the procedure. I wish you the best of luck and look forward to seeing you in a few weeks.

Sincerely,
Dr. Chakrii Anurak

Figuring out Bile's blood type was pretty easy because he was being held in captivity. Erica's father, on the other hand. I didn't even want to think about how to go about finding his blood type. Thankfully, I didn't have to think much more about what blood type Erica's father had because Bile's blood type was Type O negative, known a universal donor.

Then, I had to tell Erica that she would need to book tickets to Thailand for only her and her father because I planned to go back to Zurich before going to Thailand to ensure the money transfer was made properly. I hated lying to Erica, but I didn't want her to know about Bile. I thought about telling her about my plan for revenge because this fell in line with a guarantee that her father's heart donor would come from an evil person, but I was worried that she would find out about my involvement with Bile and the T6 Cartel.

These were secrets I wanted to take to my grave. There would be no possible way for me to explain how I found the man who exploited her and brought him all the way around the world to be a heart donor for her father. In addition to this, in order to meet Erica's moral standard of evil, simply being a pervert wouldn't be worth ending a man's life.

Thankfully, Erica bought my story and felt comfortable traveling to Ko Lanta with her father. They booked tickets departing from Denver on the afternoon of May 2nd and arriving in Phuket City just before noon on May 4th. All they had to do at that point was take a couple of ferryboats to Ko Lanta, which would likely arrive later that night.

Once Erica and her father's travel plans were finalized, I booked tickets to fly down to Costa Rica. Then, I used Bile's passport to book tickets for him and me to fly from San Jose to Phuket city.

After these reservations were made, I called Juan to let him know when I was coming to get Bile and finally relaxed for a couple of weeks.

Then, in the early morning of April 28th, Erica drove me to the Denver airport, where I boarded a three-hour flight to Miami at 11 am. After losing an hour during my flight to Miami, I gained an hour back on my flight to Costa Rica, and my plane finally touched down in San Jose at 9 pm on April 28th.

Juan picked me up at the airport that night and drove us back to his house in Quepos. After this sketchy nighttime drive, we finally arrived at his house around 2 am. I planned to stay only two days in Costa Rica before continuing to Thailand. The day after my arrival, I was invited to dinner El Tapatio Oceania, the oceanside restaurant where Juan's brother was a chef.

This dinner was something special. Not only was Juan's entire family there, but a good portion of his extended family was also there. In addition to this were the three men who worked at the illegal exotic jungle creature captivity operation and what appeared to be their extended family. I couldn't believe what I was seeing, but not a single one of these three men touched a single drop of alcohol that night.

It warmed my heart to see these three men settling into a new life free from the intense burdens of imprisonment they had experienced for the last decade. Juan, of course, dominated the conversation by explaining to everyone several times about how great of a chef his brother was, and when he wasn't talking about the admiration he felt for his brother, he was explaining his love and admiration for the rest of his family.

These two narratives were only interrupted once throughout the night, and that was when he made a toast to express his gratitude for being reunited with his daughter, to which he made a specific point to thank me for making this reunion possible. This was a very emotional experience for me and the first time in my adult life that I cried in front of a group of people. I felt pretty embarrassed about this at the time, but as the years went by, I realized that this experience was a very important step toward maturity and becoming an emotionally intelligent person.

Juan insisted I stay with his family at his house in Capos that night before driving us to Manuel Antonio early the next morning. I didn't have much time to spare at the exotic jungle creature captivity compound because I had scheduled Bile and me to fly to Thailand at 5 pm that afternoon. When Juan and I arrived, one of the three men who had spent a decade imprisoned there sat on a lawn chair near the edge of the jungle.

He was holding a remote control for an RC car he was driving around. When I walked up with a friendly greeting, I wasn't expecting to see what was lying in front of him. He pounded four big wooden stakes into the ground, and then he tied Bile's arms and legs to them. I saw Bile's naked body stretched out across the ground with a white fungus spread all across his upper legs, groin, and abdominal area. There was a large amount of this fungus specifically spread on his dick and nut sac.

Then I saw a long line of millions of giant ants walking in and out of the jungle, carrying little leaves over to chunks of fungus where they had organized their colony. What the men had done was spread a fungus called Leucoagaricus gongylophorus onto Bile's body, which was what leaf-cutter ants cultivated and digested for nourishment. This caused them to organize their colony around Bile's lower abdominal area.

These ants had mutilated much of Bile's flesh and had specifically mutilated his genitals to the point that you couldn't even see Bile's dick anymore. What was probably the most disturbing thing about this is that Bile was wide awake and conscious, so he was likely feeling every ant crawl across him as they used their mandibles to create a colony inside open flesh wounds spread all across his midsection.

As terrible as this was to see, I honestly felt delighted when I thought about what these men had done to Bile. I was glad to see that they had gotten their revenge for what had been done to them. In any case, we needed to get Bile cleaned off and prepared for travel, which unfortunately meant that I needed to reinsert the six-inch cylinder bomb back inside his ass. It took nearly an hour to get him back to a condition suitable for travel. Finally, we strapped Bile into the back of the truck and left for San Jose.

# Chapter XXVII

After exchanging warm-hearted goodbyes and promising to stay in touch with Juan, I wandered into the airport with Bile to get our tickets to Thailand. Before going through security, I checked my suitcase, which was filled with summer clothes, five rolls of duct tape, twenty grand in cash, and two electric dog collars, before going through security. This trip made me nervous.

The main thing that made me nervous was that I needed to travel around the world with unusual goals, bizarre intentions, and Bile with a bomb stuck up his ass. I was also nervous about the fact that this trip was scheduled nine months after the 9/11 terrorist attacks, which was about the time that airports started updating their security protocols and x-ray equipment. Another thing that made me nervous was that if Bile had planned to make a great escape at some point, this trip would have been the place to do it because I couldn't exactly blow the fucker up on a plane with people sitting beside him.

Luckily, Costa Rica seemed to be behind the times by a few months, so we boarded the plane at San Jose International Airport without incident at 5 pm on April 30th and surprisingly never had to go through a single metal detector during the entire trip to Thailand. It certainly helped to be traveling between two developing countries whose governments didn't seem very concerned about security. Bile didn't even have to go through a single walk-through x-ray. His ass only set off a couple of metal detectors along the way, which I explained was caused by a metal plate in his head after losing half his brain in military combat. Bile looked crazy enough that no one questioned this.

The flight back to Los Angeles from San Jose took only six hours, but we had a five-hour layover before boarding a fourteen-hour flight to the Taoyuan International Airport in Taipei, Taiwan. After a four-hour layover in Taipei, we boarded a three-hour flight to the Suvarnabhumi International Airport in Bangkok, where we had another two-hour layover before finally boarding our final one-hour flight to Phuket City. This trip took thirty-six hours, but we lost fourteen hours in flight, so we didn't reach our final destination until the morning of May 2nd.

At this point, I had to get a motel room for about an hour to do a little maintenance. This was another disgusting experience because after I duct-taped the electric dog collars back onto Bile's upper thighs, I had to remove the bomb from his ass so he could take a bio break. I thought long and hard about just blowing him up right there and then. It took a tremendous amount of willpower not to push the detonator button before I left for Ko Lanta.

Once we finally arrived at the pier in Ko Lanta, I faced another challenge, which was substantially more difficult but much less disgusting. I had to figure out how to get my extra large suitcase, Bile and myself over to the other side of the island on a single scooter. The good news was that this island was desolate, and privacy was easy to come by. So, after walking a few hundred yards, I sat Bile on the seat facing backward and duct taped his hands to the bar on the back of the scooter. Then, I put my suitcase on his lap and duct-taped it to his chest. Finally, I put a helmet on each of our heads and drove away.

Once we reached the gate at the top of the long driveway to Dr. Chakrii's home and hospital, it just so happened that Duangkamol was standing there, ready to let us in, which was great because we arrived based on a loose set of plans made a couple of weeks back via e-mail. I hadn't thought about how silly Bile and I looked on this scooter, but I was forced to take note as Duangkamol started laughing his ass off as we pulled through the gate.

When I parked the scooter at the front entrance, he told me to wait while he ran inside to grab a Polaroid camera to take a picture of us. He returned a few minutes later with other staff members and Dr. Chakrii, who all stood belly-roll laughing at us. "You sure know how to make an entrance, Oliver, holy shit!" Dr. Chakrii said after catching his breath. "Good work, my friend. You couldn't have come at a better time because I just finished my day's work. Let's get the heart donor in a holding cell and discuss what to expect in the coming days."

Unfortunately, this meant that not only was I faced with the daunting task of removing the bomb from Bile's ass, but I would also need to explain to Dr. Chakrii about the situation. Fortunately, he found this humorous, creating a lighthearted transition into a much more serious conversation. "Oliver, you are just full of surprises," Dr. Chakrii said. "I hope you plan to stick around while Erica's father is in recovery."

"Yes," I replied, "I think that is the plan."

"So, when are we to expect the arrival of Erica and her father?" Dr. Chakrii asked.

"Either the late afternoon of May 4th or the morning of May 5th, so long as everything goes as planned," I responded.

"That should work out perfectly because I can schedule the procedure for the morning of May 6th, Dr. Chakrii said. "However, if there is any delay in their arrival past May 5th, we will have to reschedule for later in the week."

"Out of curiosity... what do you do with the bodies after the operation is finished?" I asked.

"From start to finish, a heart transplant takes between eight to ten hours, and so long as the procedure goes as planned, this leaves plenty of time to remove the kidneys for donation as well," Dr. Chakrii responded.

"So, you also do kidney transplants?" I asked.

"No, a speed boat comes from Krabi to pick them up, and then they are transported to the Bumrungrad International Hospital in Bangkok," Dr. Chakrii answered.

"What about lungs and livers?" I asked. "Can you transport these organs from the same donor to save even more people's lives?"

"Unfortunately, that is not possible," Dr. Chakrii replied. "There is not enough time. A liver is only good for transplant up to sixteen hours, and lungs have an even shorter lifespan once removed from the donor. A lung transplant needs to be performed within four hours just like a heart transplant."

"So, what happens to the corpse?" I asked.

"Incidentally, there is a large population of tiger sharks in the ocean between Ko Lanta and Ko Phi Phi," Dr. Chakrii replied. "We transport the carcass a couple of miles northwest of the island and let nature do the work from there."

"Interesting," I said. "I need to ask you something else."

"Okay, what is it that you want to ask?" Dr. Chakrii replied with noticeable apprehension in his voice.

"Well, it's about Bile… the person I transported here as a heart donor. I told you that he ran a sex trafficking operation and that he kidnapped my friend's daughter at the age of twelve. Anyways, before this twelve-year-old child was removed from her home and family, Bile made my friend watch his daughter get repeatedly raped by three thugs over the next several days. Then, this psychopath held my friend and three other people in captivity in the Costa Rican jungle for four years until he was finally captured. I suspect the other children and families experienced something similar," I explained.

"With this said… before I left Costa Rica with this evil man, I promised my friend that this awful person would live the rest of his life in pain. So, I guess what my question is if this terrible, horrible man could be spared anesthetic as his heart is being removed from his chest?"

"Wow!" Dr. Chakrii replied. "I was not expecting that. Unfortunately, I don't even know if that would be possible or if my conscience would allow it to happen."

"Well, don't think of it as your decision," I answered. "Consider this a burden for me to bear."

"Even if I agreed to this rogue procedure, I'm not sure it would even be possible," Dr. Chakrii responded.

"Why is that?" I asked.

"Because a body has to be completely free from movement, and if the donor is aware of his surroundings during the surgery, it would be nearly impossible to keep him from moving around on an operating table," Dr. Chakrii explained. "Even if this were somehow possible, I don't think someone would be able to endure this type of pain without naturally passing out."

"Does the donor die immediately after their heart is removed?" I asked.

"No, it usually takes a few minutes," Dr. Chakrii replied.

"Perfect, we will just wake him up once his heart is removed from his chest."

"I don't think it'd be possible to wake someone up from a slumber resulting from this type of pain, particularly after his heart has been removed," the doctor responded.

"What if we injected him with a shit ton of 100% pure Columbian cocaine?" I asked.

"I suppose that might work," Dr. Chakrii answered. "Unfortunately, cocaine isn't something that is easily found in Thailand. If you are caught with the substance, you could find yourself in prison for life."

"Back in America, all you need to do is ask some college kids or someone like my friend, Fredrick, and you'd have all the cocaine you want," I replied. "Is there some other drug that would work which isn't so illegal to possess?"

"There is something called Dopaminergic Neuron Maturation Stimulant that would maybe work," the doctor answered. "This drug is very expensive, and the only pharmacy that sells it is in Bangkok."

"Is this drug like cocaine?" I asked.

"No, it is nothing like cocaine," Dr. Chakrii answered. "It enables maturation of excess floor plate progenitor cells to midbrain dopaminergic neurons. You'd also need the Dopaminergic Neuron Differentiation Kit to activate the stimulant."

"I see... well, I guess I'd have to trust you with this one because I have no clue what you just said," I replied. "So, how much is all this?"

"About five thousand dollars for a single dose."

"Woe!" I responded. "This shit must get people super high!"

"It's used to activate brain functions in coma patients that have suffered severe head trauma," Dr. Chakrii replied.

"Well, I do have five grand with me," I said. "If I leave now, I could make it to Bangkok tonight. Can you write me a prescription or something?"

"I guess I could," the doctor answered, lost in thought and hesitant. "That would still leave the problem of making sure he didn't move during the procedure."

"Let me handle that," I replied. "If I can't get him to lay still, then you can administer the proper anesthetic."

"Alright, I hope that I don't regret this," Dr. Chakrii responded.

"You won't," I replied. "I have just a couple more questions."

"Oh God... what?"

"Do you have a large backpack I could borrow?"

"I'm sure Duangkamol can find you something," the doctor answered.

"Are you able to bring 2x4s onto the ferryboats?"

"Like wooden planks?"

"Yeah," I replied, "exactly like wooden planks."

"Yes, you just need to buy a freight ticket."

"Awesome!"

"Oliver, you are one hell of an interesting person," Dr. Chakrii said, as he filled out a prescription for a Dopaminergic Neuron Maturation Stimulant and a Dopaminergic Neuron Differentiation Kit.

"Thanks, Doc, you are a pretty interesting person as well," I replied.

"Here is your prescription and the address for Phattamon Wetchaphan Kit Pharmacy. This place is right across the street from the Baiyoke Tower II, a hotel and the tallest building in Bangkok."

"Is it anywhere near Khao San Road?" I asked.

"No, it's on Ratchaprarop Road in the Ratchathewi District, which is nowhere near Khao San Road," the doctor answered.

"Dang! I love that place," I said, with a bit more enthusiasm than necessary. "Well, thanks for everything. If everything goes well in Bangkok, I will be back by tomorrow night."

"Good luck."

After Duangkamol found me a backpack, I drove away from Dr. Chakrii Anurak's home and hospital on my 49cc scooter, hoping to catch the last ferryboat headed back to Ko Phi Phi. Thankfully, I made it just in time. This meant that I would make it to the island in time to board the last ferryboat headed to Krabi at 6 pm. It also meant that I'd be able to board the last airplane flying from Krabi to Bangkok at 10 pm. I touched down at the Suvarnabhumi International Airport around 11 pm and then took a taxi to the Baiyoke Tower II.

I somehow managed to get a hotel room on the 79$^{th}$ floor of this 88-story skyscraper for 7200 Thai Baht, equivalent to USD

$120. The view from this hotel room was incredible! This hotel towered over the entire skyline of Bangkok. I felt very fortunate to look out my windows that night before I went to sleep and again in the morning when I woke up. This incredible view was a great way to start out the day, and the rest of the day went exactly as I had planned.

I walked across the street after eating breakfast and picked up the pharmaceuticals at the Phattamon Wetchaphan Kit Pharmacy right when it opened. Then, I caught a taxicab back to the airport just in time to board the 10:30 am flight to Krabi. This allowed plenty of time to find a hardware store and purchase a large box of wood screws, a screw gun, and twenty 8-foot 2x4s.

The only problem I ran into was transporting this wood. It took quite some time to convince a Taxicab driver to drive me to the pier with these eight-foot planks of wood hanging out the window. Thankfully, Krabi wasn't anything like the chaos found on the streets of Bangkok, or else these 2x4s would have likely killed a few people riding scooters.

I also had serious challenges transporting this wood onto the ferryboat and even more problems transporting it back to Dr. Chakrii's home and hospital. I initially had to leave the wood at the pier and drive all the way to the other side of the island to recruit Duangkamol's help. Even with his help, it took all day long to transport the wooden planks over to the other side of the island. A lot of thought, ingenuity, and elbow grease went into this project.

I woke up early the next morning with plans to build an operating table designed to attach Bile's body to it with duct tape. Duangkamol and the nurse scheduled for the procedure helped me with this project, which I thought strange, considering Dr. Chakrii's reservations about the situation. My concerns were that Erica would somehow learn about this bizarre endeavor and start asking questions. However, after hearing the stories I told them about Bile's evil life as a supervillain, they both swore not to tell anyone else and seemed to share my enthusiasm for building Bile's deathbed.

# Chapter XXVIII

WE FINISHED BUILDING THE operating table just before Erica and her father arrived at Dr. Chakrii's home and hospital at around 5 pm that afternoon, which happened to be right when the facility's chef began to cook dinner. After an extended introduction with Dr. Chakrii and several hospital nurses, everyone in this giant sixty-seven room mansion was invited into the grand dining room for dinner.

I could tell that both Erica and her father were very nervous about the heart transplant scheduled less than forty-eight hours from the time dinner was served. Neither one of them were able to swallow more than a couple of bites of food. Their fragile nerves also rendered an unwieldy silence, which seemed to have no cure. I tried to lighten the mood by describing the scheduled procedure as an opportunity that we all were waiting for, but my words seemed to fall on deaf ears, and well short of their intention. I couldn't get either one of them to say more than a couple of words.

Unfortunately, their anxious demeanor not only continued into the next day, but seemed to escalate into full-blown panic attacks at times. I felt helpless looking at the terrified expressions on their faces. After only an hour, I decided that I couldn't be in the same room with either one of them.

There was only one upside to the void of expression Erica and her father were experiencing, which was that it gave me plenty of time to tweak Bile's operating table. We finally got it to the point that Dr. Chakrii felt comfortable moving forward with my bizarre request to keep Bile conscious while his heart was being removed from his chest. Thankfully, his nurse helped me because I would have never even come close to creating an operating table for a heart transplant. This project was much more involved than just some boards, Bile, and duct tape. However, it wouldn't appear to be so if you were to look at it because once the table was built, I wrapped up the majority of Bile's body with several layers of duct tape and strapped him to a bunch of wooded boards.

I had some time the following morning to have a one-sided heart-to-heart conversation with my nemesis. I could have spent hours explaining to Bile how horrible of a person I thought he was, but this would be meaningless because he already knew this about himself. I would say that most people on this planet at least try to be good. Whether or not planet Earth creates the environment for their aspirations to succeed seems to be a variable that is not easily managed. Everyone has the opportunity to be good in theory, but not everyone has the same opportunities in life.

Unfortunately, some people are simply misguided from what would seem to be a universal goal of being a good person. The same can be said for achieving happiness, love, or success in any form. Our journey toward enlightenment is difficult to understand because everyone starts their life in a different place and pursues a different pathway through life. We all have behavioral health issues, and we are all misguided to some extent. Incidentally, this is what makes people normal.

The reason why the anomaly of Bile's life seemed to be an enigma only the devil could solve was that he was never misguided or plagued with unusual mental health issues. It only appeared to be so from the perspective of those with aspirations to be a good person. This man was born evil with a sinister goal to do evil things, and unfortunately, planet Earth created an environment for him to be incredibly successful. This man's soul was pure, and very few people on the planet can identify with this higher level of existence. Typically, when people think of someone with a pure heart or a pure soul, they think of a saint, a nun, or someone who is known for being an exceptionally good person. Bile's soul was pure just the same, except he was known for being an exceptionally evil person.

The fact that I had duct-taped him to this operating table or dragged him around the world to meet his ultimate demise didn't make me a good person, and I came to realize this more as my goal of revenge began to materialize. The idea that I sought revenge rather than peace with the world around me indicates that I was misguided and was likely struggling with unusual mental health issues from the beginning. Despite having clear aspirations to be a good person, I have often pondered whether this bizarre quest for revenge made me an evil person in some regard. Unfortunately, this question will haunt me for the rest of my life because there are no definitive answers or righteous perspectives to explain the difference between right and wrong. All we have in this world is the bible and opinions.

As elusive as my purpose in life was at this time of my life, I knew for certain that Bile's existence in this world was pure evil, which gave me a damn good reason to achieve my peculiar goal of revenge. This man's heart was being removed from his chest to save the life of Erica's father, which was the only good thing to come from Bile's entire existence on planet Earth. I cannot explain the emotions that came from my goals of heart and revenge because they were, and still are incredibly complicated. However, I am able to explain that ultimate revenge was accomplished when Bile watched his own heart beating heart removed from his chest and then carried across the room to save someone's life. This may have been the only moral endeavor to come from Bile's body, heart, mind, or soul. From that day forward, I never second-guessed the possibility of turning the worst kind of evil into something good.

"Bile, I have never explained to you what created my first goal in life. If you think back to one of our first encounters, I made an exchange for some naked pictures of a seventeen-year-old girl that you exploited on the internet. What you didn't know is that this woman is the love of my life, and she means more to me than anything else in the world. My decision to remove you from this planet, and serve you with your ultimate demise was to silently answer the collective prayers that came from the mothers and fathers of all the children you have abused. However, the reason why I decided to specifically bring you here to have your heart removed from your chest is because of my personal conviction for revenge. I want you to experience the exact same thing as I felt the moment I realized that you exploited the love of my life. It felt like my heart was ripped from my chest, and I want you to know exactly what that feels like before you die."

I left the operating room and walked down the hallway to where Erica and her father were sitting in complete silence. No words were said for almost an hour until the nurse told us that it was time for the surgery. The procedure to remove a heart is far less complicated than the procedure to insert a heart, so Erica's father was brought into the operating room two hours before Dr. Chakrii even started to remove Bile's heart.

The only words I heard Erica say that morning was when she got up to hug her father. She said, "I love you, Dad." Unfortunately, this meant that at some point, I would have to interrupt this silence to tell Erica that I planned to watch the surgical procedure of removing a heart from the donor. As expected, this wasn't reciprocated as I would have liked. She had some questions.

"Why in the hell do you want to watch someone's heart being removed from their chest?" Erica asked.

"I don't know," I responded. "I'm just interested in watching, I guess."

"What the fuck for?" Erica asked with strong conviction.

"I just find open heart surgery fascinating... that's all," I answered.

"You find open heart surgery fascinating... ok... why?" Erica asked.

"I just do."

"That isn't good enough, Oliver," Erica stated. "I want to know why you find open heart surgery to be so fascinating."

"I'm thinking of becoming a surgeon," I said. "That's why?"

"You can't become a surgeon, Oliver."

"Why not?" I asked.

"Because you smoke too much goddamned pot," Erica replied. "You'd probably drop a roach in someone's chest and kill the poor bastard."

"Well, anyway, I made arrangements with Dr. Chakrii a couple of days before you and your dad arrived, and it is important to me to see this," I explained.

"Fine, Oliver. Go watch your stupid open-heart surgery," Erica responded. "I guess I'll just sit here worrying about everything all by myself."

"Don't be like that," I replied. "Dr. Chakrii said this part of the procedure only takes a couple of hours. Then, I promise to come right back to provide all the love and support you could ask for."

"Just go, Oliver," Erica said with her eyes full of tears.

I felt awful walking away from Erica, but I had been planning for this forever and was excited to finally accomplish my goal of revenge. Unfortunately, the first couple of hours were very uneventful, as Dr. Chakrii predicted, because Bile passed out from the pain and shock caused by this procedure in less than twenty minutes.

The monotony of an otherwise boring operation ended when I saw Dr. Chakrii remove Bile's beating heart from his chest. This was when I jammed the syringe full of the Dopaminergic Neuron Maturation Stimulant into his arm. This caused Bile's eyes to open wide as saucers instantaneously. Moments later, the stimulant entered his bloodstream, and his body twitched so hard that the entire operating table appeared to jump up off the floor.

As disturbing as this was to experience, the next few seconds provided a peculiar satisfaction I will never forget. This was when I saw Bile's mortified expression and evil eyes staring at his own beating heart. The first goal I had ever set for myself was finally accomplished, and it felt good knowing that this was the last thing my nemesis experienced while on planet Earth. As his retched, wicked soul began its descent down through the flaming gates of hell, this moment in time was the pinnacle of retribution, the ultimate payback, and the masterpiece of my revenge.

I watched Bile take his final breath just as Dr. Chakrii left the donor operating room. It was a defining moment when he walked into the transplant operating room with the heart that saved the life of Erica's father. This was my cue to exit this transitory moment of accomplishment and run back to Erica's side with hopeful anticipation that her anger was short-lived.

Unfortunately, the flames of resentment were still burning when I arrived. However, her anger was allayed by only a few dirty looks before she fell into my arms, desperately seeking comfort from the pain of relentless worry brought on by her father's heart transplant. I sat there for another seven hours, trying everything I could to pacify the terror of uncertainty and the panic of anticipation Erica continued to experience. The sunlight shined through the windows all afternoon, but just as the sunset began to cast shadows across the hallway, Dr. Chakrii exited the operation room.

"I'm pleased to inform you that this was one of the most flawless heart transplants I have ever worked on. There were zero complications throughout the entire procedure. So long as your father's recovery goes well, he can expect to live a long, healthy life."

"Oh my God! Oh my God! Oh my God! Oh my God!" Erica said, as she jumped up to give the doctor a long hug and several short kisses on his face. Then, she turned back toward me and began to completely unravel. She threw her arms around me as she buried her face into my shoulder. Immediately, she began to cry for several minutes. My shirt was completely drenched in tears when she finally pulled her head up to look me in the eyes.

The expression I saw at that moment was a certain type of happiness that is impossible to describe because of the multitude of emotions that it contained. There were parts of this happiness that went missing the day Erica found out her father was dying. This happiness seemed to fade a little more each time she looked inside the coffee can she left on the counter where she worked. This happiness may have been forever lost if the procedure had not gone as planned. Thankfully, everything had gone exactly according to plan, and so the element of happiness was restored as it should be, which returned to Erica's demeanor in the form of a spectacular smile. I felt very fortunate to witness this newly invigorated emotion, and understood immediately that all the personal sacrifices that I had made to save the life of Erica's father were well worth it.

"Can you believe this, Oliver?"

"Yes... I mean, no... I don't know," I said, at a loss for words.

"Did you hear what the doctor said?" Erica asked.

"Yeah, I think so," I replied.

"He said my dad can expect to live a long, healthy life!"

"I know that was so wonderful to hear."

"Do you know what this means?" Erica asked.

"I know what it means to me," I said, pleased to have accomplished my second goal in life, "but it's hard to imagine what it means to you right now."

"It means that I'm going to continue to have a father. It means that our kids will have a grandpa. It means that... that... our grandkids will maybe have a great grandpa. Oliver, it means that my father will walk me down the aisle on our wedding day!"

This was an incredibly profound statement in the fact that I had not heard Erica talk about our anticipated wedding since the day she found out about the seriousness of her father's failing heart. This was not just unusual but eerie in the worst way possible. From the day I first met Erica back when we were just little kids until this terrible news was first explained to her, there was not a week that went by that I didn't hear a fantasized description of our wedding day. Incidentally, I never heard Erica describe her wedding day fantasy, leaving out the description of being walked down the aisle by her father.

Erica and I spent most of the next day resting, but we got up in time to join everyone for dinner that night. Dr. Chakrii informed us that it would take a week or so before Erica's Father recovered enough to have a conversation, and it would be a couple of weeks before it was anticipated that he could join everyone for dinner. He suggested that if we wanted to do a bit of traveling or sightseeing, the coming week would be an ideal time to do it.

We took the doctor's advice and spent the next few days exploring Ko Phi Phi village a little more. We also spent quality time hiking around the island. The view from the top of the tallest hill displayed a breathtaking beauty that went unrivaled throughout our time spent on the island. We traveled to Bangkok after this because I wanted to show Erica the incredible view from the top of Baiyoke Tower II. This was also an incredible place to make love. The beds were huge, and there was just something awesome about smashing our naked bodies against a window 79 floors above ground level.

When Erica and I weren't fucking, making love, or sleeping, we were exploring other parts of Bangkok that we hadn't seen before. Then, we traveled down to Rai Leh beach, which was much more enjoyable than the first time we passed through with much less time on our hands. We discovered substantially more places to visit that put Thailand's exquisite beauty on full display. Some of these places were local gems, and others were tucked away down trails that were less traveled. This was likely our favorite place we visited during our six days of exploration.

We finally returned to Ko Lanta on the seventh day, hoping that Erica's Father would be recovered enough to have his first conversation with his new heart. Erica was absolutely ecstatic when we walked into her father's recovery room and found him with his bed tilted up. From this point forward, these two happy souls were inseparable until Erica's Father was healthy enough to be discharged from Dr. Chakrii Anurak's home and hospital. By this time, we were all ready to leave the desolate island of Ko Lanta. As a matter of fact, we were all ready to leave Thailand altogether.

After thanking Dr. Chakrii for all he did for us, we boarded the Ko Lanta Pier Ferryboat on the morning of June 5th and made our way to Bangkok by late afternoon. Our flight back to America was not scheduled to depart until the following morning. There was a short discussion about going into the city that night, but at this point, we were just ready to get back home. We stayed at the airport hotel out of convenience.

# Chapter XXIX

We departed from Suvarnabhumi International Airport at 8 am the following morning and spent six hours on a flight to Narita International Airport in Tokyo. During a two-hour layover at this airport, we decided to eat some sushi. What made this sushi different than any other sushi I have ever had in my life was that it was hands down the most expensive sushi I have ever eaten in my life. I boarded the plane weighing significantly less than when I arrived because a large wad of cash was spent on sushi, and at least ten pounds of frustration, regrets, and unanswered questions about Japanese airport sushi were left on the table with the check.

We had a twelve-hour flight from Tokyo to Dallas/Fort Worth Airport, where we had another four-hour layover. It's not a typical thing to say, but this four-hour layover was perfect because we got in touch with Sherly to meet us in Denver when we touched town at 11 pm. The last flight from Dallas to Denver was only a two-hour plane ride. My seats were separated from Erica and her father, so I asked if it would be all right if I switched seats to sit next to her dad during this flight. Of course, Erica asked why I wanted to sit next to her father considering the fact that we had never really gotten along very well. However, Erica eventually gave me permission after some awkward looks and a few questions that no man could have answered correctly. Our initial conversation occurred at the gate while we were waiting to board.

"I have something I want to say to your dad."

"What do you need to say?" Erica asked.

"It's kind of personal."

"Like boy talk personal?" Erica asked, with a peculiar grin on her face.

"Yeah, kind of," I replied.

"Dad... wake up," Erica shouted.

"What? Holy shit! Is it time for another meal or something?" Erica's dad asked in a sleepy voice and with an exhausted look on his face.

"No, we haven't even left the airport yet," Erica replied. "Oliver wants to talk to you about something."

"Okay... what do you want, Oliver?"

"Oh, I don't want anything," I stated, "well, not really anyway... I just want to talk to you about something is all."

"Is this going to be something important?" Erica's asked. "Because if it is, you might be better off waiting till after we get back to Nebraska and I've gotten some solid sleep."

"It is important," I answered, while staring intently at the airport floor, "but really... well... it's just a question that I was hoping you'd be able to answer... but it can wait I guess,"

"Okay, what's the question?"

"Let's just wait till we get on the plane, and I'll talk to you then," I answered.

"As you probably know… I'm in love with your daughter, and she is in love with me."

"Is this about when I threatened you and told you to make sure not to get Erica pregnant… or when I said that I didn't know what Erica saw in you?" Erica's dad asked. "Listen, I'm sorry. I think that maybe I was having a bad day, which continued for about three or four months after our little talk, and when I said that I didn't know what Erica saw in you… this was before you saved my life. You are all right in my book, Oliver."

"No, it is not about that," I answered.

"You didn't get Erica pregnant, did you?"

"No, not yet, anyway."

"What do you mean… not yet?" Erica's dad asked. "Please tell me you two aren't trying to have a baby."

"No sir, we are not."

"Okay, what is it then?" Erica's father asked, as he pulled out a gigantic container of toothpicks from his pocket. It was hard to look this man in the eyes as it was, and the fact that he seemed to have a full sushi role still stuck in his teeth from our layover in Tokyo didn't make it any easier. To this day, Erica's dad is the only person I know who religiously carries around a giant container of toothpicks. This man and my own father seemed to be in daily competition to make every situation awkward.

"As you might know, Erica has been planning a wedding inside of her head for as long as I have known her, it seems, and she has always envisioned that you'd be there to walk her down the aisle. However, something changed about a year ago. I noticed she stopped talking about this picture-perfect moment she always used to tell me about. I think this is because when she found out how serious your heart condition was, she stopped trying to imagine what her future might look like."

"Huh, I wonder why?" Erica's father replied, as if my sentimental confession wasn't vibrating in the same frequency of emotion as his. "And she never told me about wanting to get married."

"To be honest... I think it was because she didn't know if you'd be in her life anymore."

"Well, I would like to thank you from the bottom of my heart for saving my life and giving me the opportunity to be in Erica's future. What you did for me was remarkable!"

"Yeah, well, I didn't do much," I replied, surprised with the sincerity in his voice. My response was not at all accurate. He knew it, and I knew it. This man had no idea that I had spent the past year continuously putting my life in the most terrifying situations one could ever dream of to raise money for his transplant. This, and the fact that my nemesis was his heart donor, left a lump in my throat, anxiety in my chest, and horrific memories in the back of my head that I'll never forget no matter how hard I try.

"You saved my life, Oliver, and that is a whole hell of a lot!" Erica's father responded with a raised voice.

"Well, I guess it is something," I answered. "I'm just happy that you're alive and that Erica can maybe move past all this with a smile on her face. Maybe now she can go on imagining and dreaming about the future... you know... and well... now that she knows you'll be in her future... maybe it's time to turn one of her dreams into reality."

"Maybe it is... maybe it is," Erica's father replied. These words led to a few minutes of awkward silence, which was probably only awkward for me because I was dying to ask this man the second most important question of my life. As time ticked by, I became more hesitant to ask this question, but this only caused a long pause and thankfully didn't completely put an end to our conversation. This short amount of time felt like an eternity. I spent most of this time trying to find the right words to say, and the rest of the time trying to remember what this man's name was. Erica always called him Dad, and I spent most of my life trying to avoid him. I knew it was either Tim, or Jim, but I wasn't confident enough to address him by name, or any way that would add credibility to my fiddly demeanor.

"I want to talk to you about something, and it's really important... well... actually... I want to ask you something," I finally said, with bumbling words and an assertive tone.

"Okay, man... just ask me," he replied. "You have to work on your stuttering, Buddy."

"I want to ask your daughter to marry me," I blurted out. "Will you give me your blessing?"

"You want to ask my daughter to marry you?" Erica's father responded, as if I was asking the strangest question he had ever heard in his life.

"Well, yeah, but I don't want to just ask Erica if she will marry me," I replied. "Ummm... I want to ask her to be my wife, and I want to ask to be her husband... and well... I want to make her happy. Not just happy to get married, or to be married... umm.... this is harder than I thought it would be. I want to make Erica happy every day for the rest of her life, and I want to be happy... I would like Erica to make me happy for the rest of my life, too.

I know that there will be some days that are sad. Sometimes there might be whole months that don't go as planned, and every now and then, I'm sure there will be pain... the kind of pain someone feels when they don't understand the world around them... and well... I want to be there for Erica when she is feeling this pain. I want to be there during those times when things don't go as planned, and on the days that she is feeling sad, I want to be the one she comes to when she tries to run away from whatever is making her sad... if that is the entire world... or even if it's me that made her sad. I want to be standing with my arms spread wide open when she comes back... back to a place... back to a time... back to a world where we make each other happy. Most importantly, I want to love her forever... and... ever." Time paused in this sentiment as a lonely tear of complete sincerity rolled down my cheek. "Anyway, yes, I want to ask Erica to marry me, and I want to ask you for your blessing before I do."

"Oliver, I don't know what the hell you just said, or what to say about it," Tim or Jim responded while reaching in his pocket for another toothpick. "You are an interesting person. I have always thought you were a little ass-backward when most people were facing forward. I have never been able to figure out exactly why Erica loves you so much. With this said, I have never known her to be wrong about much of anything, so I never thought that her feelings for you were wrong. I have put a lot of trust in my daughter to make right decisions even if I don't understand why she makes them. Your relationship hasn't been an easy one to wrap my head around, or approve of. You smell like a Grateful Dead concert. Your goals are either well kept secrets, or nonexistent, and you don't seem to like people very much. Then, I saw your two best buddies on the news being charged with murder! I don't know how the hell those two bozos became your friends, or how you and Erica fell in love, but I guess maybe this isn't for me to understand. If Erica wants to marry you... then you have my blessing."

"Thank you! I can't tell you how happy this make me," I answered with a big smile. "For the record, I used to have three goals in life, and I just recently accomplished all three of them. Now, I only have one goal." I didn't say another word for the rest of the flight back to Denver. I just smiled, and smiled, and smiled.

It took me a few days to think of where I planned to ask Erica to marry me. Unfortunately, western Nebraska doesn't have many romantic venues. There are many places to pursue the complex commitment of love, but I wanted to find a location that was beautiful and meaningful. I thought hard about traveling around the world looking for a beautiful place as meaningful as the love I felt for Erica, but I eventually realized that this would be impossible. Even if I were to locate the most incredible place on the entire planet, it wouldn't compare to what I felt inside my heart.

I carried Erica's wedding ring in my pocket the entire time I traveled around Thailand, thinking that remote islands, palm trees, and white sand beaches would create the perfect backdrop for a marriage proposal. Unfortunately, this trip was filled with too many emotions to concentrate on the only one that mattered to me.

I finally found what I was looking for one afternoon while taking Daisy for a walk around the farm and playing her favorite game. My English Springer Spaniel really liked to hunt pheasants, but she absolutely loved playing Frisbee. I remember the wind catching the frisbee just right and watching Daisy running down into a small valley to retrieve it. I called Erica that same afternoon.

If someone didn't share the same unique experiences as Erica and me, there wouldn't be anything to distinguish this place from anywhere else in Nebraska, but this specific location was very special to me. I could only hope that it was also special to Erica. I knew that I had chosen the right spot when I saw her gorgeous smile. We both stood looking at the heart that I had carved in a tree the day before she moved away when we were twelve years old. The heart was carved into a large oak tree with our names in the middle. It described how I imagined to spend the rest of my life... Erica + Oliver.

I remember seeing tears roll down Erica's face as I opened the little blue velvet box containing Erica's wedding ring. She suddenly expressed emotions I had never seen before. This moment meant a lot more to her than just the love she felt for me. Everything inside her heart was standing before me, and I was down on one knee. "Erica, you are the most important person in my life. I have loved you since the day we met, and I promise to love you for as long as I live... forever. Will you marry me?"

"I love you, too, Oliver... of course I will marry you!"

Stay tuned for the fourth novel in the series. Find out what happens to Adam and Billy. Get ready to read about an exciting wedding and honeymoon. All the beloved characters, including Oliver's family, Fredrick, and Sherly return for another adventure in The Identity of Oliver Series.

The estimated release is 2027.

www.ingramcontent.com/pod-product-compliance
Lightning Source LLC
Chambersburg PA
CBHW031336010826
48972CB00012B/403